The
Brightest
Light

This is for Kelly,
Bayli, Noah and Kace.

The magical crystals that help me fly.

ACKNOWLEDGMENTS

This book could not have been completed without the
support of many people. Here's a list of the main ones...
Kelly Robinson, Sharon Dunne, Jason Nahrung and everyone
from Vision Writers who looked at the manuscript and
offered support and encouragement in other ways over a lot
of years.

Other Books by
Scott J. Robinson

<u>Tribes of the Hakahei</u>
Part 1: The Space Between
Part 2: Singing Other Worlds
Part 3: When the Time Comes
Part 4: A Different Kind of Heaven

<u>The Last Great Hero</u>
The Age of Heroes
A History of Magic (Coming Soon)
An Army of Heroes (Coming Soon)

The Brightest Light

Scott J. Robinson

"Is that the end of my stupidity?"
"I'm afraid not, love."

Prologue

Lemar heard the gunshot but it was a moment before he realized he'd been shot. "Damn." Blood was soaking through his shirt, leaving a warm trail down his chest and stomach. "Damn." There was surprisingly little pain, but he leaned against the wall and slid slowly down to the floor. This was supposed to be the simple part of the operation. Nobody was supposed to get hurt. The real risks were being taken elsewhere.

At the other end of the warehouse, there was a constable half hidden behind a workbench. The man looked calm and collected as he rammed a slug down the barrel of his musket. Lemar watched him cock the gun and fill the firing pan. It seemed to take forever. Aim. Fire...

Lemar flinched and felt a line of pain lance across his cheek. He screamed but that pain was gone in a moment. He reached up and felt his face. Half his ear was missing. His fingers came away sticky with blood.

The constable was loading again, pouring powder as backup came in the door behind him. There seemed to be a lot of them.

"Lemar? Are you all right?"

Stupid question. Lemar looked back at his companions. They'd been right behind him a moment ago but had quickly taken cover. Jommy worked up his nerve, darted forward and grabbed Lemar by the arm.

When he regained consciousness, Lemar found himself propped in a corner made by two storage crates. His sword hilt was digging into his side but he didn't try to move it.

"Are you all right?" someone asked again. Donar. Big lad. Showed promise.

"How long?"

"Just a couple of seconds," Donar said.

Lemar nodded.

"What do we do now?" Jommy was obviously scared, but trying not to show it.

"How am I supposed to know?" Lemar snapped. His chest hurt now. Hurt like a bitch.

"But—" It wasn't Jommy's fault.

"Arik's in charge of the operation, remember?"

Arik was going to be a great. He was smart and talented, just not quite as much as he thought. He shouldn't have been running operations. Not yet. Lemar had known it was a bad idea from the start. He'd tried to help, but with the council looking over his shoulder, judging everything, Arik had tried to do it all on his own. Which was understandable, really. But that didn't make things any easier now, for Lemar and his squad.

So, what do we do? "Our job is to create a distraction. Simple." Consider it done, really, though two minutes wasn't going to be enough. They had to draw this out as much as possible. Lemar leaned back against the crate and tried to think. If he breathed too deeply his chest hurt. He couldn't feel the left side of his face at all.

"Lemar?"

He couldn't concentrate, but his companions were looking at him as if he had all the answers. Most were hardly more than kids but there were a few with a bit of experience; why didn't they come up with something?

"Lemar?"

"Yes? What?"

Damn Arik. It shouldn't have come down to a pitched battle with constables but it was really the only option left. Either that or turn around and go back. But would a withdrawal leave the other two squads at risk?

Why were the constables even here? It was supposed to just be some private security. Had they been tipped off?

"We have to keep going," Lemar said. Not that he was going anywhere. He tried to sound confident.

This is no way to live. And certainly no way to die. Why didn't you listen to me, Arik?

Lemar wondered what he might have done differently. Not tonight, but in general. He wondered when he might have turned aside. There had been that woman... Janessa.

"Lemar."

His mind was wondering. Lemar tried to sit up straighter but didn't have the strength for it.

"Here it is then," he said. "If we go back... We could... All we need to do is last a few minutes. Then we can get out of here." They weren't going to get out, of course. If there were half a dozen constables here there'd probably be more not far away. Arik had killed the whole squad.

Donar was on his first operation. He was sixteen, wasn't he? "How old are you, Donar?"

"What? Seventeen."

Lemar nodded. This was no way to die. "Did you ever want to be a baker?" he asked. Janessa had been a baker. Or an apprentice baker anyway. Horrible hours, but she'd seemed to enjoy it.

"No."

"I wanted to be a pilot," Jommy said.

"I wanted to be a tailor," said another, a girl who looked calm beyond her years.

An older woman grunted but had a faraway look in her eyes.

Lemar nodded again. "Here's what you do," he said, feebly pushing the hilt of his sword out of the way and looking at each of his companions in turn. "You run. Get out of here."

"But—"

It wasn't Arik's fault. Not really. He shouldn't have been put in charge. He should've listened. Lemar had spotted Arik's potential long before anyone else. He'd tried to help him but there was only so much he could do. There was only so much anyone could do with the Council watching everything.

"Don't go back," Lemar said eventually. "They won't be happy, they won't forgive. They never do." He coughed up a dollop of blood, wiped at his mouth with the back of his hand. "Split up. Hide. Or, if you want, meet up at..." He tried to think. There was a tavern across the road from the bakery where Janessa worked. "Go to the Drinking Trough at High Peak. In six months. Meet there in six months."

Lemar looked around, barely able to move more than his eyes. "This is no way to live," he said. The others tried to lift him up but he waved them away.

This is no way to die.

Tribalin:
Skyway Man

I

The hulking, cast-iron monster looked into the night over the edge of the skyland, groaning and humming with internal tension. Bolts as large as dinner-plates pimpled the dark surface. Rust, like dandruff, flecked its shoulders. Braced and chained and wedged, it strained invisibly against its bonds.

Kade felt like the winch mechanism. Standing in the inland corner of the Local Yard, he strained silently against the invisible bonds that held him to this inconsequential skyland, to its insignificant people. He was the thief, but Whiparill had stolen ten years of his life.

There wasn't anything to see but Kade knew Tribalin was close by. It was as if the other skyland had a gravity all its own or a siren song he couldn't resist. A group of boys, milling about in the dust, knew as well. They looked from the winch to Whiparill's part-time soldiers to the Watch Tower, pointing at each shift in cloud beyond the wall. But to them it was just something to gawk at, it wasn't going to change their lives.

"Be a while yet before we dock."

Startled, angry, Kade snapped his attention away from the shifting clouds and looked around. He saw Laro climbing down from his lorry near the gate.

Kade tried to calm his breathing. *A little while longer. Soon, none of this will matter.* "What?"

The old man gestured to the Watch Tower as he went through the ritual of lighting his pipe. "We'll start to see some action up there before anything *really* happens."

The average skyland docked fairly regularly, and Whiparill was more average than most, so everyone knew how it worked. Everyone had seen it dozens of times before. Even so, the awe was evident in Laro's voice. It was evident in the faux casualness of the boys and the obvious impatience of all the other spectators. Two flying islands coming together like kissing leviathans was not a sight that one quickly grew bored with. Any other day Kade might have been as excited as everyone else. But not today. Not this time.

He took a deep breath, making himself wait, as the men and women in the Watch Tower finally started to move and talk.

A broad, gentle hill slowly materialized, shouldering through the clouds. Sequins of light illuminated buildings, creating a patchwork of the seen and unseen. Steam and smoke streamed out behind a dozen factory chimneys to disappear amongst the cloud. It seemed like a different world.

A spotter plane came in low over the moving hill, crystal engine buzzing. It flashed coded messages back to those on the ground, as if Whiparill could ever be a threat, then dipped its wing and disappeared into the cloud building up on Tribalin's leading edge.

The city loomed larger. Running lights marked the top of a high, encircling wall. The spotter plane buzzed past again.

Muffled shouts. Then the huge winch thumped, a sound like a punch in the chest, and sent a hook flying into the night. A cable whispered out behind. Kade knew a hook would be arching over from the far side as well and...

The hooks from Tribalin crashed into the housing outside Whiparill's truncated wall in a sharp metallic heartbeat that shook the ground. The few gas lamps amongst the crystal lights flickered and hissed. The boys covered their ears and squealed with delight, or hung their mouths open at the immensity of the sound.

The winch went to work before any of the spectators had recovered, reeling the hooks back in. The two skylands slowly, inexorably, drew together, like fishing boats with tangled nets.

The boys rushed towards the gate as if it would open at any moment, as if they would be allowed through. Up on the wall the soldiers paid some attention to their tasks for the first time. Men and women donned the domed helmets that Kade had made for them a few years earlier. They adjusted them so the short, flared wings were at precise angles. Cannons were adjusted as well, focusing on likely targets. Powder was added to pistol firing pans, bullets rammed home once more. If it came to a fight Whiparill would be overrun in a few minutes, but pride could do strange things.

Kade smoothed the collar on his brown, coarse woven shirt and straightened his shoulders. He checked his small pack to make sure the empty box and his purse were still inside. There was a change of clothes as well, plus some gloves and a woolen balaclava that would pass as a beanie to casual inspection. He took a deep breath.

"Do you want to earn a few extra doms, Kade?" Laro had put away his pipe and climbed back into his lorry. He was warming up the engine. Dust painted the air, billowing out from underneath as the crystals spun and whirred.

"Not today, Laro," Kade replied. "Today I'm on holiday."

"Just an hour to help unload the lorry. That's all I'm asking."

"Sorry."

"Get yourself a journeyman's tattal and you suddenly think you're better than the rest of us?"

Kade ran his hand over his shaven head and the crystal hawk-design imbedded in his skin. It was still slightly tender and swollen from the implanting process. He could feel the memory spaces in his mind, though he hadn't worked out how to access them yet. "Of course I'm better than you, Laro."

Laro grunted and switched the lorry into gear. He sent a small burst of power into the crystal engine. "Don't expect any free meals next time you're sick."

Kade shrugged. Laro's wife was a terrible cook anyway and her pies generally ended up in the trash. "I haven't had a holiday in a long time, so I'm not going to ruin it before I even start." The old man annoyed him as well, chattering and smoking constantly.

As the lorry pulled away, Kade looked back through the night across the width of Whiparill, over the fields and paddocks, towards the smithy and workshop near the gate on the far side. He couldn't see it, of course, and hoped to never see it again, but it was stuck in the back of his mind like a lodestone. It was a promise. A threat. The other direction, Tribalin was the same, the opposite.

The Secretary appeared on top of the watchtower and conducted a shouted conversation with her Tribalin counterpart as the winches ground to a halt. When she was done, she adjusted the two clocks on the back of her tower.

"Two days, four hours," Kade said to himself. One way or the other, it would be enough. They may want him to go back to Whiparill for a short time after the job was done, but he hoped not. He was done with the place.

The crystal cables from each skyland were being connected. Information would soon be transferring across: schedules, entries, exits, births, deaths, marriages and a thousand other pieces of news and correspondence that were slowly making their way around the world, from skyland to skyland, like a disease.

A few minutes later, Kade walked out of the Local Yard onto the paved dock. He looked around though there was nothing to see. The covered bridge across to the other skyland had already been lowered and people were moving through. Even as he watched, the Tribalin bridge thumped onto the ground as well, thickening the storm of dust that had already built up. The Quartermaster was the first person to come through from the other side. He sat in the passenger seat of a small, enclosed crystal-cruiser. Tattals covered most of his scalp but he had allowed his hair to grow through a gap in the patterns. His official robes were missing the left sleeve, showing an entire arm covered with the curling silvery designs. A younger man was driving the cruiser and trying to sort through a bulging file at the same time. People stood aside to let them pass. Hundreds of pages, each covered in small, neat writing, threatened to fly everywhere.

By the time Kade crossed the bridge and joined the queue in the Tribalin Local Yard, customs officers were already talking to Laro. The old man produced a contract from a local merchant and allowed his wristal to be scanned. Then he had to wait while they conducted a search of his lorry.

Indicating crystals flashed green as a sniffer was passed over the sacks of grain. Two random sacks were sliced open. The papers were examined again and compared to the information, supplied by both the buyer and seller, which came up on the scanner.

Kade looked around.

A dozen soldiers lined the angled walls, creating a field of fire between them. They held blunderbusses, with short flared barrels that sprayed shot over a wide area. Everyone passing through Tribalin customs was being told that they didn't really matter; if trouble broke out, nobody would be safe. The weapons were held at precise angles. Uniforms were pristine. Helmets and the swords gleamed in the lamplight.

Finally, Laro paid the taxes and the lorry was waved through. Everyone shuffled forward. Whiparill had a population of little more than two hundred, but it seemed most of those people were in line ahead of Kade. He shuffled forward some more. And each step took him further from Whiparill.

"Why are you visiting Tribalin?" the customs officer asked Kade when his turn finally came. The man was a corporal, with a disk shaped tattal the same size as Kade's on the very crown on his head. The patterns, raised slightly above the skin, sparkled as if they'd just been polished.

"Just visiting." He remembered the first time he'd gone through customs. He had not yet broken any laws but still had trouble controlling his heart. That was two lifetimes ago, and it felt it. He couldn't help smiling at the nervous boy he'd been.

"Wristal, please."

Kade held out his left hand, palm up. The memory crystal embedded in his wrist was surrounded by a narrow band of tattals, as tender as those in his scalp. He allowed it to be scanned.

"Kade Traskel?"

"Yes."

"You've never visited Tribalin before?" The man flicked some switches on his scanner and could see for himself. There would be only one lie in the information flashing up on the scanner's LCD but, hopefully, large chunks of the truth would be absent. The secret to telling a good lie was to tell the truth as often as possible.

"That's right."

He'd grown up on Girindult, a tiny metalworking skyland. As part of the Last Chance Archipelago, it moved along the wind-lanes between Rookery Reef, High Plain and Wind Haven. Then he'd spent a couple of years on Dassellaron before moving to Whiparill to work in the skyland's smithy. In between he'd had short visits to a handful of other places.

"Why now?" The customs officer flicked another switch.

Kade smiled and rubbed his hand over his new tattal. "Celebrating my promotion."

"And you're intending to return to Whiparill?"

All the information would have been passed through from the customs officers on Whiparill who had scanned his Wristal as he entered the Local Yard.

"Yes."

"What's in the pack?"

Kade showed him. As expected the man poked through the contents but didn't look too closely.

"Anything in your pockets?"

"No."

A second officer conducted a quick search, patting down Kade's clothes, looking quickly at the soles of his boots. Finding nothing, he gave his companion the thumbs up.

"Gate tax, please."

Kade handed over the money.

"You know the count?"

"Two days and four hours."

The customs officer nodded and cleared the scanner's screen, though Kade's arrival would have been registered in the system. "All right then, on your way."

Kade nodded and walked away, keeping his pace measured and even. It was all so easy. He hadn't committed a crime in more than ten years, but it was like he'd never left. He exited the Local Yard with a knot of people and stopped in the square beyond to stare with the rest of them.

Dusk was more than four hours gone but the crystal-lamps lit a riot of color and movement. People argued and shouted and laughed. Shops and stalls lined either side of the street, striped awnings reaching out over the wide sidewalks as if to grab the passers-by and draw them inside. Despite the hour, everything was open and doing a roaring trade. There was a watchmaker and a glasscutter. The aroma of honey from a bakery vied with throat-scratching acid from a silversmith. There were cafes, supermarkets and jewel makers.

Kade felt he was being overwhelmed. He'd seen cities far larger than Tribalin, but those times were locked away behind ten years in a small town with furnaces and anvils, hammers and sparks. They had all happened to someone else, to a kid with the whole world at his feet.

But lessons learned in the dark, smoky halls of Girindult had not been forgotten. Maybe he no longer had the world at his feet, but he'd kept up his training for just this occasion. The Skyway Men had told him his stay on Whiparill would be short term and he'd spent ten years waiting to hear something else, but now they had finally called him back. With a smile, he straightened his shoulders and looked around once more.

A young trainee priestess, with clinging curls of hair, hurried past, eyes on the ground. The tiny bells tied to her robes left a shower of sound in her wake. Nearer, two hopeful looking youths, smelling of cheap aphrodisiac, leaned against a statue of a broad shouldered, imposing man. Kade examined the plaque, knowing what to expect.

"Gafol Martinol. The first to see what needed to be done. The first to do it." Kade could guess the story.

Thousands of years ago, when Tribalin had been just another town on the world below when Gafol Martinol, the mayor, or perhaps just a man of vision, had grown tired of fighting off the Wilders and decided to do something about it. So he buried ten of the largest crystal engines ever built and used them to tear Tribalin free of the world, flying it into the sky where it would be safe. Every skyland had a similar story about their little chunk of real estate being the first to break free. There was no evidence to support anyone. Kade didn't know why they cared.

Gafol Martinol may really have been great for all Kade knew, but the statue was terrible. They hadn't cleaned up where the mold seam had been and, perversely, there were rub marks all over the bronze. Martinol also seemed to have a very crooked face. Even as an apprentice, Kade would have been embarrassed to show such a poor piece of work in public.

Above the statue and the people, the awnings and the street art, the walls of the city were stark and menacing. They were covered in soot and grime that made them hard to distinguish from the darkness. Even the occasional lamp shining through a window did little more than point out the gloom. Along the street, he could see a smokestack leaving a grey smudge in the white of the clouds. Tribalin was just like Whiparill—dirty and smelly—only different. It wasn't special in any but the most mundane ways.

The sound of a lorry horn brought Kade's mind back to his immediate surroundings. He shifted off the road to let the vehicle pass, and a cruiser behind it, then tried to get his bearings. He'd memorized the location of the tavern but it took a moment for him to match the ink and paper in his mind with the reality around him.

He spotted the street he was after.

Kade turned right at the next corner, towards the aft end of the skyland. The street was narrower here, barely five metres across, as if impressing tourists was no longer the aim of the urban planning. All the authorities wanted here was fit in as many buildings as possible.

Crystal-lamps punctuated the darkness. Balconies on either side leaned out so far they almost touched. Clotheslines went from wall to wall like giant spider webs, waiting to snare unwary blouses. Windows had been thrown open, trying to entice the stifling, still air of the street-canyon inside.

A lorry nudged out of a parking garage. The driver, half asleep, leaned out the window as he swung the wheel and tried to miss the opposite wall. The crystal engine, long overdue for a reshaping, whined and rattled. Standing in a wedge of space between two buildings, back against a dripping down-pipe, Kade waited until the street was clear then continued on.

The route he followed led generally up hill and at one stage he stopped to look back. Nothing was really visible, just the sharp, dark lines of buildings slicing through cloud and diffused lamplight alike. He sighed and walked again.

Around one corner and down an alley with piles of rubbish underfoot, walls crowding close on either side. Kade ran the tips of his fingers along a wall for a moment and brought them away slick with grease and dark with erstwhile smog. Around another corner. Across a square with cracked cobbles and an open drain. A crystal air-conditioner, at least fifty years out of date, whined and clicked in a corner.

The tavern wasn't much further. The *Leaf and Stone* was a tired looking place with a sagging porch on the front and a small, full parking area on the side. The patrons were tired and sagging and full as well. A couple looked up blearily as Kade entered but most didn't pay any attention.

With only a cursory glance, Kade knew his contacts hadn't yet arrived. They would blend in, but would still be obvious enough to someone who knew what to look for. The clock above the bar said it was almost twenty-two bells past dawn; he was early. Finding a vacant table at the back he sat down and ordered a drink.

The table, the seat and the glass were all dirty. It looked like they hadn't been washed in days. The drink, on the other hand, tasted like soapy water. Kade sat back to wait, letting the feel of the tavern wash over him. There was none of the friendly banter that filled both of Whiparill's two small taverns at all hours of the day but, if you were the type who wanted solitude, that wasn't a bad thing. There were spider webs near the ceiling and dusty spirit bottles behind the bar. There was a broken floorboard in the corner with a weed growing up through the gap. But there were strangers. He could sit there and know there were people in the room that didn't know all the details of his life. For the first time in many years Kade was with other people and still alone. It was a wonderful feeling to be completely anonymous.

Nursing the same drink half an hour later, Kade was starting to wonder if he would ever get used to the stench. It was like someone had thrown up a week ago and nobody had bothered to clean up, which was entirely possible. Everyone was watching him suspiciously. He was hungry and thirsty but unwilling to fix either problem in the *Leaf and Stone*. And he couldn't leave until contacted.

Looking at the clock on the wall he decided he should have been on his way to do the job some time ago. Either the Skyway Men were much more relaxed than they had been or something had gone wrong...

Kade waited another fifteen minutes then got up and made his way slowly to the door. He examined each of the tavern's patrons as he went, giving an inconspicuous signal to anyone who caught his eye. Nobody returned the signal. Outside he breathed deeply, trying to clear the stench from his nostrils. He didn't know if that would ever be possible.

"What the hell am I supposed to do?" he muttered. He had the box in his pack so he could go to the address that was written on it and tell the person there what had happened. It was probably the local Operations Manager and they'd obviously know what to do. But he also knew the address of the job. Instead of turning up and asking for help, he could do the job, save the day and be back in the good books for fixing someone else's mistake. Kade smiled. That sounded like a much better plan. He knew a way for one man to get into the laboratory, he knew what they were after. He knew what success would get him. If he failed, on the other hand...

But he wouldn't fail.

II

It wasn't far to the laboratory. Further up the long, low hill, along narrow ancient streets. It was on the first floor with a factory beneath and another above. The building, with no others adjoining it, looked much the same as every other Kade had passed, except there were no windows at all and two guards stood outside the only door. There was another man atop a small, raised platform on the other side of the street. All three held muskets and racks behind them kept lines of blunderbusses ready and waiting. It was unlikely they'd ever have to use the swords, gleaming like a strip of dawn at their sides.

Kade continued to climb the hill, wishing he had a weapon of some kind. He should have bought a dagger, or stolen one.

Two of the guards watched him approach, the other, towards the aft, kept an eye out for trouble coming from the opposite direction.

Kade smiled at one of the men as he breached the triangle and nodded a silent greeting. No reply.

The next street was 'one way' and hardly a street at all. Small lorries wouldn't have a lot of room to move. Kade turned right, around the end of the laboratory. He went to the building across the other side of the street and tried the door. It was locked, but the mechanism was simple enough. Pulling his purse from his pack he removed one of the smaller denomination doms, had a quick look around, and cracked the fake crystal against the corner of the doorjamb. It crumbled, revealing the three small, dark metal pins of a lock-pick.

The lock gave in to his ministrations in less than a minute, just like old times, and Kade slipped through into a stairwell that seemed to echo back even the smallest sound. He climbed, slowly, carefully, pausing on each landing to cock his head and listen. On the first floor, the lamp lighting the four doors whined and spluttered, flickering fitfully with a cracked cylinder. On the next floor the lamp didn't work at all, but illumination fought its way through the dirty window overlooking the street and a door was underlined with light. Muffled voices came from beyond. Laughter. Life. Next level, the lamp showed a door off its hinges and graffiti scrawled on the wall. *Kerig's moved. Don't bother me.* And, *She's like the air to me— foul and thick.*

The fourth floor was dark as well. Kade leaned out the window at the top of the stairwell to look. A pair of lovers strolled along the street below. A lorry, laden with barrels, one crystal headlamp broken, edged between the crowding walls. When it was gone, nothing else moved.

Kade pulled on his gloves and mask and shifted his pack around to wear on his chest. He climbed out, standing on a ledge with his toes hanging out over nothing. He calmed his breathing. This was nothing he hadn't done before. It was exactly the type of thing he'd been dreaming of for ten years. This was where he was meant to be. This was the life Lemar had stolen from him.

A lot of the city was spread out below, but most of it blended into a smudge of grey and black that was barely visible through the clouds. At the very front of the skyland, the Flight Tower and Administration Complex blazed brightly. To the left, to port, Kade glimpsed Whiparill through the haphazard constructions. It was about a kilometre away. From his position it just looked like more of the same. Another skyland was away to starboard. There was nothing to suggest which one it might be, but it seemed to be preparing to undock.

Down on the street three green-robed Pundits paused to lean against each other and sing a bawdy song that never seemed to get far past the chorus. Someone shouted at the men, but they took that as encouragement and sang all the louder.

Kade decided they wouldn't see him even if he fell from the ledge and landed at their feet. He closed his eyes for a moment then slowly sidestepped along the wall. Eventually, he reached a balcony and climbed the rail. His hands were covered with grease and grime. His back must have been black with the stuff, but there was little he could do. He switched his pack back again.

The roof of the laboratory building opposite was almost level with Kade's position. The distance wasn't great, but with no room for a running start it would be a close thing. Kade inspected the rail that came out from the wall. It was a fairly basic thing with simple curling balusters and bad welds. He would have done better in the first year of his apprenticeship, but at least it would give him two steps...

Kade had studied maps and plans supplied by the Skyway Men and knew there were no other realistic options to enter the building unnoticed. There were several things he could've done to make the task easier but he hadn't thought he'd be doing this without assistance. He climbed onto the thin metal rail, got his balance, "Here's to simple men and simple plans," and surged forward. The first step made the rail shake and screech in protest. The second brought a loud crack and a thrum of vibrating metal. He pushed off into the nothing as the rail collapsed beneath him.

And he was gone.

He wanted to close his eyes, but that was stupid.

He closed his eyes.

For a moment.

When he opened them again he wondered if he'd moved at all. The laboratory roof didn't seem to be getting any closer.

Then he *was* moving. Too quickly. Sailing through the air. Not going to make it.

Kade slammed into the edge of the roof. Winded, legs hanging over nothing. He tried to breathe, scrabbled for purchase, gritted his teeth against the pain of damaged ribs. The singers in the street below fell suddenly silent as Kade continued to search for something to hold onto. Reaching. Desperate. He slipped lower.

"What was that?" one of the Pundits asked.

"What was what?"

He found the edge of a tile with a flailing hand, grabbed on and stopped. Still. Silent as well. He tried to look down. Had he been spotted?

"What was them words you were singing, Marat?"

"My pappy taught me them words when I was a boy."

"Was he drunk when he did it?"

"Probably." Marat didn't seem to care. He started to sing again and the three men continued their loud, discordant stagger down the street.

Kade breathed a painful sigh of relief and carefully pulled himself up onto the roof. Over the edge and onto the tiles he curled into a ball. Struggling to control his breathing he wondered if he could stay right where he was. But he couldn't. There was work to do. He crawled to the cell cluster arranged in the centre of the roof.

A noise.

Kade paused, listening, and almost yelped in surprise when a handful of pigeons launched themselves skywards from among the cells. He waited, breath held, hand to his aching chest, to see if anyone had noticed the commotion. Seconds ticked by and he started to breathe again.

The cells—metal boxes that housed the crystal arrays— made up a security system that would be beyond most thieves. But Whiparill didn't have a permanent crystal-engineer so Kade had done what he could over the past ten years, reading books and learning as he went. He didn't have any qualifications, but he knew enough.

He spent five minutes locating the tamper array and, reversing one of his lock-pick pins, started to work on the screws. When the side finally came away, the crystals were revealed. A power cube, two cylinders, a cone and pyramid were bonded to a sphere. The whole arrangement hummed softly.

A minor change in the alignment of crystals could completely change the nature of an array and therefore the nature of a machine. It might turn the tamper array into a light, or a plate warmer, or something that didn't yet have a name. It could also set the alarm off or turn it into nothing more than a group of pointless crystals.

Holding his breath, he carefully spun the pyramid to the right. Not too far. The humming stopped. Nothing else happened. Kade started to breathe again and went to work on the next step. Black marks from his soot-covered gloves told the tale of the work he'd done. Fifteen minutes later he had opened five cells and rearranged seven crystals. Nothing had happened in the meantime and he took that as a good sign.

Finally done, Kade took a deep, painful breath and started to remove one of the roof tiles, gently wiggling it back and forth until the joiner broke and he could pull it clear. Three more quickly followed, leaving a hole large enough to climb through. Ribs screaming, Kade lowered himself into the ceiling cavity. He broke through some plaster and three minutes later was on the top floor, crouching in the shadows near a large, crystal-run loom. Strips of light stretched away from arrays set into the wall. He could hear nothing over the sound of his own ragged breathing. Nothing moved.

There was another cluster beneath a bench in the centre of the room. Kade pushed himself to his feet and went to look. When he pulled apart the first cell it took him several seconds to work out that the alarm wasn't even turned on.

With a shrug, Kade undid the eight screws that held the cluster to the floor and carefully dragged the whole thing out of the way. Beneath was a hole and, with a prophetic wince for his ribs, he ducked down under the bench and put his feet into the laboratory below. As he lowered himself, he was too busy thinking about pain to take much notice of anything else. It wasn't until he was crouching on top of a table that he heard anything at all. It was a moment longer before he realized there was someone in the laboratory with him.

Swearing silently, Kade slipped down to the floor and tried to assess the situation.y lights.

The room took up the entire level of the building. A dozen solid workbenches were arranged in several groups. Centrifuges and moulds, lathes, a crystalis and naked arrays threw crazy shadows. Temperance clusters guarded each corner of a platform used to keep experimental arrays under control. Shelves lined an entire wall and three men, dressed in black, hooded, were examining the contents.

Kade hadn't been spotted and he wasn't about to announce himself. These men had to be those he was supposed to meet in the *Leaf and Stone*, but that didn't really help. The men would probably react quickly and violently if they saw him, not waiting to check his identity. Kade was one wrong move, just a couple of seconds, away from death.

Looking down at his hand, he noticed that his fingers were shaking. He was sweating beneath his balaclava. His heart was racing. And he finally realized that things *had* changed while he lived on Whiparill. *He* had changed. Fitting back into his old life was not going to be a simple matter of just turning up and doing the things that needed to be done.

Kade took a deep breath and watched the men as he tried to think.

One of them collected a cell about the size of a large book and stuffed it into a pack while the others rifled through a filing cabinet. They found what they were after, a thick file held in a black box.

Kade wondered what he should do. Wait until they'd left? Then slip out and tell the Operations Manager that he hadn't been contacted? Or announce himself and risk a sword between his ribs before anyone had a chance to think? Trapped by indecision, trying to control his breathing, he crouched in the shadows. His fingers still drummed a silent tattoo against his leg. He thought he was going to throw up.

When they started to leave, any options Kade thought he had suddenly disappeared. They walked right past his hiding place.

"What's that?" The soft lisp of a dagger being drawn.

Kade's first reaction was to freeze, hoping the men would not see him. That was never going to work. His second reaction was to jump to his feet and charge. That wasn't much better.

He dropped his shoulder into the first man's solar plexus, knocked him to the ground. The knife clattered away. Kade's ribs screamed some more and he almost blacked out. But he kept his feet and spun.

"I'm Kade Traskel," he said, blocking a lunge from the second man. Kicked high. Gasped with pain.

The man snapped out a punch.

Kade swayed out of the way. Instinct made him grab the hand and twist. A finger cracked, bent all the way back. The man hissed. Kade pivoted, drove his knee into his opponent's stomach. He followed up with an elbow to the head, a knee to the head—unconscious—and spun again.

He stared down the barrel of the pistol.

"I'm Kade," he said again, sucking in air. "I waited for you at the *Leaf and Stone*."

"I know who you are." The man's eyes, all that could be seen behind his mask, flickered away, went wide. "Shit."

Kade swallowed.

But the man wasn't looking at Kade. He shook his head, "Sorry," he whispered, tensed and fired. The gunshot rang out loudly in the confined space, echoed back.

Kade jumped and felt a flash of pain. It was his ribs. Only his ribs. As acrid smoke drifted up from the pistol, he turned around and saw a guard hitting the ground near the door. The shooter had already discarded his useless pistol. His companions were armed as well.

Kade didn't move. The man he'd knocked down in his original charge was upright again, muttering something as he helped his semi-conscious companion. Kade already forgotten, the three men headed for the door; apparently they thought they had bigger problems.

"I was supposed to meet you," Kade shouted, desperate.

They were gone in moments with just one glance back, and Kade still wasn't sure what had just happened. He looked at the shelves. The cell he was after was still there—they had taken the wrong one—but it was the size of a scooter engine. It was supposed to fit in the box he had in his pack. He had no idea what was happening.

"Thorn, damn it." The Skyway Men definitely weren't going to be happy, one way or the other. And the god of thunder and lightning wasn't likely to help, one way or the other.

Gunshots rang out. Two of them. Three. A scream. A shout of inquiry from out on the street. Reinforcements would be on their way.

The job wasn't going as well as it might. *Just like old times,* he thought. His bosses weren't going to be impressed, but maybe they wouldn't be surprised. He was on the edge of hysterical laughter. Everything was going to hell.

Kade collected a pistol from the fallen guard. Checked it was fully cocked and the firing pan was still full beneath the frizzen. He pushed out through the door onto the landing. No sound. Down the stairs, slowly, one at a time, pausing now and then to listen. A guard lay dead at the bottom in a pool of blood. His twisted right leg held open the door to the building's ground floor factory. The door had a lock. It should have been locked. Kade inched forward, pistol at the ready. He heard something, a scraping, and carefully poked his head around the corner.

He was just in time to see square of concrete flooring drop down into a hole and fit snugly in place. It was indistinguishable from another couple of dozen such squares that made up the entire floor. For all intents and purposes there was nothing special about it at all. From close up, Kade could see tiny scratches on the floor where the block had slid along, but nothing else. Nobody would know. And there was no way to get the block up again from this side.

He swore again and wondered if he could salvage the situation. If the guards hadn't been alerted. If he hadn't been injured. If he had more time... But there wasn't time. No time. He was out of options but the fact that secrecy was obviously no longer a concern gave him the best chance of getting out alive. Ten years out of the game had taken away his edge. He had a lot of work to do to get back to where he had once been but first, he had to do was make it out of this mess alive. He laughed. *Easy.*

Kade returned to the guard blocking the door. He picked up the man's pistol and slung his bandolier over his shoulder. He quickly loaded the weapon, spilling powder all over the floor and ramming the ball home with unnecessary force. He tried to hook the half empty powder bag back onto the bandolier but his hands betrayed him. He discarded it and clamped his fist around shaking fingers.

"Now what?"

There was at least one man remaining outside. Soon, there would be more. Kade's heart was pounding.

Grunting in pain, eyes watering, he heaved the dead man to his feet and stood him in front of the door that led onto the street. For a moment, he balanced the guard with one blood-slicked hand on his shoulder. Then he pushed him forward and crouched back out of the way.

A shout from outside. A single shot from the podium across the street.

Kade dived through the still open door, rolled painfully down the two stairs. He came up onto his knees on the worn cobbles of the street.

The guard had thrown down one blunderbuss and collected another. He didn't have time to use it. Kade aimed with his right hand. No sign of shaking now. Solid. Steady. He fired.

The guard screamed and fell but Kade had already forgotten about him. Gun smoke stung his eyes. The bitter taste clogged his throat. It hurt to breathe. He shifted his focus to the pistol in his left hand and scanned his surroundings.

Nothing.

Shoving the used pistol in his belt Kade changed the other to his right hand and moved quickly to the man he'd shot. The guard had taken the primed blunderbuss with him when he fell. Kade collected it and scanned his surroundings again.

Movement. Just down the hill, an old man trying to hide in a doorway. Huddled in the shadows, eyes wide with fear.

A witness. Kade aimed and fired without thinking.

Second pistol in his belt, blunderbuss ready, he looked around. Nothing to see, but at least a dozen men were coming; he could hear the heavy tramp of their feet.

Turning quickly, he strode down the hill, sparing a glance for the old man and the rivulets of blood that ran between the pavers. He quickened the pace until he was almost running. His heart was thundering in his chest.

Kade's first job in ten years had *not* gone well.

III

He chose streets at random. He didn't care where he went, as long as it was away from the laboratory. This way, that. Through a short, narrow alley. Across a patch of bare dirt. Each shadow hid potential enemies, each patch of light exposed him.

As soon as he was sure there was no immediate pursuit, Kade dumped the blunderbuss and crouched in the shadows to reload the two pistols. He scanned his surroundings as he worked. He spilled more powder, then dropped the bag of shot. A dozen balls rolled out onto the road. They looked like pearls of blood in the dim streetlights.

A cruiser hummed past.

Forget the scattered balls. Move. Don't think about what happened.

Through a residential area where narrow houses butted shoulder-to-shoulder and sick, drooping plants crowded the dooryards. Between two rows of factories. Past a brooding, boarded-up warehouse and across a canal via a hump-backed bridge.

A siren blared back the way he'd come, cutting through the night and smog. A bi-plane buzzed overhead, so low it almost clipped the top of a building. Another followed a moment later. How they'd help from up there was anyone's guess.

Kade was back amongst houses again. These ones were larger but in no better condition. Smoke and grime coated everything with dark, gritty reality. Death crouched in the corners and clung under the eaves.

Don't think.

The street ended in a small square. Wrought-iron seats and tables, all rusting and badly made, huddled beneath umbrellas. There were half a dozen huge ceramic pots, two metres across but only half a metre high, spread about on the worn cobbles. It looked as if they'd once contained plants and shrubs, but now they were filled with decorations that could better handle the conditions. One sported Mer Poles, the ribbons and bells hanging limp in the still air. No god was likely to notice at all. No god would help. Kade swallowed, licked his dry lips. In another pot a cheap light-array walked lazy circles on the back of a wheeled cell. It sprayed random flashes of sickly, half-light—now lighting up the front of a foundry, now painting the underside of the clouds, now attempting to bring life to the Mer Poles. In a third pot were statues. A bronze soldier stood guard while a second checked an injured companion. They were life sized, and in the darkness could almost have been real. The injured one probably wouldn't make it.

Kade gagged, doubled over, threw up. He leaned on the back of a seat and spat bile. He heaved in a breath and hardly even noticed the pain from his ribs. He spat again and closed his eyes.

Last week he'd been working with the farmers on Whiparill, repairing ploughs, making fancy candlesticks to sell in the market and working with crystals when he had to. Ten years he'd done that. Ten years, waiting for the Skyway Men to call him back again. Ten years of slowly, day by day, wearing away his sharp edges. He'd given up hope years ago, though he'd kept telling himself to wait for just one more month. Just one more. And they'd called him back and nothing had changed but it wasn't quite as he remembered. He'd seen men killed, he'd killed, and all of it hurt. The two pistols were still in his belt, the cold hard touch of them a reminder of the night. Kade pulled one of the offending objects out and threw it at the feet of the guarding soldier. He pulled the bandolier over his head and threw that as well. The second gun was in his hand before he finally started to think. He was most probably the only suspect in a crime that he didn't actually commit. Well, he *did* kill two people. That was something that was going to take some getting used to.

He laughed at that. It was a painful, strangled sound. "The Skyway Men are going to kill me anyway." He had only survived ten years ago because not even the Skyway Men could hold him completely accountable for what had happened. But, even then, a second chance had been highly unlikely. And now he wanted a third chance?

He took a deep breath and fingered the shining silver lock of the pistol. He pushed the frizzen out of the way and pulled the trigger. The hammer fell home, going though the motions with no spark to make it meaningful. Even so, the click was loud in the still air. If echoed back off the buildings. Gunpowder flew from the pan, wasted.

"Thorn." He didn't want to talk to his superiors. He didn't want to tell them he'd failed again but didn't see that he had a choice. He could either try to convince them he could fix the problem or return to Whiparill to await his execution.

Kade wiped his mouth on his greasy, grimy sleeve and almost threw up again. The smell of the city clung to him like a dying rat. He spat and wiped his face on the front of his shirt instead; it was cleaner than the rest. With a deep breath, he half-cocked the pistol again, snapped the frizzen back into place, and shoved the weapon into his belt. He collected the discarded items but then wondered what to do next. It was all very well deciding to talk to the Skyway Men, but he had to find them first. He knew nobody on Tribalin and he...

The box was still in his pack. He was supposed to use it to post the cell. There was an address already printed on the front. Pulling the box free he strode from the square in search of someone who could give him directions.

Back at the Local Yard only one café remained open, though nobody sat at the sidewalk tables. It was still and quiet. How the world had changed since he'd first boarded Tribalin.

An old man sat on the step in front of the bakery. He didn't look anything like the old man he'd killed, but still Kade looked away quickly. There was a lorry was parked outside the supermarket and three men were unloading.

"Excuse me," Kade said, crossing quickly to the truck. He was surprised his voice wasn't shaking. He was surprised the man standing on the tailgate could see past all the blood on his hands.

"What can I do for you? We don't need any help."

Kade managed a short hollow laugh. "Actually, I need help. I'm after some directions."

If the man was at all suspicious he didn't show it. "Right then. I might be able to help." He lifted another box down to one of his companions then dusted off his hands on his dusty shirt. "Where are you going?"

When Kade named the street he was given detailed directions as only a delivery driver could give.

"Thank you."

Kade headed towards the centre of Tribalin, looking for the aerodrome and every step he took seemed to make breathing easier. When they had originally broken free of the world below people had quickly realized that fumes and smells were swept to the aft of skylands more often than not. About five minutes after that, everyone started trying to move forward. Soon, it became a way of life. On Tribalin there were still factories forward of the keel, but that was slowly changing. Every little bit helped.

When he found the aerodrome he paused to look at the twin-engine bi-planes parked in a neat line along the fence. Two were warming up with pilots listening to shouted instructions from the ground crew. Then they were gone, out onto the runway and clawing their way into the air. Down the far end, a zeppelin was preparing to lift off as well.

Suddenly, a foghorn sounded, seeming to shake the night. Four long slow blasts, a mournful cry in the night. It was the signal for an Emergency Undock. Within half an hour Tribalin and Whiparill would be separating, despite the days and hours still remaining on the Dock Count. Kade had a horrible feeling the undocking was a result of the robbery. He had a horrible feeling he was way out of his depth.

He looked back the way he'd come, as if he was actually considering running back to his old way of life. He could use any form of public transport for free to get back to his home skyland on time. But he wouldn't find any public transport at this hour. He could walk the distance easy enough; it was no more than a kilometre as the crow flies. But he wouldn't do that either. He had to clean up the mess or all the running in the world wouldn't help at all.

A security guard, loaded down with weapons and leading a dog, wandered a path between the line of planes and the fence, watching suspiciously.

Instinctively, Kade staggered and grabbed onto the wire. "Hey," he said, slurring his voice. "Can you give me a lift home?" The fence trembled along with his hands.

The guard grunted and shook his head. "Go home, you idiot."

"What d' you think I'm trying t' do?" Kade looked one way along the fence then the other. "Where am I, anyway?"

The guard kept walking and Kade went the other way. When he was out of sight he made sure the pistols were still properly hidden beneath his shirt and picked up the pace.

Half a kilometre further and he found himself in a park with plants that actually looked healthy. His mind told him to keep moving but his feet slowly dragged to a stop. He stood beneath an oak tree with roots that broke the ground all around like veins on a wrist.

Life.

Kade could smell it. It was fresh and cool. He could taste it, green on his tongue. Flowers and shrubs gamely held back the stench. The sting was gone from his eyes. He had never felt settled on Whiparill, always waiting for a call from the Skyway Men to move him on, but the garden brought back memories of the small forest near Whiparill's tail fin, the fields, and the quiet of the village. He closed his eyes, breathed deeply and wished for home.

The horn sounded again, three times. Fifteen minutes till undock. Time was slipping away. Kade crossed the park, took his bearings on the spire of the Flight Tower, and turned slightly to starboard.

The horn had blown the double repetition and then the final undocking signal before he knew exactly where he was. Ten minutes after that he found the house he was after; the mark on the top right of the doorframe confirmed it. It wasn't a large place but it was semi-detached and there was enough room for a small cruiser to be driven down the side.

Kade stood across the street in a pool of darkness between two humming lamps. He thought of waiting, but not for any sensible reason. He just wanted to delay the inevitable. Perhaps he wasn't completely to blame for this failure, just like the last time, but it certainly felt like it. It was doubtful anyone would care. But he'd spent too long waiting for the opportunity to give up now. He could fix the problem, if he could work out what was going on. He could make the Skyway Men see that he could still be useful. He could at least get to keep breathing.

With a sigh, Kade stepped out of the shadows and headed for the narrow driveway. A light appeared in the neighbor's widow.

A woman, getting an early start to the day, drove past. The cruiser, not yet warmed up, hummed too loudly and lurched down the street.

More lights came on.

Kade nervously crossed the street and made his way down the driveway to a small yard around the back. It looked over the still, green waters of a canal. There was a battered, single seat cruiser parked beneath a tilting, tile roof. A water barrel occupied the corner near the door.

Kade knocked on the door, wondering if the timid blows would be heard. He scooped water from the barrel with a bucket and washed his face and hands while he waited. He was about to knock again when sounds from inside reached him. He stood back and waited.

The door opened a crack.

"Mistress Kiri Mirani?" Kade said into the heavy silence that ensued. "I'm Kade Traskel. Wif sent me."

The door opened a little bit more and a woman's face was revealed. She was about fifty years old with a double chin and a three-haired mole on her cheek. A garland of tattaled flowers encircled her head.

"Wif sent you?" She straightened her shapeless green and brown dress over her large form.

"Yes, ma'am." Kade stared at his shoes.

"That code's well and truly out of date." Kiri disappeared from view, letting the door swing slowly open of its own accord.

Inside was a low roofed kitchen. Kiri started working at a scarred, stained table, mixing batter with huge jiggling arms. A sparkling tattal circled her entire forearm. Pots and pans hung from the wall behind her like a constellation of full moons. She set another pan on the ancient gas stove to heat.

"Not the most sensible time to turn up, you know, love," Kiri said as she continued to work.

"Sorry, ma'am." He noticed the front of his shirt was stained with blood.

"Well, I suppose we can say you were looking for Roker." She shrugged. "Come on, come in. Standing on the steps won't help." She gestured at his shirt. "I assume that's someone else's blood?"

"A bit of both. Mainly someone else's." Kade lifted his shirt as he stepped into the warmth of the kitchen. A dark, livid bruise marked the left side of his chest. The skin had been broken and a stream of dry blood led all the way down across his stomach.

"Ouch," Kiri set down her mixing spoon. "Could have been worse though, if you didn't have all that muscle." She cocked her head to the side. "Broken rib?"

He shrugged and winced in pain.

"Here, cut a lemon." Kiri gestured to a bowl of fruit with her chin as she went to pour batter into the pan.

Kade found a knife and did as he had been asked, nearly slicing off the tip of his finger in the process. The knife continued to shake after he'd set it down.

"Plates are above the sink."

"Oh. Right." He got a plate and put the four slices of lemon on the edge. "I didn't get the array," he said a moment later, concentrating as he adjusted a wedge to a more exact angle.

Kiri looked back over her shoulder, examined him with a strange expression. "You don't like pancakes?"

"I love pancakes."

Kiri raised her eyebrows and looked pointedly at the single plate on the table. Kade got another.

"There's syrup in one of those tins near the cooler if you prefer."

"Thank you, yes." Kade felt like a boy again, though neither motherly women nor pancakes had featured during that part of his life.

"Good. Well, get rid of those pistols and get us two stools."

Kade took off his pack and set it on the floor, then took out the weapons. He didn't immediately put them down, wondering if she just wanted to get him unarmed. Eventually, he did as he was told and sat down at the table. A moment later a plump pancake slapped down onto his plate. Steam rose enticingly and his mouth started to water. He suddenly felt as if he hadn't eaten in a week. He spread around a big dollop of the thick, golden syrup, rolled the pancake and took a bite. It was just about the best thing he'd ever eaten. He didn't stop until his fingers were sweet and sticky and the last soggy crumbs had disappeared.

"Hungry?" Kiri asked as she sat down as well. "Why don't you tell me what happened while I eat this."

Kade suddenly became nervous again.

"I like you, Kade," Kiri said as she squeezed a wedge of lemon, releasing a bitter tang into the air. "You've got more manners than most people who knock on my door. And the fact that you're here at all says a lot as well. Just tell me what happened."

"I waited at the tavern but nobody contacted me. I thought something must have happened to the others but decided to do the job anyway. There were a few minor problems with the entry, but nothing major."

Her pancake done, Kiri returned to the stove. "We'll have a look at your ribs after breakfast. Keep going."

"Then, when I got into the laboratory, the others were already there."

"Really?"

Kade didn't reply.

"Sorry. So the others got the cell then?"

"That's the strange thing; they took something else." There was more than one strange thing about all of this.

"They stole something else?"

"Yes."

"And yet you're here empty handed?"

"Yes."

Kiri raised her eyebrows.

He took the box from his pack and sat it down on the table. "I was supposed to put whatever I stole in here and post it to you. But the thing I was supposedly sent to steal was as big as a scooter engine. Either the information was wrong, or the location changed. I'm not sure. If I knew what I was actually after..."

"What about the other men?"

"They stole something smaller, about book sized. Then they killed a few guards and disappeared through a hole in the floor. And a short while after that Tribalin and Whiparill emergency undocked."

"Really? Well, that *is* interesting."

As he started on his second pancake, Kade examined the woman's face, trying to work out what her strange tone meant.

"Do you want to know something even more interesting, Kade Traskel?" Kiri was back at the stove. She looked over her shoulder. "You've been set up."

Kade stopped chewing.

"Actually, *we've* been set up. Well and truly."

Suddenly the pancake was cold and tasteless in his mouth. He swallowed. "What makes you say that?"

"First of all, I'm the Operations Manager for Tribalin and I have absolutely no idea what you're talking about."

"Well, sometimes jobs are managed elsewhere because it's part of a larger operation."

"You're right, but the local manager is usually informed anyway. It's just polite, if nothing else." Kiri sat down with another pancake. "Secondly, you were sent on what is an extremely difficult mission when there was really no need."

Kade shook his head. "You don't even know what I was after. I assume if they sent me there then there was a need."

"We have an agreement with the manager of CRG, Kade. I assume it's CRG you're talking about because none of the others really have anything worth guarding. Why go sneaking in through the roof—I assume that's how you went in; quite impressive, really—when all we have to do is ask?"

"Oh."

"Yes, 'oh'. And thirdly. You were given a parcel with my name and address on it."

Kade sighed. It was obvious really, when he thought about it. "If I was caught, the constables would be led straight to you."

She nodded. "My records can withstand casual enquiries easily enough but if someone got serious about searching they would come across a few inconsistencies... This tavern you were sent too, I assume it was the *Leaf and Stone*?"

Kade was pretty sure he hadn't said the name. He nodded.

"The constables had a tip off that some Skyway Men would be meeting there at midnight last night. The reason you weren't arrested was pure good luck."

"So they question me, I eventually admit who I worked for and what I was going to do and they assume my accomplices did the job without me?"

"That's my guess."

"So, is that all? Is that the end of my stupidity?"

"I'm afraid not, love."

"Let's have it then."

"Very well. Fourthly. Finally. Of all the people on all the skylands, you, Kade, are the least likely to be offered a job."

Kade examined his hands. "What makes you say that?" he asked.

"They use your name, your real name, during lessons to warn of what can go wrong. You're a legend. A legend with a moral, which is even better. *See what can happen if you aren't careful? See what hubris can do?* After what happened, you were lucky to live. There's no way they'd call you back."

After what happened. Kade had been a rising star of the Skyway Men, a shining light. The brightest light of them all. He pulled off jobs nobody had thought possible, cleaned up messes made by people far more experienced. He'd been touted as the next leader before he was twenty years old. And less than three years after that, after a couple of jobs went wrong, he'd been shipped off to Whiparill.

Kade cleared his throat and looked around. "It wasn't my fault," he said. "The constables were tipped off. They were everywhere. And Lemar didn't even..." Kiri was about as impressed by his excuses as he'd expected. "I just want a chance. I waited a long time. I just want to prove I can still do the job..."

"Can you?" Kiri sighed and finished off her pancake. She licked lemon juice from her fingers. "I'll have a look at your chest, then we'll see about getting ourselves extricated from the mess at CRG. We'll worry about the rest after that."

Kade ate another pancake while Kiri cleaned the dried blood from his chest and strapped it tightly, painfully, with pristine white bandages she pulled from a medical kit under the bench. It still hurt to breathe, but as a reminder of his stupidity it was pretty mild. He should have known. He had been too keen to impress that he hadn't seen what was obvious. He realized that he could turn the situation to his advantage though. If not for the set up he'd be sitting in Whiparill. Now, he had his foot back in the Skyway Men door.

"The bandage won't do much," Kiri said when she was done, "but it might give a bit of protection."

"Thank you."

"My pleasure, love. Now, let's see if one of my son's shirts will fit you."

The shirt Kiri returned with a minute later was not quite what Kade would have selected. She seemed to catch his expression and held the shirt up to look for herself. It was a pale blue blouse with a lacy collar and a tie-ribbon down the front.

"Sorry, last season's, I know, but it will have to do. Roker is quite a bit slimmer than you, so this season's tight shirts wouldn't fit."

"I don't care about fashion," Kade said. "It just looks ridiculous."

Kiri shoved the shirt at him. "Ridiculous, perhaps. But it certainly isn't bloody."

Kade sighed and painfully pulled on the shirt. It was too tight across the shoulders, but it would have to do.

"Come on." Kiri straightened her dress and led the way.

IV

Outside, the sun was up and rain was falling. A sparkling curtain of water hung before the door, overflowing from a gutter. The barrel in the corner was spilling a torrent onto the pavers. A growing stream crossed the cobbled yard toward the canal.

"It's going to be a beautiful day," Kiri said.

Kade shrugged, wished he hadn't, and followed the big woman out into the shed. She moved surprisingly quickly, dancing around puddles in her soft leather slippers, holding her dress up off the ground. "We'll have to be quick if I'm going to make it to work on time," she said. "I can't afford to be fired."

Kade stepped under the shelter and examined the cruiser. It wasn't even two metres long with four serving-platter-sized wheels and an awning over the top. There was only one seat.

Kiri gave him a smile. "You'll just have to make yourself comfortable on the carrier tray."

Kade shook his head. "You're the one who loves the rain," he muttered. "Why don't you sit out in the open?"

Kiri smiled some more. "I really don't think you want to see me back there."

Kade thought it best to hold his tongue.

Ten minutes later, the crystals were warm enough. Kiri moved the cruiser out into the slap and sting of the rain and headed to starboard, towards the city's commercial district.

Rush hour was starting. Pedestrians dashed along footpaths. They bumped into others, apologized, danced between puddles and gurgling flood-drains. Vehicles sent out arcs of spray or waited patiently as the traffic tied itself in knots. A scooter and a lorry came to grief at an intersection but apparently that was no reason to slow down. Kade hung onto the tie-rails as Kiri squeezed the cruiser through a gap that was surely too narrow.

The streets were wider than those further to aft. The buildings were set back several metres. Even the industrial buildings—aging harlots with fresh, gaudy coats of paint—sheltered behind low walls and small gardens. Kade didn't look. He closed his eyes and wondered if Kiri could do either of her jobs from a hospital bed.

Eventually, the cruiser juddered to a halt. Kade opened his eyes, checked to make sure they weren't going to take off again at any moment, and unclamped his hands. He wiped them on his soaking shirt, trying to tell himself he was only shaking because of the cold.

"Doesn't anyone regulate the speed of traffic?"

The crystal engine fell silent as Kiri shrugged and hauled herself out of her seat. "People only complain if there's an accident."

"Uh-huh." Kade was happy to get his feet back on solid ground. He wiped rain from his face.

They were parked in front of a large, plain building that looked out of place amidst the ostentation that surrounded it. Next door, leaf-carved columns held up a vast portico that, on its own, covered more area than any building on Whiparill. Across the street, a carved skyscape with rain-blurred edges covered an entire facade.

"This is the place?" Kade asked, looking at the building that seemed to be their destination. There was just a large, arched door on the ground level. On the four floors above that, plain, blank windows stared silently.

"No, I just thought you'd like to stop here for a while first to admire the architecture." Kiri shook her head. "Come on."

Through the door was a passage with bare stone walls and nowhere to hide. Two guards waited silently in protective embrasures at the far end. They held blunderbusses like they knew how to use them and had a collection of other weapons close to hand. The men watched them pass but said nothing.

They stepped out into a lush garden with full sized trees. It was as if they'd become lost and found themselves in a different building entirely. A small stream led to a rain-stippled pond. The buildings around the outside gleamed as if they'd just been scrubbed. More plants were placed strategically on porches and windowsills. It seemed as if the rest of the city had disappeared. Kade hurried through the rain after Kiri, crunching along the winding gravel path in her wake and taking in the heady aromas of the flowerbeds.

Kiri gestured towards one of the doors in the wall. "This place belongs to Madam Chanise Larinal, the manager of the Crystal Research Guild. CRG is completely owned by Tribalin Administration and is one of the most powerful organizations around the world. They have been responsible for the discovery of more useful crystal arrays than everyone else put together."

"So we're going to visit the woman we tried to rob?"

"As I said, we have an agreement with Madam Larinal. We have to clear up the mess with her, make her understand what actually happened, before we can move on with anything else. She isn't someone we want as an enemy. Let me do the talking. Answer any questions she asks and don't interrupt."

"Great. Thanks." He wiped his face, flicking the rain from his fingers.

A servant answered Kiri's knock at the door. She was in her mid twenties and was tall, slim and striking. She wore a fashionably tight blouse and skirt to her knees. There was a teardrop tattal surrounding her wristal and another on her forehead.

"Mistress Mirani. It is good to see you again."

"Likewise, Tilli. Sorry for calling so early."

Tilli had a smile that suddenly made Kade aware of his too-small, out-of-fashion blouse. He plucked ineffectually at the soaking material then stilled his hands. He didn't stop staring, giving her a nod and a smile when he caught her eye. She smiled back. Living on backwater skylands with populations of barely more than 200 had more disadvantages than Kade had remembered. He tried to straighten his clothes when the maid turned back to Kiri.

"I'm sorry, but Madam Larinal was called out in the middle of the night. I'm not sure when she—" Tilli stopped mid-sentence when noises emerged from deeper in the apartment. She cocked her head to listen but made no other move. Kade watched her, the curve of her neck, the fall of her hair. Her smooth, pale skin glowed. She ran the tip of her tongue along her lips.

When she moved, turning to look over her shoulder the spell was broken and Kade examined the apartment. There was a staircase along one wall, carved timber balustrade perfectly matching the entrance door, and a regiment of severe portraits lining the other. The sounds that held Tilli's attention seemed to come from beyond an arched doorway squeezed between a fading matron and young child.

"I believe that may be her now. Please wait here a moment." Tilli glided away across the plush carpet.

Kade watched her go, staring for long moments after she had disappeared from sight. "Do you—" He started to say eventually, but Kiri nudged him with an elbow as Tilli returned.

"Come this way. Madam Larinal will be with you shortly."

"Thank you."

They went up the stairs. Kade, last in line, stared at Kiri's back and envied the mistress her view. He smoothed down his lace collar and breathed in the golden, tacky scent of the beeswax-polish from the balustrade. He ran his fingers along the smooth, cool timber.

When Tilli ushered them in a study on the first floor, she left the door open and turned to continue up the next flight of stairs. The last Kade saw of her was when she glanced back at him and smiled.

Kade could see Kiri almost laughing. "What?"

She shrugged in reply. "Nothing, love. Nothing at all."

"Good."

Hardly any bare wall remained in the study. There were ancient swords and chipped daggers. A shelf behind the huge desk a held an ornate double barrel pistol in a wooden rack. A yellowing map with tattered edges looked down over that. Fading tapestries molted onto the carpet.

"Don't like this place much," Kade said softly.

"This room is worth more than my house and cruiser and job put together."

"No, it may cost that much, but that doesn't mean it's worth it."

He snapped his mouth shut as a woman, presumably Madam Larinal, strode into the room. She was as tall and slim as Kiri was wide. Her bald head was completely covered by tattals. They ran down her neck, across her shoulder and joined with those on her arms.

"Am I being extorted?" she asked in a deep, sonorous voice, sitting down in the creaking leather chair behind the desk. She gripped the armrests as if to stop the fury from leaking out through her fingers.

"No, Madam," Kiri replied.

"Then where is the cell?" For a moment it seemed she would launch herself to her feet, but she subsided.

"I guess that answers my first question." Kiri sighed and glanced back over her shoulder as if she thought there might be spies. "Madam Larinal, the Skyway Men had nothing to do with the theft of your cell."

"I think... What? I just came from the laboratory. Three men are dead, the cell is gone and here you are."

Kiri looked embarrassed. "I believe we've been set up. I'm almost certain of it, though I don't yet know who's responsible."

Madam Larinal looked from Kiri to Kade and back again. "And you expect me to believe this? Who is *he*?"

"Kade worked for the Skyway Men some time ago but was contacted again recently with a new job. He was supposed to be caught so he would lead investigations to the Skyway Men while the real thieves got away."

"And Kade would have talked?" Madam Larinal looked across at him as if he were something nasty stuck on the bottom of her shoe.

"None of our cover stories are perfect."

The woman shook her head. She picked up a small wooden box from her desk and examined it. "I'm sure you can understand why I'm having a hard time accepting this."

Kade watched as she spun and twisted the wooden box in her fingers. There was a switch on the side and a carved grille on the front. He'd never seen anything like it before.

Kiri shook her head. "Why would we steal something when we can just ask?"

She finally seemed to accept what Kiri was saying. "You don't have the cell?"

"No."

"Three men stole it then left through a hole in the ground floor," Kiri said. "Three men I know nothing about."

"Explain."

"Kade seems to think there's a passage under the building."

"You do realize that cell will do nothing on its own? It needs to be clustered with a dozen others."

"We don't have the array."

Kade thought of the files the men had also stolen. Had Madam Larinal checked on those yet?

"You don't have it..." Madam Larinal sighed. She rose from her seat and went to look at the map on the wall. She leaned against the shelf and traced a line on the map with a long green fingernail. "In that case," she said softly, "no more can be done. We will wait."

"Wait? For what?"

Madam Larinal looked back over her shoulder for a moment. "Matharzo Skyland undocked during the night. We are in pursuit. I don't think any further assistance is required from the Skyway Men. In fact, I think it's time we ended our relationship permanently."

Kiri raised her eyebrows.

"I have other customers who are much less trouble than the Skyway Men. Much less," Madam Larinal searched for the word, "conspicuous."

Kade had seen the skyland undocking *before* he'd entered the laboratory. As he tried to decide if he should say anything, Madam Larinal spun back to face the room, the ornate pistol from the wall now in her hand. Instinct drummed into him as a boy threw him to the left. He heard the gun discharge, smelt the smoke, and immediately knew he hadn't been hit. In one smooth motion he rolled to his feet, crouching, hoping he was ready for whatever came next. Madam Larinal wasn't in sight.

The only movement was Kiri, hauling herself to her feet on the far side of the room. "Are you all right?" she asked.

He wasn't sure. "Yes."

"Good. Hurry up, we don't have much time."

They didn't have any time at all. Kade could hear heavy footsteps on the stairs outside, at least two men. Kiri went towards the door; he went the other way, darting around behind the desk. Larinal was dead, Kiri's dagger protruding from her left eye socket. Blood spread away from her, staining the thick carpet.

The door burst open behind him and Kade snatched up the pistol. One barrel was still primed.

Two guards. Not the men who'd stood at the gate.

Kiri was right on them. She batted away a blunderbuss, unbelievably quick. Punched twice. Ripped the weapon from the man's hand and used the stock to knock him unconscious. The second man had been standing back, waiting for his partner to finish the old, fat woman, but that wasn't going to happen. He raised his blunderbuss, but not quick enough. Kade got him first, a lead ball in the chest. A disbelieving look skittered across his face. Kiri's as well.

"Come on, love."

Kade finally moved towards the door and scooped up the remaining blunderbuss. But there, he stopped again, attention riveted on the cold, staring eyes of the man he'd killed. An innocent man, just doing his job. Just doing what he thought was right. Maybe he had a wife, children. Kade stared back at him, willing the man to blink first, waiting for him to draw in a breath. The old man outside CRG probably had a family as well. Grandchildren who would no longer get to sit on his knee.

"Kade!"

Kade snapped his attention to where Kiri stood near the door.

There were more guards. The ones from the gate. Kiri took out the first with the booming blunderbuss. A scatter of shot bit into the man's chest. He fell and scrabbled at the floor, breath gargling.

The second guard, hiding behind the questionable protection of the balustrade, raised his weapon. Fired. Kiri dived for cover, but Kade stood his ground, firing from the hip. Splinters of wood flew. The man screamed, clutching at his face as he tumbled down the stairs.

"Come on," Kade said softly, staring at the weapon in his hands. "Let's get out of here."

He stepped towards the door, but Kiri didn't move.

"Mistress Kiri?"

She was lying on the floor, barely breathing, blood soaked hands clutching at her stomach. Her eyes were glazed and staring.

"Mistress Kiri?"

The woman blinked, focused her eyes.

"I'm sorry," Kade said, crouching down beside her. "I should have..."

Kiri shook her head. "A decade out of service." Each word seemed to take a lifetime. "You've done well." She coughed a dollop of blood. "Wristal." She reached into her robes and drew forth a second dagger.

"No, I..."

"Do it." She pushed the weapon into his hand. "I'm finished."

And she was. She stopped breathing and the last of the tension drained from her body.

Kade blinked away tears. Eventually, he looked around as if help might suddenly present itself. There was nothing. Taking a deep breath, he pushed the dagger into Kiri's wrist and dug her wristal free. It came away with a sucking sound. The fine filaments that connected it to her tattals came free as well, silvery and glistening with blood.

He might have stayed there all day, staring at the blood, but the sound of quiet, furtive footsteps came from outside the room. Wiping away the tears, he jumped to his feet, pocketed the wristal and grabbed the one primed blunderbuss that remained. He dived out through the door, rolled to his knees, fired...

Tilli was standing halfway down the stairs from the second floor. A look of surprise was etched onto her face. There were spots of blood on her neck. Her cheek. Blood started to spread across the front of her fashionably tight blouse. Red polka dots, probably ten years out of date, that blended and merged.

Kade swallowed, stood, went up two stairs. "No..." He reached out to her but she shied away. "I didn't... I'm sorry."

He thought she was going to say something. Her mouth moved but all that came out was blood, dribbling down her chin, dripping onto the floor. Then, still staring, she toppled forward, bounced down a couple of stairs and ended up at his feet, face down, dead.

Kade dropped the blunderbuss and fell to his knees. He sucked in heaving breaths, hands hovered over Tilli as if there might be something he could do, if only he could think, if only he could clear the tears from his eyes and stop his hands from shaking.

But once again, there was nothing he could do. Nothing he could undo. A whole life that he couldn't undo.

When he could think again he pushed himself to his feet and headed for the ground floor, one slow step at a time, hand leaving a glistening red trail on the carved timber balustrade. The smell of beeswax and cordite, fear and blood.

A dead guard had tumbled halfway down the stairs. Kade stepped over him without seeing, continued down. A moment later he stumbled out into the garden. Mist was gathering in the courtyard, clinging to plants and buildings. Soft noises came from out on the street beyond the entrance passage. People. Kade went the other way.

Blood and fear. And flowers. A heavy, cloying commotion of scents. He crunched along the gravel path towards another apartment that was still and quiet. He knelt to pick the lock on the door.

Shouts behind him.

A gun fired. A musket, not a blunderbuss. The ball hit the wall beside the door. Stone shrapnel stung Kade's face. He flinched but he kept his concentration. Don't look back. Don't let them see. It would be hard for them to see through the mist. Keep working. No shaking now. Calm. Still. But it was hard to see through the tears and if he'd been thinking properly he would have gone directly out onto the street from Madam Larinal's apartment.

More shouts, coming closer.

Finally, hours later, the door opened. Kade slipped through and locked it behind him. Musket balls knocked, death trying to get in. Men charged across the garden. Other than that it was quiet. Hopefully if anyone was in the apartment they'd be sensible enough to stay out of the way, though Kade wasn't exactly sure what he'd do if confronted.

Stairs along the left wall, as at Madam Larinal's, arched door halfway down the right.

Wiping blood and tears from his face, picking out a piece of stone, Kade went through the arch then through another door on the far side of the room. He found himself in an empty parking garage. He took a rag from a shelf and wiped his face and hands then opened the large door that would give a cruiser access and stepped out onto the street. Rush hour was drawing to a close, but it was still relatively busy. Nobody noticed him as they hurried about their business.

Kade closed the door and had a final look around. He took a deep breath. Hands in his pockets, head down, he walked away. He couldn't stop shaking.

V

Kade checked over his shoulder as he walked. He turned right at the next street and left at the one after that. He didn't care where he was going, as long as he went. Beyond the third corner he started to recover. His breathing was back to normal. His heart had slowed to merely a gallop. Tilli was a witness; she had to die. It was easy enough to say, harder to believe. Surely he could have thought of another option if he hadn't... Surely... But it was too late now. It was done.

He paused in front of a bookshop. Office buildings and stores had taken over from apartments and factories. The windows were huge and clean, the balconies nonexistent. Men and women, most with a dark fuzz of hair or gleaming first stage tattals, sat at desks or served behind counters. They wore bright, tight clothes and smiles much the same. Cruisers lined each side of the street, nose in to the deep gutters. Pedestrians rushed about with files and memory crystals. Or they wandered at a more leisurely pace with purchases in bags or tucked under their arms.

Kade had a chance to go unnoticed in the crowds of the commercial district but splatters of blood marked his blue, out-of-fashion shirt and there was a smear of it down the side of his trousers.

If anyone *did* notice... A woman looked him up and down as she passed, shaking her head and mumbling to herself.

"Thorn." Kade turned aside, making his way through a narrow alley, across another busy street and through the alley beyond. He came to a small park, sat down on a cast iron seat and tried to think. He clutched Mistress Kiri's wristal in his pocket. Covered in congealing blood, it was all that was left of the only person he knew in Tribalin. He rubbed at the smooth, hard surface. If he could get the information out of it, it might help him find other members of the Skyway Men, but doing that could take him a week. It wouldn't help *now*. It wasn't likely the Skyway Men would be inclined to help anyway.

He tried to think, to pull his thoughts away from Tilli's shocked face and point them in a useful direction. It wasn't easy. He wondered if it would ever be easy. He examined the scrollwork of the seat, let his eyes trace the swirling patterns. He scratched at the neat soldering, as if picking apart those joins might also pick apart the places where his two lives met.

A Pundit spotted him and started towards him. The man seemed to think better of it and took his pamphlets elsewhere.

Breathe. Think.

The first thing he needed to do was find some clean clothes. Obviously. He could get some more from Kiri's house—he had some in his pack that he hadn't even thought of earlier—but that was a long way from his current location. Rising to his feet, Kade started to walk again. *Look calm. Nothing to see here.*

Tribalin was ascending, racing desperately upwards as the Captain chased the phantom thief from Matharzo. It was getting colder, almost by the moment. The mist was now so thick it cut visibility down to a few metres. Pedestrians were overtaking cruisers. Kade wiped a slick of moisture away from his face and bald scalp. Or was it sweat? He noticed he was almost running and managed to slow his steps.

A couple of minutes later he saw the first apartment building and, across the road from it, something even better. A laundry. A longhaired, tattless lady left with a bulging package and a child in tow.

Without changing stride, Kade made his way to the alley around the back. He reached what he thought was the right spot and stopped to lean against the high stone wall beside a scratched red door. There was nobody in sight and no noise from beyond the wall, so he opened the door and had a look through into a small courtyard. A bakery, heavy with the smell of smoke and fresh bread. Firewood everywhere, stacked in crazy piles, filling almost every available space. Kade moved on.

The next door was locked so he grabbed the top of the wall to haul himself up and have a look. There were no clothes but a dozen clotheslines, on three different levels, divided the yard. Kade pulled himself up to the top of the wall, ribs complaining, eyes watering, and dropped silently down the other side. He dusted himself off, which was about the most pointless task he had ever undertaken in his life, and unlocked the door back out to the alley. Then he crept across to the back of the building. It felt as if each step was a monumental decision. Just minutes earlier he'd hardly been able to slow himself down, now it was all he could do to move forward.

The back door of the building was flung wide. Kade hid outside, trying to see through the wafting steam. It was raining inside. The top half of the room was filled with more lines and crystal engines blew dry, warm air onto the rainbow of clothes hanging there. Water dripped down onto the outside of canvas chimneys that carried away most of the steam rising from the huge tubs on the floor. More crystal engines worked propellers in the tubs, mixing a thick stew of shirts and breeches and underwear. A man with a tattal all the way to his elbow was working his way through a huge pile of dry, clean clothes. He held up each garment and examined it critically. From there, they went into one of two piles or were folded with precise economy and placed into canvas bags that hung from a rack above his head. He worked steadily for some time.

Waiting outside the door, Kade began to wonder if he'd have to sneak in and hit the man over the head. Finally, a bell rang from the front of the store. The man grumbled, lowered the green and blue dress he'd been examining and made his way to the counter. He left a swirling wake of mist behind. Kade slipped inside before the man had gone from sight. The first thing he did was dip his hands into one of the tubs. The water was hot, making him wince, but he quickly washed away all trace of blood then moved to the pile of clothes. He wiped his hands and face on the green and blue dress then started to work on the pile. A dress. A skirt. Too big. Too small. Too pink. A white shirt with laces on the front and a stiff red collar. He stripped off his old shirt and donned the new one. Perfect fit.

Ribs aching.

Back to the pile. He found some tough blue breeches and struggled to get his old, bloody ones off over his boots. Would've been quicker to do it properly. Before he could get himself redressed the bell sounded again and Kade heard footsteps heading his way. He grabbed his clothes, old and new, and darted out the back.

It was cold. Kade wished he'd stolen a coat. He shivered as he finished dressing in the corner of the yard. When he was done, he bundled his old clothes under his arm and walked out through the gate. A block away he dumped the clothes in a garbage bin then had to dig them back out to take Kiri's wristal and his purse from the pocket. It wasn't the discreet operation he'd planned. He couldn't think. People watched him as they passed. He shrugged in reply and smiled apologetically. With his shaking hands in his pockets again, he strode away, taking corners at random, trying to put distance between himself and his crimes.

After half an hour he paused at the corner of two wide streets, apartments and houses on either side, and looked around. Occasional cruisers. Pedestrians rugged up against the cold. Mist thinning out again as the skyland climbed clear. No wind. Or lots of wind, but they were moving with it. There was no chance of catching Matharzo any time soon.

There was a public altimetre on the side of a building nearby. Almost three thousand metres. Soon, it would be hard to breathe. At five thousand metres businesses would shut down. People would be warned to stay at home... Kade had no home on Tribalin. He needed to register at the Administration Complex or he'd be branded an illegal immigrant. They were probably going to question his tardiness as it was.

With a destination finally in mind, Kade got his bearings and set off for the front of the skyland. It wasn't far away, which didn't leave him much time to think. Why hadn't he returned to Whiparill before the undock? Why had he waited so long before trying to register? It took a while to get his mind moving in the right direction but, in the end, the answers were obvious.

Kade knew he would have to think quicker if he had any chance of the Skyway Men taking him back.

"They aren't going to take you back, Kade," he said softly to himself. They had never been going to take him back. And now? Now he'd ended a very lucrative relationship with Madam Larinal and been involved in the death of an experienced Operations Manager. They would probably think his former mistakes paled in comparison. Remembering Mistress Kiri, he could hardly argue. The Skyway Men were not going to take him back. They were going to kill him as quickly as they could. Kade's needed a plan, something that would let him live through the next few days at least. Hopefully, by then, he'd be able to come up with something else. "Sounds easy," he muttered as he quickened his pace.

The Administration Complex was housed in the Forecastle. It perched at the very front of the skyland, looking out at nothing but wind and sky. The central section—the Control Tower—was twenty metres wide and ten storeys high. Eight storeys of offices and departments stretched fifty metres to either side. The stone was dark with years. A colony of terns occupied the cliff of the port wing, with nests on windowsills and ledges. They were a never-ending squawk, a constant flutter and swirl that softened the building's harsh lines. The biting smell of bird shit was almost as palpable as the cloud.

Twelve wide, white-veined stone steps led up to the glass doors. There was a worn rut in the centre and a phalanx of life-sized statues stood to either side, watching over all who entered.

Gafol Martinol was there once again. Kade stopped to look, wishing he could just plant a crystal engine and fly away from all the danger like Martinol had. He laughed. If he was going to believe in the fantasy of Gafol Martinol he might as well start believing he was going to survive the mess he had created.

"No loitering."

"What?" Kade spun and saw a guard standing half in-half out of the door at the top of the stairs. He'd left a big greasy handprint on the glass.

"No loitering. Go about your business."

"Oh... Well... My business is here." He didn't have to act nervous. "I come from Whiparill. I couldn't get off when the emergency undock was signaled."

The guard grunted and held the door open. "Get to it then. There's been trouble and the Captain is keeping a tight hold."

Kade hurried through and stopped in the foyer. There were four lifts in the far wall, reception to the left and a wide arch to the right. He headed for the counter but the guard called after him, telling him to go to level one.

A minute later, Kade was standing in front of a small, tidy desk waiting for an old woman to acknowledge him. Eventually she looked up and clasped her hands on top of a pile of documents. She had a narrow band of tattal around her wrist and a flower on her crown.

"Who are you?" She adjusted her spectacles but still had to squint.

"Kade Traskel."

"What do you want?"

Kade looked around. He was in the Registration Office. "I need to register."

The old woman grunted and pointed to a door. "Through there."

"Yes, Mistress." But the woman had already turned her attention back to the papers on her desk and had forgotten all about him.

The small man in the next room had probably never forgotten anything in his life. If he *had* forgotten there was a note in his filing system that would remind him. His desk was immaculately tidy, as were the shelves that lined the walls.

"Hello," he said, his face creasing into a smile. "My name is Damin. Why don't you take a seat." The receptionist seemed to resent her lowly rank and menial job but this looked like a man who reveled in what he did. His blue and white shirt was crisp and clean. The tattals on his arm gleamed in the soft light coming through the window.

"I'm Kade. I come from Whiparill."

Damin checked an LCD screen hardwired into his desk. "Kade Traskel? Let me scan your wristal."

Kade held out his arm.

"And why are you only coming in to register now? You should come in straight away, you know."

Kade ducked his head and tried to look embarrassed. "It's my first holiday in a long time. I may've had a bit too much to drink."

"Oh, I see."

"I didn't wake up until a couple of hours ago and I didn't know we'd undocked."

"Right then. That's understandable, I suppose. And..." Damin's eyes narrowed. "What's that on your collar?"

Kade reached up to feel. There was something pinned there. A little piece of plastic. The laundry must use them for keeping track of clothes. Kade tried to undo the pin quickly, as if hiding the evidence would hide the crime.

"It's..." he tried to think. His fingers were shaking. He was sure Damin would see. *Say something.* Keep his attention away from the collar. Keep the lies small. Tell as much truth as possible. "It's a tag from a laundry, sir. As I said, I drank too much last night and... Well, I was sick. I had to get everything cleaned." Kade held out the tag, hoping the man would ignore it or give it only a cursory glance.

Damin didn't bother taking it. "A very big night."

"I didn't know there were so many types of alcohol." Kade slipped the plastic into his pocket and ran his fingers around the top of his breeches to find the one pinned there as well.

Damin smiled and shook his head. "It says here you are a metal worker."

"That's right."

"You should be able to find work then. Your best bet would be the aft-port quarter." He checked his screen again. "You haven't checked in to any accommodation yet?" Obviously not a good thing. "Here's a voucher for a hostel in that area. It's good for one week. After that, if you still need help, you'll have to come back and convince us."

"Thank you."

"If you don't register at the hostel in the next six hours we'll expect you to come and update us on your living arrangements."

"Of course."

"There are no zeppelins heading in a likely direction any time soon so at the next docking the Secretary will make enquiries about getting you back to Whiparill." He entered information into the system memory and saved it with a decisive tap on the screen. "That's all done then. Good luck."

Out on the street, Kade stopped at the bottom of the stairs and shivered. The day was clear and bright now. Kiri's beautiful day. The altimeter on the Control Tower indicated 3900 metres. It was a long time since he'd been that high. Trying to rub some warmth into his arms, he looked at the voucher he'd been given. There was a map for the location of the hostel on the back...

Kade suddenly wondered why Madam Larinal decided the thieves were on Matharzo after examining the map on her wall.

"I need a map." There was sure to be one at Kiri's place and, now that he was wearing clean clothes, getting there wouldn't be a problem. He turned to starboard and hurried away.

When Kade neared Kiri's he walked slowly, looking for any signs of life from inside. All was quiet. The curtains were drawn tight. The neighboring properties stared blankly as well. Kade, as casual as he could, made his way around the back and paused beneath the cruiser shelter to look again. Water rushed along the canal beyond the back fence, blocking out any other sounds.

No movement, but Kade didn't like it. Something was wrong.

He shook his head. "Thorn." Last night he'd dropped into a room full of armed criminals and today he thought he could sense trouble in a silent, locked house.

He crossed to the back door and started working on the lock. As expected it was an advanced mechanism. He wondered if he should try to break in after all. He didn't want to. He wanted to sit in the glowing warmth of his workshop on Whiparill and... Licking his lips, barely able to hold his lock picks, Kade set to work again. He was just starting to think it was beyond him when it clicked open and he slipped inside.

The smell of pancakes still hung in the air. The dirty bowl and frying pan sat in the sink. Pieces of lemon, like bright, tangy shards of sunshine were scattered on one plate. A dribble of syrup drew random patterns on the other. Beyond the next door was a narrow hall with bare ceiling beams. On the right, he passed a door to a small, dark sitting room. At the far end was the door out onto the street. A set of steep, narrow stairs started near the door and led back parallel to the hall. Kade was about to start climbing when he heard something. He crept back towards the sitting room and reached the door just as a member of the constabulary, blue uniform jacket unbuttoned, stepped out of the gloom.

"Who are you?" the man asked, even as he reached one hand for his pistol and the other for his sword.

Instinctively, Kade lunged forward. The other man forgot his weapons, blocked crisply and replied with a low kick.

Kade half retreated, half stumbled as his knee twisted. He flicked out his fist as he went. He struck his opponent flush on the chin, but barely. Kade continued to back away, trying to shake some feeling into his knee. The constable pressed forward. They exchanged a flurry of blows that all amounted to nothing in the end. Apart from Kade's ribs sending a sharp reminder of their delicate condition.

They paused for a moment near the foot of the stairs.

"You picked the wrong house to break into," the constable said. He was only a few years older than Kade but his epaulettes announced him as a detective. Most of his arm and scalp were covered with tattals, except where there was one long plait on his very crown. A dragon marked his neck and left cheek. He was tall and slim with a strong nose and clear blue eyes.

Kade shrugged and attacked, thankful his opponent seemed to have forgotten his weapons completely. This time, he pushed hardest and they went back the way they'd come, into the shadows of the hall. Past the sitting room. Towards the kitchen. He was sweating but continued to press, forcing the pace. He was stronger, but only just. His opponent was quicker. But only just.

A punch got through. Another. The constable rocked back, stunned, and countered while still off balance, snapping out an arm and leaving it there a moment too long. Kade grabbed the arm—one hand inside the wrist, the other outside the elbow—and tried to break it. But the man went with the force, shifting sideways, and they were facing each other across the narrow hall, backs against the walls. Another whirlwind of blows before Kade spun away.

He stumbled into the lemon and pancake scented space of the kitchen. Stayed on his feet, barely, with a hand on the cold flags of the floor as he tried to get upright again.

Footsteps behind him. A pistol being drawn. He remembered his own stolen pistols. He'd put them on the bench at breakfast, near the syrup. Near where he was. He reached blindly as his momentum carried him past. Fumbled one. Got the next.

Kade went with his stumble, spun. His ribs screamed but he landed on his back looking along the barrel of the pistol, suddenly unsure if he could use it. It didn't matter as it was only half cocked anyway.

Tribalin:
Constable

I

The constable stared along the barrel of his own pistol for a moment before glancing at the pistol that rocked back and forth on the bench, stirred by Kade's attempt to grab it. "Where did they come from?" He smoothed his plait, threw it back over his shoulder. "They aren't my mother's."

"Your mother?" Kade's voice was hardly audible. He cleared his throat and sat up, keeping the pistol trained on the other man's chest. "Kiri was your mother? You're..." He tried to think of the name she'd used. "You're Roker?"

The constable lowered his pistol. "Only my mother calls me Roker. Everyone else calls me Roke." He held out a hand and helped Kade to his feet. "I should have known something was up. No common thief would fight as well as you. You seemed a bit rusty though. I may have been in lot of trouble otherwise."

Kade shook his head ruefully. "It's been a while. I'm Kade." He dusted himself off, though the floor was clean, and sat on a stool to try to massage his knee. As expected, his hands were shaking. He tried to breathe.

Roke continued. "But you said 'was'. Kiri *was* my mother?"

"Yes. Sorry. Today isn't quite going as well as it might have." He closed his eyes for a moment and took a deep breath. "We went to see Madam Larinal about the robbery—"

"I don't know the details of my mother's business, Kade."

"You aren't a Skyway Man?"

Roke shook his head. "No. I helped my mother occasionally but the Skyway Men get along fine without me. More often than not, she was helping me. You don't get to be a detective at forty without a little help, but I'm basically honest."

"Oh. Well, I suspect you're going to have a busy morning." Kade tried to order his scrambling thoughts and explained the events of the past few hours while Roke sat and took it all in. Roke stayed silent when Kade described his mother's death but the pain was obvious in his eyes, in the tightening of his jaw. Kade wiped away tears for a woman he barely knew.

There was a moment of silence after the tale was done, then Roke cleared his throat and blinked away tears. "You don't think the cell is on Matharzo?"

"No. The skyland was undocking before I entered the laboratory. I actually came here to look for a map. Madam Larinal seemed to think something she saw on a map was important."

"Let's have a look then."

Roke went upstairs and returned with several sheets of paper all rolled together. The outer one was almost filled with a light brown circle that represented the skyland itself. The other papers were clear overlays. One showed prominent buildings and places of interest. Another showed streets and the next had patrol routes and traffic management systems. Another three detailed Tribalin's underground. Roke put the prominent building overlay in place and located the CRG laboratory.

A moment later he shook his head, mumbling to himself, and found the sheet showing the second underground level. "Well, *that* mystery was easy to solve," he said.

Kade examined the map. Like most skylands, Tribalin had four Crossing Yards spaced evenly around the edge with passages linking them all at the Hold. Whenever an archipelago formed there were merchants, tourists or migrants who wanted to simply pass across a skyland to get to another. To save time, they could avoid customs officials on the intervening skyland by using the Crossing Yards and the underpasses. They could also use the skyland as free transportation, staying in the Hold until they were ready to leave. These underground systems were supposed to be completely sealed but that was rarely the case.

The laboratory was situated about twenty metres from an underpass with utility passages even closer.

"So the cell is probably in the Hold," Kade said.

"Possibly. That doesn't help us much though." Roke sat down and stared at the map. He spoke absently as he tried to think. "Tribalin's Hold is two hundred metres to a side. There's a whole town down there. The latest official estimate is a permanent population of about two thousand with that many again intending to disembark during the next month. And you forget, Matharzo undocked too soon, but Whiparill didn't."

"So, what are you going to do?" Kade stared at the map as well, though without really seeing it.

"Maybe nothing. I might not be involved in the case yet. Either case."

"You mother's cruiser is parked outside Larinal's apartment." He didn't look up. "When they check—"

"No. It has a false registration. Without the wristal it could take them a week to work out who she is."

Reminded of the wristal, Kade pulled it from his pocket and handed it over. "I'm sorry. I..." He wiped at his face.

"Thank you." Roke spun it in his fingers, watching the filaments twirl. "The main problem is, as soon as I see mother's body I'll have to admit who it is, otherwise, when they eventually find out..." He stood up and straightened his clothes. He did up his jacket and took his kepi from his pocket. He took a deep breath. "I may have to organize some body napping. For now, as far as I know, my mother is staying at a friend's place."

He spoke about it calmly but Kade suspected he was holding his emotions in check.

"What about you, Kade? What are you going to do?"

Kade shrugged. "Get a job, I suppose. I've registered. I have a housing voucher."

"What was your story for missing the undock?"

"Drunk. I got a little bit excited at the beginning of my holiday. Things got out of control, which is true enough."

"You're sure there are no witnesses?"

"I suppose I can't be one hundred percent sure but..." Kade thought of Tilli. The look in her eyes as he shot her. And the old man. "Well, I did my best." He cleared his throat and looked at his fingers as he picked at the edge of the table. Then he realized what he'd just said. No witnesses. Nobody to tell the Skyway Men he'd even been on Tribalin. They weren't likely to randomly check the system for his name to see if he might be involved.

"Good. Well, stay here, if you like. I went out last night as well. We can say we met at a bar." He paused. "I don't suppose that tavern you were at last night was the *Leaf and Stone?*"

Kade nodded.

"That explains that then. But anyway, I'm a good enough alibi to dissuade any casual witnesses."

"But if we met in some bar surely we would simply have parted ways at the end of the night. Would I even know where you live? Would I—"

"Kade, I'm known to roam in certain circles." He looked Kade up and down. "You're a bit older than I normally like, but I'm sure people will understand."

"Right." Kade nodded. "As long as I don't have to go deep undercover."

Roke laughed, but his heart didn't seem to be in it. "No. Not unless you want to."

"Thanks."

"It will mean you won't have to find a job straight away either." He smiled some more. "I can afford to keep you for a while. And maybe you can help me out. The faster someone finds a suitable solution to this mess the less chance there is of anyone digging too deeply."

"Umm..." What Kade really wanted to do was disappear, to slip away into the shadows and never emerge, if that was possible. But Roke was helping him, as his mother had tried to do. Ten years ago that wouldn't have mattered, he would have felt no obligation. But he had changed. Every moment he was discovering that he'd changed more than he had realized. He sighed. "All right. I'll see what I can do."

"Good. I don't know of any criminal who'd be willing to set up the Skyway Men; that's just asking for trouble. Something very strange is going on here." Roke put on his kepi, adjusted it to a different angle, and wiped his dragon tattal until it gleamed. "Go to a bar call the Tail Sail and see if you can find Leni Miklor. He may be able to help. My mother has money under a loose board in the corner of her bedroom, if you need it." He paused. "*Had* money." With that, he collected his pistol and was gone, down the hall and out the front door.

Kade sat at the table, alternatively rubbing his knee and ribs. The smell of breakfast drifted around him until he finally got up and went to the sink.

"I'll make a good wife for Roke," he said a moment later, watching water bubble amongst the dirty dishes.

As the name suggested, the Tail Sail bar was near the back of the skyland. Worn stairs led up the outside of a paper-manufacturing factory to the second floor. There was an enclosed, smoke filled room at one end and a huge open balcony at the other with a thumb of bar in the middle. Even at midday there was quite a crowd. Some were sitting with their heads over their drinks while others played pingo machines. A group of men and women were lined up at the bar, smoking cheroots. A man and woman sat at a table in the corner and studied their drinks with silent, awkward concern.

Kade straightened his jacket. It was brown leather with a wool lining. Not very fashionable at all. He'd bought it from a second-hand store not half an hour earlier but was starting to wish he'd bought something even warmer.

Doing up another button, he made his way to the bar and leaned against the warm dark timber at the end of the line of smokers. Eyes watering, nose itching, he waved away thick swirls of smoke as the barman approached.

"What can I get you?" He was tall and gaunt with a crazy eye and forearm marked with cheap, back-alley tatts.

He cleared his throat. "I'm looking for Leni Miklor."

"Who's asking?"

"I am. And my name won't help either you or him."

The barman pulled out a scanner that was as illegal as his tatts. "Show me."

Kade held out his arm.

The other man examined the data that came up on the screen and grunted. "Outside. In the corner."

The balcony offered views across a heavy concentration of industrial buildings. A hundred metres to starboard, a row of chimneys leaned against a factory, billowing smoke from invisible cheroots. Closer, acrid fumes rose in lazy drifts from a sludge pond. Lorries and cruisers jammed the narrow streets. The tail sail, from which the bar took its name, was only a block away. It was a fifty-metre high rigid fin that helped with the steering of the skyland. At the moment it threw a dark, jagged shadow across the city.

Leni sat on his own, looking out at the view, drink cradled against his potbelly. His feet were up on the lichen-covered rail. There were other people on the balcony, but they all seemed to make a point of minding their own business. Some of them might well have been Skyway Men. Kade had been one once, but now he felt like nothing more than a metal worker from Whiparill. He felt out of place and Leni would spot that in an instant.

Standing amidst of the tables, fiddling with his buttons, Kade was more out of place by the moment. People were starting to watch him openly, wary glances that set his nerves on edge. He could imagine them fingering pistols and knives, wondering if they'd have to use them. Setting his shoulders, he quickly made his way to Leni's table. The chair scraped and clicked across the pavers as he pulled it out and sat down.

"I don't believe you were invited," Leni said in a reedy voice without looking around. He was past middle age with a pockmarked face and uneven ears. "I'm saving that spot for someone."

Kade didn't know what to say, so he said nothing. *Sit still. Act calm.* He put his hands on the cast-iron table and stared at the other man.

"Beat it, before someone nasty comes along."

Kade cleared his throat. He'd once *been* one of the big, nasty someones so all he had to do was pretend he still was. "Have you ever heard the story of the three billygoats, Leni?"

"Yeah, I know it."

"Right, well why don't you think of me as that first little goat."

"Well," Leni said, "maybe us trolls have got bigger brothers as well." He still hadn't turned from his inspection of the city.

Kade swallowed. He picked at a fingernail without looking, working at a tiny spur. "Who said you were the troll, Leni?" The unexpectedness of the comment got the other man's attention. Kade smiled. Coldly, he hoped. "Maybe you're just the bridge and I'm going to walk all over you until I get where I want to go."

Leni still wasn't scared but he was interested, and that was enough. "Very nice," he said with a small smile and a nod of appreciation. "Do you mind if I use that?" He took his feet off the rail and turned his chair to face the table. "You aren't from around here. Who sent you?"

"I got your name from..." Kade examined the other patrons on the balcony, unsure how well Leni and Roke's situation was known. Nobody was paying any attention. Or, at least, they didn't seem to be. After a moment he decided it didn't matter. Like Roke said, something very strange was going on and it needed to be sorted out. "I got your name from Roke."

Leni nodded as he looked around as well. "And what do you want to know?"

"Last night?"

"Ahhh, yes. Last night." Leni laughed and tugged at the lobe of the higher of his ears, as if unconsciously hoping the treatment would create a balance. "Everyone wants to know about last night."

"What have you heard?"

"I heard the Skyway Men were somehow involved but have reason to be unhappy."

"I heard that too," Kade said. Those simple words , and Roke's involvement, would probably lead Leni to some wrong conclusions. That suited Kade fine.

"So you want to know about the robbery?" Leni leaned in close too. "There's a couple of stories going around. One, the buyer found a cheaper option and was trying to get out of the contract." Leni paused there and Kade shook his head. "Ahhh... Very well, number two then. The Green Sea Raiders."

"The Raiders?" Kade sat back and let out a grunt of laughter. "There's no proof they exist. They're a myth." The Skyway Men had invented the Green Sea Raiders about a hundred years earlier as a smoke screen.

"There's no proof the Skyway Men exist either. Just whispers from you and a hundred other would-be-players. The Green Sea Raiders, that's what I heard."

"That's it?" Kade shook his head. "That's the best you've got?"

"They're the only bedtime stories I've heard. It's only been a few hours though, so who can tell?"

"So where are the Raiders now?" Kade couldn't believe he was asking. He felt like getting the Bogeyman's address while he was at it.

Leni shrugged. "Matharzo, perhaps."

"No chance."

"Whiparill then," Leni said, not questioning Kade's certainty. "Or they could be sitting inside at the bar for all I know. News of the robbery was bound to spread, it couldn't be helped, but a disappearance isn't all that helpful if there's news of that as well."

"Whiparill's run isn't taking it anywhere interesting for the next few weeks," Kade said, "I think they're still in the city somewhere." The Hold was the most likely option, but Leni didn't need to know that.

Leni spread his hands. "It's my job to pass on what I hear, not to speculate."

"A least not without a price increase," Kade said, handing over twenty doms. He wasn't sure of the going rate on Tribalin, or the going rate *anywhere* these days for that matter, but if there were any complaints then Roke could handle them.

Leni smiled, hardly even looking at the money.

"You know where to find Roke if you hear any more bedtime stories?"

"Of course, little billygoat."

Half way down the stairs, Kade stepped aside to allow a young girl to pass. She was so busy watching her bare feet slap against the worn stone that she didn't see him until she had almost gone past. When she finally did notice, she stopped so suddenly she almost fell over. He reached out to steady her.

"Thank you," she mumbled, eyes on her wiggling toes once more.

Kade watched her toes as well. They were dirty and calloused.

"That a hawk on your head? Are you Kade?"

Kade thought about that. Was he Kade? It depended who was asking. He looked around, trying to see if he was being watched. "Yes. Do I know you?"

The girl shook her head. "No. But your friend says he has important work to do today and you should organize to meet Kiri on your own." She shoved a small slip of paper into his hand. "She'll be at this address but should be gone before the close of business. I had to say those words exactly."

Administration Centre. Starboard Wing. Basement Level 1. Room 32. "Are you sure?"

"Of course."

"All right then. Thanks."

Still she didn't move. "Your friend said you'd give me a dom."

Kade doubted Roke had said that at all, but he went through his purse and pulled out a five dom piece. "Don't spend it all at once."

The girl snatched the money and raced down to the street. Kade stayed halfway down the stairs, paper in his hand, back against the wall. "Thorn." He had to break into what he assumed was the morgue and steal a body in the next four hours? He wouldn't even be afforded the luxury of darkness. He didn't know if he could. After last night...

The sound of footsteps disturbed him and he looked up to see Leni standing at the top of the stairs.

"Are you still going?" Leni asked. "Or are you coming back?"

Kade cleared his throat and closed a shaking fist around the paper. "A bit of both, Leni," he replied eventually. "I need some help." Thorn, did he need help.

II

When the cruiser came to a halt in the shade of a textile factory, Kade stayed where he was, staring through the dirty windscreen. There were a dozen other vehicles nearby, from a battered, pug-nosed lorry to a shining new scooter sheltering beneath some external stairs.

They were only a hundred metres from the Administration Centre.

"Are you doing this?" Leni asked from the driver's seat.

Kade nodded. "No choice." Any activity he undertook increased the chances of the Skyway Men noticing his presence but there wasn't much he could do; Roke needed his help. He shook his head and sighed.

"No time to waste then."

He nodded again and looked over his shoulder. Peata and Dolik were a rough looking pair with matching studded collars around their necks. They both had ink designs on their arms, as if they'd gone in to have tattals but had to leave before the crystal could be imbedded. For the two hours Kade had known them they'd always seemed more interested in each other than the task at hand. Now, they were serious and focused. Professionals with a job to do. For the first time, neither of them had the little buds plugged into their ears.

"You two ready?"

Peata laughed, a surprisingly feminine tinkle of sound considering her scarred face and broken teeth. "Give us another day and we might be ready."

"No can do."

"Then don't ask pointless questions. Come on." Peata opened the creaking cruiser door and stepped down to the cracked macadam of the parking area. Dolik slipped across the seat and followed her out.

Kade watched the two of them together. He was huge, nearly two metres tall and built like a lorry. He hulked over her tiny form.

"Can they be trusted?" Kade asked Leni quietly.

"Can *I* be trusted?" He shrugged and smiled, tugging at his higher ear. "It was short notice. They aren't the best but they're good. Professional."

"And they owe you a big favor..."

"That's right. And now *you* owe me a big favor."

"All right. Let's do this."

Leni leaned over and opened the door. "I'm already doing what I'm supposed to be doing. We're all just waiting for you. Good luck."

Kade collected two double-barreled pistols, a dagger, bandolier, mask and gloves from the floor near his feet, took a deep breath, and climbed out to join the others. He adjusted the bandolier across his chest, slipping a torch into a free loop. He holstered the weapons. Peata and Dolik were checking each other's equipment silently. They rolled down their sleeves, touched each weapon, tightened each buckle and knot. It looked like a ritual. They moved with gentle precision, one at a time.

"Come on."

They walked away without looking back, out of the shadow of the building and into the sharp, late afternoon sunlight.

There was a canal beyond the gap-toothed fence at the back of the parking area. Dirty water splashed and gurgled along the bottom, but a small ledge was visible. It was no more than a kink in the steep, paved wall.

Dolik broke two loose palings, climbed through the fence and slid down. He shuffled downstream and a minute later Kade was by his side, examining the wide mouth of a storm-water pipe. A trickle of foul smelling water glowed faintly green, like a trail of moldy breadcrumbs leading into the darkness.

"This is the one," Dolik said, crouching down to get a better look. He wrinkled his nose in distaste.

"Guess I'm going first."

"Guess so."

Kade squared his shoulders, took a deep breath, wondered what the hell he was doing, and crawled in. He went forward a few metres then paused to make sure his equipment was still secure. Anything to delay just a little bit more; the smell was worse in the confined space.

"You *are* good for the money, aren't you, Kade?" Dolik was still in the canal. He face was bathed in sunlight. He had his hand on Peata's hip and was guiding her into the pipe.

Kade nodded, brushing his head against the cold, slimy concrete. He resisted the urge to wipe his scalp. "You may not get it immediately, but you'll get it." *As long as Roke or I survive this mess,* he added silently.

For a moment, the other man didn't move. The look on his face eloquently suggested what he really thought of promises, but eventually he nodded as well.

Soon, Kade was in complete darkness but didn't bother with the torch as he didn't really want to know what he was crawling through. He groped out in front with his hands, wincing every time he made contact with the thick, slow moving water. He began to think the slime was eating away at his skin, starting at the tips of his fingers and moving up his arm. It was hard to breathe. Air gathered on his tongue like acid-soaked cotton wool. His eyes watered. He began to think he was never going to see again.

After what seemed like hours, but could not have been more than a few minutes, soft light seeped back into the world. The water started to glow again. He could hear people. Footsteps and voices.

Kade poked his head out into an intersection where pipes came in on three different levels. Strips of sunlight marked a section of rough concrete wall. Shadows flickered as pedestrians walked over the grate above.

Someone nudged him from behind and Kade climbed out into the open, standing up to his full height and stretching his back. Peata and Dolik followed silently.

A thick sludge covered the floor. It released a new stench each time someone moved, tried to suck off boots with every step.

Automatically checking his equipment, Kade gestured to a pipe. Dolik nodded confirmation.

Kade took another deep breath, almost gagged, and wiped at his watering eyes with the back of his arm. When he ran out of excuses, he hauled himself up and crawled some more. He might have kept going all day, moving into the darkness like an automaton, but somebody hissed at him from behind.

"This should be it." The voice echoed and rumbled, gathering slime and darkness as it went. It was unrecognizable. "Should be just ahead."

Kade groped for the torch and clicked it on. There was a hatch just a couple of metres further on. The locking mechanism, attached to a handle on the outside, was stuck with age and grime. Kade took a spanner from his pack and fitted it in place over the nut at the end of the shaft. When it was in place contorted himself in the confined space, grunting and heaving as he worked at it with gritted teeth. The spanner shifted once, slightly, then moved no more.

The voice again. "Move up. Let me have a go." Dolik then.

Kade did as he was asked, shuffling further along and shining the torch back the other way. Dolik, at the end of the queue, set to work, lying on his back in the slime. Kade thought he could hear the quivering of the other man's muscles, feel the tension coming off him in waves. He held his breath.

"Thorn that's tight. Hasn't been moved in years. I don't know if—"

There was a crack.

"Wait a second."

Squeaking... Grinding... A sliver of light. Kade breathed again as Dolik used his feet to swing the hatch open. When there was a full circle of light, the big man poked his head through the climbed out into the open. A minute later, Kade was out as well, crouching on the pipe, coughing and sucking in air, looking around at a small grey room. Tools hung from hooks on a wall. Other pipes and cables crossed the space overhead. The light was only dim, but he turned off the torch.

"Thank Thorn for that."

Peata smiled. "Yeah, and that was the easy bit. Now all we have to do is go up one level and through about fifty metres of the Administration Complex."

"Will it smell?" Kade asked, wondering if he could find something to scrape the remains of the drain off his tongue.

"No."

"Then let's do it." He gently closed the hatch as if that would mean they didn't have to go back out that way very soon. "Come on." He jumped down to the floor and headed for the only door.

"Check your weapons first," Dolik said, even as he suited action to words.

Kade unholstered his pistols. The frizzen on one was loose, the pan beneath empty. He nodded his thanks as he used the tools on the wall to make a quick repair. When he had reloaded he went to the door.

"Mask," Peata said.

"Thorn." Kade pulled the black woolen hood from his pocket, dropped it, snatched it up again and pulled it violently down over his head. Then he got the gloves on as well. "Am I ready now?" He felt like a schoolboy on his first day.

"You look great."

"Gee, thanks."

"Been a while has it?"

"You have no idea." *And hopefully it would be a while before the next time.* His hand shook as he opened the door. He wondered if the others could see. But it didn't matter. Fear was only relevant if you let it stop you doing what needed to be done. Action and reaction was all that mattered, not how you felt about it. He kept telling himself that as he looked into the next room.

A huge, humming crystal pump took up most of the space. A rat's nest of ancient, rusting pipes surrounded it. Shining, oily puddles covered the floor. Water dripped. Lamps threw knots of shadow. Kade ducked and wove his way across the room.

"Let's try not to kill anyone," he said as he bent to look at the alarm cells clustered by the door. Twist this crystal here. Turn that crystal there. Disconnect another over there.

"If it's a choice of them or me..."

"Yeah, I know. But last resort, all right." He hoped they couldn't hear the shaking in his voice. "This whole thing is messy enough as it is."

The alarm was ten years out of date and easy enough to bypass. It took just a couple of minutes. Kade wondered if it was supposed to stop people getting into the room or getting out.

Out into a wide, dull hallway. Ancient crystal-lamps spluttered on the wall; the whirrer caps were wearing thin if Kade knew anything at all. The metal brackets that held them were well made but rusting. Pipes and filaments traced patterns on the ceiling. Dust hung in the still, heavy air. Tired doors on either side. The pump, furnace and waste management on the right according to the plaques. Crystal powder, cleaning equipment and the laundry on the left. Only the laundry showed any signs of life with a constant mumble of sound coming from beyond the door but, according to the building plans, the huge room's main entrance was elsewhere.

Kade moved quickly down the hall, stooped and watchful, with his companions close behind. Stairs at the end.

They climbed the first flight, two at a time, almost silent. A hall, bright with light, running from left to right. Busy to the left with domestic staff from the hospital one floor up. Cooks and cleaners coming and going, sitting on benches along the walls, legs stretched out before them, chatting and smoking.

Nobody to the right.

Kade pulled off his mask, took a deep breath, and walked out into the passage. He turned right. Let them see the back of his bald head. Could be anyone. Less suspicious than a mask. The others followed.

Four doors in this direction—a stairwell, tool locker, storage room and the morgue. It was locked.

Kade cursed, took out his lock pick and started to work. The lock wasn't intricate but it would only take a few seconds for someone to notice.

"Hurry it up," Peata hissed. She stood between Kade and the hospital workers and was pulling her mask on as someone started down the hall towards their position.

Kade worked blindly, watching the man approach. A tumbler dropped and he looked back to his task. The lock gave a moment later.

Mask on. Open the door.

Kade's shoes squeaked loudly on the tiled floor as he stepped inside. Sparkling white. The bite of acid and alkaline. Disinfectant scratching at his eyes. The familiar, heavy smell of death. There were four examination tables, all of them occupied. Another six bodies, covered with white sheets, lay on wheeled beds around the walls. A bad night in Tribalin.

"That's her over there," Kade said, staying near the door to keep watch. Kiri looked peaceful. She might have been sleeping.

Dolik squeaked across to her and paused to look. "We've got to get her back through the pipes?"

"Unless you have a better idea. There'll be enough guards around here in a minute without trying to go past the constables upstairs as well." He didn't want to think about the constabulary headquarters, about fifty metres away.

Dolik examined his options and, grabbing the end of the bed, rolled it towards the door. In his rush, he bumped against another of the beds. That, in turn, clunked against the wall, sounding impossibly loud. An arm slithered out from beneath the sheet, hanging limply. It swung back and forth for a moment, a badly broken finger pointing at nothing.

"Don't just stand there," Peata said, nudging Kade.

Dolik approached and Peata went out into the hall. After a moment, Kade tore his gaze away from the crooked, pulpy finger and followed. People milled about down the far end of the corridor. It wasn't immediately obvious if anyone had gone to get help.

"Come on."

Kade headed for the stairs, drawing his pistols as he went. He considered telling everyone to remain where they were but decided they'd get the idea. He pointed his weapons in their general direction and the shifting, nervous group became suddenly still and even more nervous.

But there were other problems. Men were coming down the stairs. Heavy boots and rattling weapons.

Nearing the stairs, Kade put a slug into the wall.

Someone swore. The sounds of movement stopped.

Kade took two steps forward. When he could see the sleeve of a uniform, he fired again. The slug sent shards of stone out from the wall.

More cursing. A cautious retreat.

"There's no way out of there," someone shouted.

Kade handed his empty pistol to Peata for reloading and turned his attention to the hospital workers. "All of you into the kitchen," he said, roughening and deepening his voice. "Next person who steps back out after that will get themselves shot."

"You know we can't go to the kitchen," the man on the steps replied.

"Not you lot." Kade sighed and shook his head. "There's people in the hall, idiot. I'm sending them into the kitchen." He waved his gun like a traffic controller.

The people didn't quite stampede for the door but it was close.

"Nobody needs to die," the man on the steps shouted.

"Good to hear," Peata mumbled, handing the gun back to Kade.

Kade took another couple of careful steps forward. He fired close to another arm and caused another slow retreat. The process was repeated twice more before the stairway was completely clear.

A head poked around the corner at the top then ducked back out of sight.

"I'll shoot the next thing that moves," Kade said. He knelt in the middle of the hall, looking up the stairs, and motioned for Dolik to go.

Peata crouched as well, covering as the big man hoisted Kiri onto his shoulder, staggered, then hurried down the stairs as best he could.

Something moved. The barrel of a rifle stuck out into the hall. Kade fired. The ball clanged against the barrel. Lucky shot. Someone cursed loudly.

"Just to prove my earlier shots were deliberate misses." Kade changed the fully loaded pistol to his right hand. Single shot left in the other. The weight was starting to tire his arms.

"Clear," Peata said softly.

Kade backed across the hall, weapons ready, and started down the stairs. He paused before he lost sight of the enemy position above and called Peata through.

Downstairs, Dolik was leaning against the wall near the pump room. "This will take us a week," he said when Kade reached the bottom of the stairs. He pushed away from the wall and staggered further down the hall. "I don't know if I can do it."

Kade didn't know that he'd get very far at all. "Well we... Thorn..." He looked around as is the answer to the problem would be right there in front of him. It was. "The furnace. Quick, up here."

The door to the furnace was locked. Kade didn't bother with his picks. He kicked once near the lock but did nothing more than hurt his knee. He shifted his effort to the hinge side and the door clattered to the floor a moment later. A wave of heat washed over him, reminding him of his little workshop back on Whiparill. But there was no time to think. Dolik shouldered past him into the room.

Kade opened the door to the furnace, burning his fingers on the hot metal.

"Out of the way," Dolik said through gritted teeth

Kade helped shove the body in through the small door. Kiri's dress caught fire, blazing high. Then they had her in and were dancing away from the flames, shielding their faces.

"Come on." Dolik wiped sweat from his forehead. "Let's get out of here."

"Wait. We have to stoke it up a bit first. It's only her dress on fire now." Kade took a few pieces of wood from a supply in the corner and threw them in. He found a poker and livened the glowing coals, sending a shower of sparks out into the room. "More wood." He repeated the process and got the fire blazing high. Then coal as well to keep it going longer. Shadows danced. A patch of wall on the far side of the hall glowed bright.

Kiri was going. Her lips were gone, showing her teeth like a grimace of pain, and her eyes boiled. Hardening tattals shattered. Soon there would be nothing recognizable left. The taste of burning flesh hung heavy in the air. Almost overpowering. Kade thought he was going to throw up but a gun shot from the hall distracted him.

"Pea?" Dolik said.

"They won't wait much longer. They're getting curious." Another shot.

Swallowing bile, Kade said a small prayer and slammed the furnace door closed.

"Here they come."

Kade and Dolik raced out the door. Without looking back, they headed for the pump room. Peata followed.

When he reached the door, Kade turned. Men were coming down the stairs, weapons ready. Kade fired two shots into the stone near their feet but it didn't slow them this time.

"No use waiting here," Dolik said, dragging him through the door towards the pipe.

Kade threw his mask into the canal. He stripped off black jacket and gloves and they followed. The first wisps of evening ran icy fingers up his arms, reminding him of the earlier heat. He dipped his red, tender hands into the water for a moment. The scum and dirt wouldn't help but the moisture did. When his breathing calmed, he scrambled up the wall and through the gap in the fence. Shadows pooled in corners of the parking area, shrinking away from the street lamps like wild animals.

Leni had parked close to the gap in the fence. The cruiser's crystal engine hummed quietly, hardly louder than a flutter of moth wings. Leni was inside, feet on the control panel, eyes closed. He jumped when Kade opened the door.

"You're back."

"You didn't expect us?"

"Well..."

"Have a little faith, Leni."

"And the others?"

Kade ignored the suggestion in the question. "They made it as well, Leni." Just then Dolik hauled himself through the gap then helped Peata.

"Ahhh..." Leni craned his neck to look. "Weren't there supposed to be four of you?"

"Easier options became available." Kade stashed his bandolier and pistols under the seat, breathed in the chill air.

"But it's done?"

Kade nodded. "Yes. It's done." He thought the shaking had passed, but his legs would hardly hold him. He collapsed into the seat and closed his eyes.

"Are you two getting in?" Leni asked Peata and Dolik.

"No." Peata came over to lean on the open door. "We should probably split up as quickly as possible. You know where to find us when that money becomes available, Kade?"

"Of course."

Peata flashed her broken teeth. "I reckon we'll be hearing about this job for a while to come, Kade. See you around."

"Thanks, Peata." He leaned outside and gave Dolik the thumbs up. "Thanks, Dol."

The two thieves walked quickly across the carpark, putting the buds back in their ears. Peata started to sing.

"Where to, boss?" Leni asked. He put the cruiser into gear and moved slowly to the street.

"The first thing I have to do is wash; they'd smell me coming a mile off. Take me to Roke's place."

"And after that?" Leni tapped his finger on the steering wheel, keeping beat with music only he could hear. "A celebratory drink, perhaps?"

Kade watched the drumming finger. The finger. "No," he said absently. "The day isn't over yet."

"Not over?" Leni smiled and shook his head. "This job may well go down in history, Kade."

Kade sighed. Not the discreet operation he'd planned. He leaned back in the seat and thought of broken fingers.

III

Kade gripped the edge of the counter, drumming his fingers against the cold timber. A short, plump woman with swirls of tattal on her scalp stumped out to meet him as if he represented an hour of paper work. Her uniform looked like it hadn't been washed in a week.

"This had better be good," she said, slapping down a pile of files and looking up with mock interest.

"Ummm..." Kade stilled his fingers with an effort. He wondered if he should have stayed at home. There probably wasn't much chance of getting in to see Roke anyway, not with a crime spree in full bloom. But there were questions that needed to be asked. Mysteries that needed to be solved.

"Cat got your tongue?" the constable asked.

Kade tried to put on a look of mock concern to match her mock interest. "I suppose that would involve a lot of paper work? A crime like that?"

The woman smiled. Just. She adjusted her pile and smiled some more.

"I'd like to see Detective Mirani. Please. If I could."

"Do you know what's going on here today?"

He'd started with the light-hearted banter so it would probably look strange if he didn't continue. He tried to think. "Ummm... Paper work is being avoided? Pastries are being eaten?"

"I wish." She shook her head. "Thorn, do I wish. No, Tribalin is going to hell, right before our very eyes."

"Oh. I..." Kade gestured vaguely. "Roke just said I should..." He must have looked suitably pathetic for the woman took pity on him.

"Come on through and I'll see if I can find him." She came around from behind the counter and led the way out the room's third door.

The desks in the next large, long room were lined up with military precision but everything else was in a state of chaos. Files were piled twenty centimetres high, threatening to topple to the floor at any moment. People came and went, squeezing between chairs and desks and open filing cabinets. Everyone seemed to be on the brink of hair pulling, teeth gnashing frenzy.

Down the far end of the room, almost twenty metres away, a group of officers were gathered around a chalkboard. Though they were almost perfectly still—slumped in chairs and on desks, hands clasped before them—they seemed closer to the edge than anyone else.

"It isn't normally this bad," Kade's escort told him. "We had a busy night last night."

"Oh."

"It looks like Roke is with the task force. I'll see if he has time to talk to you."

Kade could see Roke in the centre of the calm pool, pointing to a list on the chalkboard, apparently handing out assignments. If he was in charge he probably had the toughest job of them all. He had to solve the crimes without actually giving away his mother's involvement.

Before the woman was halfway down the room, Roke saw Kade and nodded. He held up five fingers. Five minutes, Kade assumed. His escort came to the same conclusion.

"Well, that's sorted," she said. "I've got things to do."

"I'll be fine. Thank you."

The woman headed back the way they'd come and Kade sat on the edge of a desk. He succeeded in upsetting a leaning stack of files.

"Thorn." Papers broke free of the confining folders. They slithered across the floor, hid under desks. A constable, single star on her epaulette, put a boot print in the middle of one as she tried to skip through the flurry.

"Damn it," she said. "Who are you? Are you supposed to be back here?"

"Sorry." Kade crouched down and started gathering sheets. "Ah... Yes. Sort of. I'm Kade. I'm here to see Detective Mirani."

The woman examined the snowdrift of papers for a moment then sighed and stooped to help. She looked like she'd been up all night. "Detective Mirani is busy."

"Yes, I know. But he's already indicated he'll see me in a couple of minutes." Kade stood up, a rough, shuffled pile in either hand. "Ummm... Where..?"

"Seeing you upset them you can help sort them out if you like. Just until the Detective gets here."

"Of course I'll help. Thank *you* for helping. You must be busy with... everything."

She gave a soft, tired laugh. "My day hasn't actually been all that different to usual. I normally just run errands anyway, go where people tell me. One of these piles was bound to topple eventually and I'd have been the one cleaning up the mess."

"That's obviously a serious waste of talent," Kade mumbled. He was continuing with the banter of earlier but wasn't actually sure if he wanted to say it out loud. She was very attractive—with sharp blue eyes, long dark hair and a full mouth that seemed to hover on the edge of a smile—but now was hardly the time for flirting.

But apparently the woman heard him. She looked up and smiled.

Kade cleared his throat, examined the files he was holding. "So, what am I doing with these?"

She slapped a pile down on a desk and polished the tattal on her temple with the tip of her finger as she tried to think. The flesh around the butterfly was still red and puffy from the implanting procedure. "There should be a number on the top corner of each page. That's the case number. Find the folder with the same number. Easy."

"Right." But Kade didn't move.

The woman was already concentrating on the files, holding them between different fingers, swapping them, switching them around. She looked up. "The black number. Don't worry about the red bit."

"Yes." He gathered his thoughts and move to stand beside her. "Right."

"Good. We'll get the folders in some sort of order first." She set to work again.

"I'm Kade," he said again.

"I know. You said already."

She worked in silence after that while Kade concentrated on her long, slim fingers.

Eventually, the woman paused to look up. Kade could feel her breath on his cheek. Her blue eyes were clouded with fatigue. She smelled faintly of lavender and vairen.

"I'm Lana."

"Nice to meet you, Lana." Kade turned his attention to the pages he still held. He was creasing them and loosened his grip.

"What have you got there?"

Kade spun his pile of pages around and looked at the number in the corner. "It's..."

"Kade, what are you doing here?"

Roke grabbed his shoulder in a friendly fashion and Kade wondered how far he was going to have to take his cover now they were together in public.

"You said I should come to visit," Kade said. "I was—"

"So I did. It's just been so busy today." Roke looked around, as if wondering if his presence could be spared for a couple of minutes. "Why don't you come into my office? You're right with this Lana?"

"Of course, Detective."

Kade could feel the eyes of many of the constables on him as Roke led him towards the end of the room. He wondered if he was the latest in a line of men being shown to Roke's office. He looked back at Lana. She was watching him and he mouthed "Sorry," at her. She shrugged in reply and returned to her work.

When the door was closed behind him, Kade breathed a sigh of relief. "I'm sorry if this is..."

"I'll reserve my judgment until after I hear why you're here." Roke sat down behind the desk and motioned Kade to another chair. "I assume this isn't just a social call. It's safe to talk."

"Firstly then, I'm sorry, but we had to burn Kiri." Though he'd been reassured, Kade checked to see if anyone was snooping. "She was..."

Roke waved a hand to silence him. "I know what she was, Kade, the good and the bad. It might have been nice to say goodbye but things don't always work out the way we planned. I didn't have to see her in the morgue is the main thing." He straightened an already straight pile of papers. "I realize I was at more risk than you or anyone else, so I thank you for your efforts."

"She didn't deserve to..." He couldn't think of how to finish the sentence, but he was sure it was true anyway, whatever he'd been going to say.

"No, she didn't. But that's not why you're here either. Let's get to the point."

"Right." Suddenly Kade wasn't sure. He was wasting time. He was... He rubbed his thumb along the tips of his fingers.

"What is it? Come on."

"Well, there's a man in your morgue with a broken finger."

Roke nodded slowly. "Right. But if he's in the morgue then I assume a broken finger is the least of his problems."

"I think I'm the one who broke his finger. Maybe."

"You're painting a lovely picture here, Kade, but it isn't in any language I understand."

"The last time I saw the man with the broken finger, his buddies were carrying him out of the laboratory."

"All the guards were killed, Kade. The only people who left that building were you and..." Roke leaned back in his chair and pulled on his lock of hair. "Oh," he said. "I see. Are you sure?"

Kade shrugged. "It's just a broken finger but I'm pretty sure."

Roke suddenly surged up from his chair and went out the door. "Wait here," he said, just before it closed behind him.

He returned several minutes later and slumped back to his previous position. "Apparently the broken finger belongs to a merchant who was beaten and robbed in the Hold last night. A business associate named Merik Bolkin took him to the customs station, alive but unconscious. He died in hospital."

"He died from blows to the head?" Another one to add to his list.

"Yes. You don't take chances, do you? Remind me to just shoot you next time we get into a fight."

"So the cell is still in the Hold..."

"Possibly, but the Hold is out of our jurisdiction. And there's no way I could link the death to my case."

Kade tried to think. "You could say you don't like coincidences," he said eventually. "A dozen dead people in one night and only one of them isn't related?"

Roke shook his head. "No. It would be even stranger if that one death *were* related. People get mugged every day, especially in the Hold, so why would this one make me suspicious?" He flicked through the papers on his desk, lost in thought. "There is something I know, though," he said after a while. "I know what our strangers were stealing."

"You do?"

"It's a light."

"What? A light? But that's—"

"It wasn't just any light, my dear Kade. It was a very powerful light. The brightest light ever. A light so powerful you can feel its heat from a kilometre away. It will singe the hair off your arm at eight hundred metres and burn a hole in your chest at five hundred. It's a weapon like none we've ever seen."

"In that one cell?"

"No. In total, ten arrays are needed but the others are all fairly basic, if you know how to cluster them." Roke leaned forward resting his arms on the desk. "But Kade, that weapon I described could be carried by a man, if he was feeling energetic. Imagine what a larger one would do."

Kade didn't want to imagine. There were rogue skylands that wouldn't hesitate to use such a weapon. "Imagine what a smaller one could do," he said.

Roke nodded, giving the idea some thought. "I can't go to the Hold," he said after a while, "but you can. Go ask some questions. See what you can find out."

"I don't know anything about investigating crimes." From all the recent evidence he no longer knew much about committing them either.

"Neither do half the people out there."

"Why should I do anything at all?" Kade said. "I like your mother, Roke, and I like you, but right now the last thing I want to do is hang around acting suspiciously where the Skyway Men might find me."

Roke thought for a moment then shook his head. "How about this then—do you want them to be in possession of something like that? How about another group who isn't afraid of setting up the Skyway Men? Do you want them to have it?"

"You're appealing to my good nature and sense of community spirit?"

"I guess so."

Kade almost laughed. Except he *didn't* want criminals having a weapon that powerful. He knew what the Skyway Men were like. He knew what they'd do given the opportunity.

"And as you said," Roke continued, "my mother didn't deserve..."

Kade held up a hand. "All right. Thorn, I'll do it."

Roke leaned back in his chair, sighed. "Sorry. Thank you." He straightened the papers on his desk again. "My mother may have been a criminal, but she was basically a good person. She was a good mother."

"I'll go first thing tomorrow morning." He didn't want to go anywhere. He wanted to sleep. He wanted to wake up on Whiparill. Every moment he was discovering that he'd changed more than he had realized. "I'll need some more money."

IV

Merchants packed the small inspection area and the short passage to the Crossing Yard. They waved contracts and memory crystals in the air, shouting about lost profits and unhappy clients. A line of soldiers stopped them advancing any further.

A customs officer, scalp tattals gleaming in the early morning sun, slipped out of the Customs Post. He stood at the top of the stairs overlooking the crowd and held up his hands to little effect. After a minute, he shouted into the riot. "Please, unless you wish to come through to Tribalin, go back to the Crossing Yard." It was doubtful anyone could hear. If they could, they took no notice. "There's nothing we can do. Messengers are at the Administration Centre at this very moment trying to find out what's happening."

But of course, the scheduled run of a skyland was nothing more than a guide. No guarantees were made. The Captain could change course on a whim, though he might answer to the council afterwards. The events of the past day were a more than acceptable reason.

The crowd pushed forward again, shouting and waving, but the soldiers held their line. Some had arms locked and feet set. Some used the butts of their muskets to quiet the more forceful of the protesters. Others waved swords threateningly.

Kade waited behind the line with a junior official, hands stuffed in his jacket pockets to keep them warm.

"Are you sure you want to go through there?" the woman asked, smoothing the front of her uniform as if the very thought of such a venture was crinkling it.

Kade nodded. "I don't have any choice. My friend is expecting me." There was no friend, of course, but he wanted find the weapon array as soon as possible. Every hour he delayed made the task harder. He'd also had an uneasy feeling all morning, as if he was being watched... He glanced back over his shoulder.

When the skyland was docked, Nost Square would be bubbling with activity. Now, there was a casual atmosphere. The local merchants offered genuine smiles and bantered happily with competitors and customers alike, watching the scenes in the inspection area with wry amusement. They sat comfortably, legs stretched out in the sun, colorful scarves wrapped tightly around their necks, and let the money come to them.

There was nothing suspicious, so Kade turned to regard the shouting mob once more. The public altimetre on the back of the watchtower had climbed to 4300 metres and was now holding steady. The merchants would probably tire quickly in the thin air, but more would come to take their place. Kade didn't have the time to outwait them all.

"Well, here goes," he said to the woman by his side, taking a deep breath of the cool, crisp air. "Wish me luck."

"Good luck." She pressed the button that sent Kade's details, and the fact he was entering the Crossing Yard, through to the skyland's systems. If he returned within four hours and wasn't carrying anything he would avoid the tax.

Kade nudged between two soldiers and plunged into the fray. It was bad in the inspection area. The crowd surged and shifted, jostling, shoving. They took no notice of those around them, merely trying to get the attention of the man in charge. If he was a pickpocket, Kade could have made a small fortune by the time he'd moved five metres. Beyond the inspection area, in the passage, it was even worse. It was all

Kade could do to make headway. Men and women were crammed between the walls like sacks in an overloaded grain lorry. It was hard to breathe. The smell of sweat and strange spices and tobacco made him gag. Somebody trod on his toe. He swore and blinked tears from his eyes when somebody elbowed him in the ribs.

"Watch it," Kade said through gritted teeth. But he couldn't identify the offender and could hardly hear his own complaint anyway.

It was almost fifteen minutes before he fought his way clear of the passage and burst out into the Crossing Yard like a cork from a bottle. He gasped for breath and rubbed bruised limbs.

The Yard was relatively quiet. Merchants were gathered around the fire drums, chatting and trying to keep warm. They might have come to protest as well, but they couldn't see what was happening and couldn't be seen. Vehicles were lined up in neat rows: lorries and cruisers, handcarts and scooters. The owners were close by, or somewhere in the apartments and dormitories set into the walls of the Yard.

The gate to the dock was on the right. The passage to the Hold was on the left. The Hold was almost at the centre of Tribalin and the passages to the four Crossing Yards radiated out from there like spokes. This was the case on most skylands. Because of this, the group that controlled the mainly itinerant population was called the Spokesmen. They were in every Hold and had been for as long as anyone could remember. They had probably started somewhere as a group of standover men but eventually turned to more peaceful means. They still had no *official* powers but that didn't mean much.

Kade examined the Yard but could see none of their red uniforms. He went to see who he could find.

Once, long ago, the passages had been nothing more than tunnels carved into the stone, with rough timber support beams overhead and dusty ground beneath. There'd hardly been enough room for two lorries to pass side by side. Now, parking spaces lined the concrete walls and there were fast lanes and slow lanes going each direction. A café filled a wall niche. Merchants wearing fine silks and fancy hats sat shoulder to shoulder with burly lorry drivers and wary, weary travelers, sipping strong, aromatic coffee and nibbling pastries as they argued about the strange turn of events. Scheduled runs might just be a guide, but they were guides that were followed more often than not.

Kade hurried along the footpath, hemmed in between lorries and the wall. The feeling of being watched persisted but when he glanced back he never saw anything to confirm his suspicions.

The crowds thinned as he continued towards the Hold. He'd gone about half way down the long slope before he finally found a Spokesman. The woman was sitting in a little tiled alcove with several memory crystals and an LCD hardwired into the walls and a reader on the floor by her chair. She straightened her uniform when it became obvious Kade was heading in her direction.

"How can I help?" She had pale skin and large, dark eyes.

Kade check over his shoulder again. "I'm looking for a friend of mine," he said. "His name is Merik Bolkin."

"A friend?" She shook her head but took up her reader and held it to a crystal on the wall. "The details are none of my concern; I just give out information." She went onto a different crystal and scrolled through several screens on the reader. "Here we go," she said. "A wealth of information."

Kade handed over fifty doms, the standard price for information from the Spokesmen. A wealth, indeed.

The woman slipped the money into a pouch at her belt and started to read. "Merik Bolkin. Timber merchant. He's been living in the hold for six months. Rat Alley, between Dust and Grime. Blue Stack. Level 5. He also has a truck parked in Bay 7 of the port wall. It hasn't moved since he arrived, apparently."

"How old is the information."

"About two months."

That wasn't too bad. He wondered what else he needed to know. He looked up and down the tunnel, trying to think. "Known associates or affiliations?"

She shrugged. "Nothing of interest according to this."

"Thank you." He'd probably forgotten something. "Can I buy a dagger here?"

The Spokesman pulled a box out of a slot in the wall. It was filled with a jumble of knives and stickers. Kade had a quick look through, chose a small, relatively rust free, double-edged dagger, and paid the exorbitant price.

"A pleasure doing business with you," the woman said.

"I bet."

"We can handle that for you too, if you like."

The Hold was two hundred metres square. The passage Kade was following came out near the forward, starboard corner. Like in the Crossing Yard, there were apartments set in the walls with narrow windows and balconies. Here, they were prime real estate and guarded fiercely. Near him were empty spaces and parked vehicles with makeshift campgrounds scattered between. To the aft was the town Roke had mentioned. There was a buzz of activity that echoed dully off the old red brick walls. The smell of stagnation was choking and smoke hid the ceiling, swirling lazily as it searched for the chimney holes.

Kade headed aft, head down, hands in his pockets. He followed the road that linked the two starboard tunnels letting ,the flow of traffic take him along. It was mainly pedestrians, but now and then a cruiser or lorry would nudge past, heading for who knew where. For the most part, the road stuck close to the wall but detoured once for a jumbled, ancient palisade protecting a rough camp that looked to have been there for decades. The ramshackle town loomed large. It was a strange place of huge metal and timber packing crates piled haphazardly like a child's building blocks. It looked like it might fall over at any moment.

By the time Kade moved off the road and between the first of the stacks, he was moving at a leisurely stroll. A sign painted on the side of a metal crate announced 'Crooked

Alley' though the thin, wavy script lacked any real conviction. He knew he was being followed now and finally had the opportunity to do something about it. He leaned against the wall to wait. A steady trickle of people moved past. Merchants in colorful robes to long-term beggars in scraps of cloth and artisans in everything between.

"What do you want?"

An old woman poked her bald, tattless head through a window and flashed Kade a picket fence sneer.

"None of your business. I—"

Kade cocked his head at the sound of hurried footsteps, out of place amidst the slow pace of the Hold. He drew his new dagger, pushed away from the wall and readied himself. Someone rushed into view with the strange careful-hurrying motions of a tail about to lose their mark. Kade grabbed an arm, spun his pursuer and threw them against the wall. The metal crate boomed like an out-of-tune steel drum and something clattered to the floor inside. The crowd on the street drifted away as if they'd never been there. The old woman at the window disappeared, slamming a pair of rotting, lopsided shutters so hard they almost fell apart.

"What do you want?" Kade asked.

It was a woman. He held her against the wall with a forearm across her throat and the knife pricking the skin just below her rib cage. He didn't know if he could use the knife if it came to that.

"Who are you?" Their faces were close, noses almost touching. He breathed in the scent of lavender and vairen.

Kade's tension leaked away slightly and he leaned back to get a better look at the woman's face, at the tattal on her temple. It was a butterfly, the flesh around it still red and tender.

"I... I..." the woman said, swallowing. Her sharp blue eyes flickered this way and that as if the answers to Kade's questions might be painted on the wall like the unconvinced sign.

"Lana?"

The constable nodded slightly, hesitantly, and bit her bottom lip.

"What are you doing here? You shouldn't be here."

She breathed deeply and rubbed her neck when Kade released her. "I know something's going on."

"So? That doesn't mean you should... That doesn't answer my question."

"You and Detective Mar—"

Kade gave Lana a looked that silenced her immediately.

She cleared her throat. "You're up to something. A farmer from Whiparill wouldn't—"

"I'm a metal worker."

"Whatever. You shouldn't have noticed me following you—I was very careful—and if you did notice you would run, not attack."

"I was just—" He looked at the knife and slipped it under his belt.

"Don't bother, Kade. I won't believe you anyway."

Kade held back a sigh and looked around. The foot traffic was flowing again, moving steadily along the narrow alleys.

"I'm tired of hanging around the office, making coffee and running errands," Lana whispered. "I want to..." She didn't finish.

"You want to what?" He tried to hold on to his anger but she kept cocking her head to one side, looking at him.

"I want to *do* something." She straightened the ruffles at the collar of her blouse. A plain dark green, it had a high neckline and was pulled tight across her breasts.

"Well..." Kade blinked, tried to gather his thoughts. "Well, go to a market and catch a pickpocket then."

"I want to help. If you don't let me help I'll go back and suggest someone looks into your history."

"You think I'm scared of being investigated by the constabulary and yet you want to help me?" Anger would have hidden his unease, but she was still right there, head cocked to the side, butterfly tattal glowing a soft, warm silver.

"I don't think you're a criminal. I know..." Lana glanced at he people nearest. "I know your friend and I trust him."

"So where's the threat?"

"You're... undercover, part of some bigger investigation."

Kade shook his head and walked back out onto the main street with Lana following close behind, as if unwilling to let him go *anywhere* without her. The apartment set in the wall opposite had been converted into a little café so he went across and sat at one of the rough tables set up on the raised footpath.

"You can't help," Kade said, leaning in close to whisper. The chair creaked, sounding as if it was about to fall apart. He could smell her perfume, even amongst the coffee, spicy rolls and cheroots.

A girl with only one arm and a greasy apron loomed over them. "What can I get you?"

"Nothing," Kade said.

But Lana held up a stalling hand. "Two coffees, please."

The girl nodded and sauntered away, apparently not all that excited about her job.

Kade turned to Lana. She had pushed back her hood, exposing her creamy skin to the light arrays. "You can't help," he repeated. "This is not a..." He examined his hands where he gripped the edge of the table. What was it not? What was it? "This is a dangerous place."

"Well then, you'd better keep me close so you can protect me." She rubbed at her tattal with the tip of her finger.

"Don't keep touching it. It won't set straight."

"Don't change the subject," she said, clasping her hands on the table. "One way or another, I'm going to find out what's going on."

"Nothing's going on." It sounded stupid, even to Kade, like a child, pilfered jam clinging to his face and fingers, proclaiming his innocence.

"You aren't a metal worker." Lana shushed Kade before he could even start to protest. "You aren't *just* a metal worker. And you like me quite a bit more than you like... your friend." She smoothed the front of her already smooth blouse and smiled teasingly.

Kade examined his hands, rubbed at a stain on the table's scarred surface, tried to think of something to say that wasn't stupid or dangerous or both.

Lana laughed softly then continued. "And you aren't down here to visit a friend or conduct business. I questioned the Spokesman. You're looking for Merik Bolkin, who happens to be involved, in one way or another, in a murder."

"Maybe I'm down here to pay Bolkin for a job well done."

Lana hesitated, looking suddenly nervous as if she hadn't given the possibility any thought before that. The moment was broken by the return of the waitress. The girl set the cups on the table, sloshing the thick, dirty coffee over the side.

"Three doms."

Kade took out his purse and paid before Lana could. When they were alone again he said, "You don't know me. You think there's some amazing investigation involving secret constabulary or something but haven't given any consideration to what that really means."

"I don't want to spend another year hanging around the office. I enjoy serving coffee as much as our waitress."

"Maybe they keep you hanging around there for a reason. Lana..." He wanted to protect her, but the best way to do that was to get her back up above ground. There were a lot of arguments Kade could use but he knew none of them would make any difference, especially since he couldn't convince himself that he wanted her to leave. He sighed. "Stop poking the tattal," he told her and she wrapped her hands around her coffee mug.

"I'll just keep following you and you know it."

Kade sighed. "Come on then."

"Let me have some coffee."

"You don't want it."

Lana tried it anyway, taking a hurried sip as she rose to her feet. She winced, spilled half the cup as she quickly clattered it back to the table, then hurried across the street as Kade stepped into the shadows between the stacks.

V

The town was a strange, haphazard place that looked as if it had fallen randomly from above and might continue its downward journey at any moment. Some of the rough, twisted, haphazard stacks went all the way to the ceiling twenty metres up. They were made from crates either two or three metres high and were painted with different colors and patterns like a garden gone wild. None of the individual crates, made for the backs of huge lorries, seemed to be aligned properly with the one above or below. Doors and windows were cut into the walls. There were sharp edges or peculiar shapes with curtains or shutters or metal grilles. Ladders, dangerous conglomerations of timber and nails, were bolted and tied to walls so they'd be harder to steal. Knotted ropes hung limply, offering access for the more nimble. Rickety bridges spanned the narrow alleys on every level.

Kade asked several people for directions and eventually found himself at the end of a narrow, winding alley. The words 'Blossom Lane' were visible on the wall, though they were faded and crossed out. 'Rat Alley' was in fresher paint below.

"It doesn't look like a friendly place," Lana said softly, as if finally realizing what she'd gotten herself into.

She was right. It was so narrow that barely any light from the arrays in the ceiling got to the ground. Piles of rubbish gathered in corners like snowdrifts. Small, scurrying creatures could be heard, if not seen. No people were visible either.

"'Rat' does seem more appropriate than 'Blossom', doesn't it?" Kade cleared his throat and peered into the gloom.. He felt as if he was being watched again, but would've been surprised to walk through the stacks without someone taking an interest. "Come on."

They moved slowly, carefully, keeping an eye out for trouble and trying to avoid stepping in anything unpleasant. Several times they had to turn sideways and squeeze between crates that jutted out into the alley, all but blocking the way.

Finally, they found Grime Alley and ten metres beyond that, a stack painted patchy blue on the bottom three levels. The only way to the fifth level seemed to be via a bridge from the green stack opposite. And the only way to there was... Kade examined the surrounding structures, trying to follow the bridges and ladders that would get him where he needed to go.

Lana stood by his side, looking around as well. With every noise, she shuffled closer until finally her arm was pushed against his. "I suppose you're used to places like this," she said softly, blue eyes scanning the cracks and crevices, the shadows. "How can you not be scared?"

He *was* scared. Ten years seemed longer and longer by the moment. And he couldn't think straight. Kade breathed in Lana's scent.

"If you don't want to be here..."

She shook her head. "I feel safe with you."

Kade turned to look at her. She was close. He could taste her breath. She smiled and he stepped quickly away, looking at the stacks again.

Lana laughed slightly. "How about up there," she said.

"What?" Kade followed her pointing finger to a wooden stack beside the blue and from there traced a convoluted route up to where they wanted to go. "All right." He climbed a rope ladder to the top of the first crate, which was three metres high, then boosted Lana up onto the second, which was only two metres. He scrambled up behind her and squeezed past on the small triangular ledge—bodies touching, her hand on his arm, steadying him against the drop behind—and leapt across to a similar space on the far side of the alley. He paused there to look around and catch his breath. Lana was straightening her ruffles as she examined the gap. A young boy stuck his head out a door to see what the commotion was just as she jumped across.

"What do you want?" the boy asked suspiciously.

"We're just trying to get to level five of the blue stack." Kade pointed.

"Oh. I think the best way to do that is from the next street over." The boy pointed as well, back over his shoulder. "I don't think the guy there likes visitors too much."

"Right. Well, we're here now."

The boy shrugged and went back to whatever he'd been doing.

Kade examined the route again. It didn't look good at all, but he boosted Lana up onto the second three-metre high crate of the yellow stack opposite where they needed to go. From there, it was up a tilting, lopsided ladder, then between two crates towards the street the boy had indicated earlier. They climbed a knotted rope then went back the way they'd come.

Kade was half way up the final ladder, climbing carefully to make sure it didn't pull away from the wall, when he saw movement. Two men exited the fifth level crate of the blue stack and stood on a small porch created by the perpendicular alignment of the crate below. Both men were wearing backpacks and had small canvas bags in their hands.

When Kade stopped moving, Lana bumped into him from below.

"Come on, keep going. This ladder could fall apart at any moment."

The two men, tall and muscular and with tattals on their arms, turned to look. They froze for a moment and Kade froze as well. He'd never seen one of them before but the other... Then they were gone, leaping across a wide gap to the neighboring red stack.

"Damn it."

Kade scrambled to the top of the ladder and raced across to the far side of the alley. The bridge wobbled and creaked beneath him but he took no notice.

Lana tried to keep up.

The men were three stacks away by the time Kade jumped across to the red.

Jump down to a lower level, along a ledge, climb down a series of sharp-edged hand-holes cut into a wall. Across a bridge, then down and down all the way to a busy, relatively wide street. The men were out of sight but angry shouts told Kade where they'd gone. He pushed through the crowd in their wake, leaving his own trail of curse-crumbs for Lana to follow. She wasn't far behind.

Around corners. Through narrow alleys. Up a ladder and through a short, metallic tunnel. Jump to the ground again. The baggage slowed the men down. Kade was pushing through the crowd like a bi-plane through cloud, gaining with every step.

Then his quarry broke into the open for a moment. They crossed a street, raced up some stairs and into one of the apartments in the hold's wall. Kade followed, three steps at a time, boots slapping on the worn stone, and burst into a room.

There was a table to one side, lounging chairs to the other and a kitchen up the back. Flight of stairs on the right.

Five men in all.

Two of them were crouched inside a small passage in the back wall, moving a shelf to cover the opening.

A big man, solid muscle, was standing stupidly by the table. He had a thick slab of bread in his hand, steaming bowl of stew on the table in front of him. The final two were already aiming pistols.

Kade dived without slowing. Rolled to his knees. Grabbed the closest man's groin before he could move. Seized the pistol above his head. He pulled down and threw the gunman like a bag of grain, ramming his head onto the floor. The weapon clattered away across the dirty tiles.

Seconds gone. No time. Kade moved again, rolled away, came to his feet near the table.

Without thinking, he scooped up the stew and hurled it at the remaining gunman. In a reflex action the man threw up a protective arm, but too late. Stew splattered across his face. The bowl glanced off his temple and shattered against the floor behind him. He dropped his pistol as he tried to scrape watery, boiling gravy from his eyes. It was a while before he started screaming.

The big man had exchanged his bread for a sword and came around the end of the table. Kade dodged the first thrust, kicked. He slapped away another unwieldy stab. Danced back.

His opponent stared silently for a moment. Then he smiled, nodded and came again.

Kade stepped inside the swing, blocked with his forearm, punched. But the man was already gone, spinning away. Quicker than was proper for someone that big. Kade spun the other direction. He heard the sword slash close to his head. Too close. His opponent had come in again, was right behind him. Kade spun back in without thinking, ducked. Too late. He took a blow on his jaw, staggered. He tripped and landed hard on his back, right near a fallen pistol. He stared at the weapon. It had gravy on the barrel like congealed blood. It was loaded, cocked.

Kade stared until a shadow fell across him. He reached for the pistol, grabbed at the handle, swung it around. The crack of the shot was loud in the confined space. His ears rang.

A surprised look crossed the other man's face and he stumbled back, blood blossoming on his blouse. He fell backwards then didn't move again.

It was less than a minute since Kade had entered the room.

Lana was standing in the doorway, pointing a loaded gun at the spot where the swordsman had been a moment earlier. How long had she been there?

"Is he dead?"

"Yes."

"Oh." She was crying. After a few seconds, she lowered the pistol, wiped at her eyes and looked at the chaos around her. Kade looked as well. A thin stream of gravy was running away from the broken bowl to join with a trickle of blood. Kade wondered how long it would take to get used to the killing again. He wouldn't be much use if he balked at every death.

But he didn't want to think about that now. Better to move. Kade hauled himself to his feet. "Come on." He went to the back of the room and reefed the shelf out of the way. Pots and plates bounced and clattered across the floor, wild animals heading for cover. It looked like Lana wasn't going anywhere. "I'm not going to wait for you." He knew how she felt. He could hardly control the shaking of his hands, his mouth was so dry he could hardly swallow, but he crawled into the tunnel without looking back. About five metres later he found himself in a utility passage with pipes and wires covering the walls and ceiling like strange, cold undergrowth. It was a dead end to the right.

"Wait..." Lana climbed out to stand behind him. There was a haunted look in her eyes.

"No time, Lana. Keep up." He went to the left without looking back.

Kade raced down the passage. Three doors, all on the right, were locked tight. Straight ahead ended not far away so Kade turned at an adjoining passage. From there, there were no turns or intersections—not that could be negotiated by humans at any rate—for more than fifty metres. There were more doors but they were locked as well. And then he stopped at the joining of five passages, looking first one way and then the next. He cocked his head to listen. Nothing. Lost, desperate, he was about to pick a direction at random when he noticed a hatch set in the floor. The dust surrounding it had been scraped aside recently... He set his fingers into the handles and lifted just as Lana arrived, puffing and sweating.

Kade gave his companion a questioning look.

"I'm all right."

She didn't sound it. She leaned against the wall, trembling slightly, and wiped a sleeve across her pale face. Kade nodded anyway and started to climb down the creaking ladder, hands reddening with rust. At the bottom was another tunnel, this one dominated by a large concrete pipe down one side. He stopped to listen again.

Lana clumped clumsily down the ladder behind him.

"Shhh..." Kade could hear the hiss of gas and the hum of crystal water-pumps merging like whispers, but there was something else. A rhythmic banging. He spun, listening some more. "This way."

A hundred metres down the passage, the lock on a door had been broken. It could have been done to put them off the trail, but Kade doubted his quarry would slow long enough to do something like that. He pushed through and found himself on a metal walkway bolted just above the high-water mark of a mould covered, stone canal. Brown water gurgled and frothed, heading towards one of the huge purifiers. But there was only one way to go again, against the flow, towards the outer edge of the skyland. The walkway was shaking, shivering. Dust danced on the rail.

Lana leaned against the wall, breathing deeply, staring at nothing. Kade didn't know what to say to her, so he ran. After a moment, she followed without saying a word.

They ran for what seemed like a long time, stopping now and then to touch their hands to the rail and feel the continued movement.

"I see them," Lana said eventually, gasping for breath. "I see them." It sounded as if that was the last thing she wanted.

Kade nodded as he ran. "They turned aside."

Another timber door, another broken lock, and beyond it, a narrow staircase, merging into darkness as it descended. Kade didn't slow. He gripped the rail and swung himself around the corner at the landing. A gunshot rang out and the pellet grazed his arm, smacking into the ancient brick wall behind.

"Thorn!"

He skidded to a halt, waiting for a follow up shot. It never came. Lana ran into him, almost tumbling him headlong down the stairs.

"What is it?"

"I've been shot." Kade leaned against the rail, breathing deeply, and put pressure on the wound. It stung and burned all at once. Blood seeped through his fingers. He couldn't control the shaking of his hand this time. He wondered if his legs would hold him. "Didn't you hear it?"

Lana shrugged. Nodded. "Are you all right?"

A door, half hidden in a pool of shadow, was swinging back and forth at the base of the next flight of stairs, banging against the wall, echoing dully. Either the shooter was standing just around the corner reloading or not. Either way, staying on the stairs wasn't a good idea.

"What do we do?" Lana asked. "Perhaps we should go back."

Kade wanted to go back. He looked up the stairs, tensed, ready to go. But he stayed where he was. "You can if you like," he said, lifting his hand away to examine his arm. The sleeve of his shirt was soaked in blood.

With a deep breath, he continued at a more sedate pace, hand holding his arm, and poked his head out through the door. There was a tunnel with bare, ancient stone all around and a rut worn in the floor. Spluttering lights painted rainbows on oily puddles. The two thieves were fifty metres away and running again. So close.

Kade forgot about his arm and ran, moving from darkness to light, splashing through puddles, breathing hard, running on automatic. When he looked up from his feet a few seconds later, he saw one of the thieves standing in the middle of the passage, just on the edge of a circle of light, working quickly to load a pistol.

Increasing his pace, pumping his arms, Kade tried to calculate. How long to load? How long to run... He arrived in time, skidding to a halt as the man tried to pour powder into the firing pan.

"Too slow," Kade said, lashing out with his foot.

The thief scrambled out of the way, eyes wide in the dim light. He discarded the powder bag in a rain of fine grains and snapped the frizzen into place. Kade pushed forward, fists flying. But the other man stepped back and prepared to fire from the hip, keeping the weapon out of reach as he aimed.

Kade danced to the side, still swinging, moving quickly. He tripped on a jutting flagstone, half stumbled...

The thief pulled the trigger.

Kade flinched as the hammer fell home sending out a shower of sparks. But there was no powder in the pan. The man grunted in disbelief, threw the weapon and ran out through a low, narrow doorway.

Kade ducked, spun to watch the pistol strike the wall behind him. Lana was standing in the door, motionless, caught on the edge of running.

"Great help you were." His heart was racing, through fear or exertion, he didn't know. He wiped sweat from his forehead and set of in pursuit once more.

He didn't have far to go. Around the next corner the two thieves were back together again, working at a large metal door, pulling and grunting, swearing loudly. It was swinging open slowly. They started working harder but even if they opened the door Kade would catch them in a moment.

One of them looked back. Kade froze again. "Lemar?" But Lemar... Part of his ear was missing. There was a scar on his cheek. But there was no doubt it was Lemar.

The other man turned away but they wouldn't get far. Kade got his feet moving. He was running with the wind, only metres away.

Wind?

Momentum and ancient, grinding gears kept the door moving and the two men slipped through the gap moments before Kade arrive.

Kade rushed to follow, around the edge of the still moving door...

But beyond there was nothing. Kade stood on the brink, swaying, waving his arms as he tried to keep his balance, looking out at blue sky and racing clouds. The wind sucked at him, pulled at him, tugged him over the edge. He snatched for something, anything. His hands slipped on the doorframe, caught a curve of pipe.

His legs went out the door, almost horizontal, flapping like flags. His eyes watered and his hands were freezing. He banged his knee and his elbow against the huge metal bowl that held the skyland together, and again, as the wind tried to tear him free. He could hardly breathe.

Clinging to the freezing metal of the pipe, watching as his fingers turned blue, Kade searched blindly for something to hold his feet and legs still. He hooked them behind a pipe then lay against the wall, cheek against the cold metal. Secure against the buffeting for the moment, he looked down as he tried to catch his breath. There was more sky and more clouds and, far below, a skyland gliding silently across the dark, restless blue of the world beyond. The two thieves were there as well, falling away from him like stooping falcons with their arms pulled back to their sides and clothes flapping.

Then, huge squares of cloth streamed from their packs and blossomed above them, filling with air in an instant like a sail catching the wind.

Lana stood in the doorway, holding onto a handle in the wall. "Thorn, what was that?"

Kade really didn't want to talk about that at the moment. He searched around for the safest way to climb back inside. Nothing looked safe. The long fall tugged at his consciousness as much as the wind tugged at his clothes. He slowly walked his feet downwards, from pipe to bracket to bolt, until he was vertical again. Then stayed where he was, staring at his blue fingers, wondering if he would be able to loosen them. Fear and wind alike had frozen them. "I think I'm going to need some help," he called. He licked his lips, but the moisture was gone an instant later.

Lana stood for a moment, swaying in the wind, then licked her lips as well and sat on the floor. She braced herself, and took his wrist. He stared at her fingers while he worked on unclamping each of his.

"What are we going to do?"

Kade shook his head and gritted his teeth against an angry reply. At least she was distracting him.

Once he was safely on solid ground Kade didn't know if he ever wanted to move again. He knew he should probably go back to the apartment in the hold to see if he could find any clues, unlikely though that was. Instead, he sat by the door and watched the thieves land on the skyland far below.

"I don't think they were amateurs," he said.

VI

Kade sat in the angled sunlight that came in through the window over Kiri's kitchen sink.

Lana was examining the gunshot wound on his arm. "This isn't as bad as it looks," she said, dabbing on some antiseptic. "It's only a graze."

"Is it as bad as it feels?" The arm throbbed. He was just starting to get used to his injured chest and now this.

"It's going to need some stitches though."

"Can you do it?"

"The constabulary training includes basic first aid..."

"Good," Kade said. "I assume Kiri's first aid kit is fairly advanced."

"What did you do to your chest?" Lana asked as she found a needle and thread.

"Bruised some ribs. Possibly broke them."

"Yes. And... How?"

"I fell."

Lana grunted and shook her head. "Are you ready?" She started without waiting for a reply, chewing on her bottom lip and concentrating fiercely. From all indications it hurt her more than it hurt Kade. He hardly felt anything more than the burning that had been there since he'd been shot.

"I wasn't much help today, was I?" Lana said when she'd completed the final stitch and started bandaging. "Sorry. All I did was slow you down."

Kade watched her fingers, wincing as she tied off with a tug that was a bit more forceful than absolutely necessary.

"Sorry," she said softly. She left her hands on his arm for a moment, skin against skin, shaking, then clasped them in her lap.

"You've never had to think about killing someone before, have you?"

A shake of the head, and she looked up from her hands. "I've thought about it. You know, in training or whatever. But I've never actually been faced with the choice. Do you get used to it? Does it hurt less the second time?"

Kade almost laughed. "It gets to the point where you don't have to think about it at all," he said, thinking of Tilli and the old man in the street outside the laboratory. "That's when it really starts to hurt." He started to repack the first-aid kit, shoving rolled bandages and jars of ointment into the box.

"We should report it, really. I suppose."

"Report what?" He did laugh then. They'd backtracked and entered the hold by the secret passage and done a quick search of the apartment. There was nothing there, of course. Two groups of people had been out the front, arguing about who'd been there first, about who was going to move in.

"We can at least tell them about the tunnel. To stop stuff from happening in the future."

"You can do that if you like. I'll wait here."

"Then, what do we do?"

Kade wished he knew. He stood up and, flexing his arm, paced around the kitchen. "Lemar won't have..." He paused.

"Who's Lemar?"

"Ah, one of the thieves. The other one used the name."

"Oh."

"So, they've got multiple identities, so it's unlikely we'll be able to find them by just checking the systems."

"We could find out where they went though. We just go and find out the name of the skyland we saw passing beneath us."

"And then what?"

"We could get Captain Gusarpo to chase them?"

"By telling him what?"

"The truth."

"And which truth would that be?"

"Well, that you're..."

"Working on a secret investigation?" Kade laughed. "No, we can't tell him that." He sat back down and sighed.

"Why not? If he knew—"

"If he knew the truth there would be all sorts of trouble."

"But you're—"

There was a knock at the door, sharp and authoritative. It was the type of knock that seemed to echo through the house like a church bell and expected to be answered. Kade and Lana looked at each other and didn't move. The knock came again then the door started to swing open. Kade's pistols were on the other side of the room.

The man who came through the door was tall and thin, with a flock of tattal birds covering his left arm and a fuzz of hair covering anything that might have been on his head. He wore a short sword at his waist and carried a pistol that was almost as long. The furious look on his face quickly changed to one of caution when he saw he wasn't alone. He glanced from Kade to Lana and back again when it became obvious who was in charge.

"Who are you?" he asked.

Kade sighed and tried to work out his story. The Skyway Men could check entry records so... "I'm Merik Bolkin," he said, giving a signal that might be ten years out of date. "I'm an Inquisitor."

The man gave a small nod.

"And who are you?" Kade continued.

"I'm Londar Oloudis. You got here quick."

Kade nodded. "I've been living in the hold for the last six months."

Londar raised an eyebrow. "Just in case?"

Kade laughed. "You think there's nobody keeping an eye on things? There's always someone around 'just in case'."

"Well, everything is under control." Londar carefully closed the door.

"Under control? Really? So, what's happening?"

"Well..."

"Apparently, I'll be back in bed in half an hour."

No reply.

"What's your position?"

He cleared his throat. "Operations Liaison."

Not Kiri's superior, as such, but the one who keep communications flowing up and down the chain of command. Someone who Kade couldn't just blow off.

Keep things moving. Kade nodded and gestured to Lana. "This is Tegan. She's been answering some questions for me. She was working with Kiri."

Londar glanced at Lana but didn't say anything.

"Could you leave us alone for a minute, Tegan?"

"Of course." She looked around the kitchen as if thinking she may have forgotten something, then headed for the door out into the back yard.

Londar watched her go. When the door closed behind her he turned on Kade. "So, Merik. This is just about the biggest mess I've ever seen."

"And you probably don't know half of it." That was a silly thing to say. *Keep it simple.* Too late now, though.

"So, what do we know so far?"

"Well, it's been an interesting couple of days."

Londar grunted.

"The constabulary received a tip off about some Skyway Men meeting at the *Leaf and Stone.* Fortunately for us, the tip off was given to Mistress Kiri's son, who passed the message on. Kiri went to the *Leaf* instead and found one of the men in question. And he told her about the operation he was involved in."

"Before we continue, let's just be clear on one thing— neither Kiri nor I knew anything about this job."

Kade held up his hand. "We know that, Londar. Nobody is accusing either of you of anything."

Londar grunted and gave a small, relieved nod.

Kade tried to stay calm. Things were going well and he didn't want to ruin it with a simple mistake now. "Anyway, this operation was supposedly to steal something from CRG. Which we both know is stupid. I think Mistress Kiri was trying to clear up that mess when... Well, the mess just exploded."

"So, you know what happened. Do you know why?"

"We were set up. The agent Kiri was talking to was supposed to get caught to point the constables in the wrong direction."

What Kade couldn't work out was why. What was the point? It looked like Lemar would've gotten away clean anyway, so what was the point of the charade? *Maybe he just likes making trouble for me.* He was certainly very good at it. He'd abandoned him last time, left him in the factory with just two squads and no diversion. It was a miracle anyone had made it out alive.

"Do you know who did it?"

"No yet."

"So, that's all you know?"

Kade looked at the other man. "At the moment. It hasn't been that long."

Londar nodded. "Right." There was a definite change in tone. "Well, let me tell you what *I* know."

"All right."

"I know you aren't a Inquisitor."

"Really?"

Londar stood up and pressed the cold tip of the gun barrel against Kade's forehead. His eyes narrowed. "Really. And I know this because... Can you guess?"

"You're physic?" He licked his lips and glanced towards his pistols. Unless they were in his hands, he didn't think they'd be much use.

Londar smiled. It wasn't a friendly smile. "No. One last guess?"

"Because *you're* an Inquisitor?"

"That's it. Well done."

Kade winced. "I didn't really think of that at the start."

"It's obvious enough, when you *do* think about it. And now we're clear on who *I* am, so that means it's your turn."

Kade didn't say anything.

"Talk, Merik, and make it good."

Kade licked his lips. His heart was beating so hard he was surprised it wasn't hurting his ribs. His hand trembled on the edge of the table. "Well..." He cleared his throat. "Well, that's an interesting story."

There was movement in the doorway as Lana slipped back inside. She had a pistol, holding it as if it were a snake. Before she had a chance to aim, possibly before she had a chance to think, the floor creaked beneath her feet. Londar turned to look, but didn't move the pistol. The barrel still pressed coldly against Kade's skin.

Lana raised the pistol, holding it in two shaking hands.

"You aren't going to shoot me," Londar said with a grunt of disgust. "I've seen killers. They have a look in their eyes. You don't have that look, girl."

As Londar started to turn back, Lana fired.

Londar jerked. His eyes went wide, his jaw slack. He fired as well, splitting the timber wall behind Kade. Then he dropped the weapon, slumping against the kitchen table. He fumbled for purchase with one hand, scattering a small pyramid of apples, and with the other hand he tried to find the wound, clawing weakly while dark blood stained the back of his shirt. He kept trying even as he slowly, slowly, slipped to the side and toppled over. He bounced off the table and fell to the floor, eyes staring blindly.

"He was going to kill you," Lana said, staring as blindly as Londar. The pistol was hanging limply in her hand, smoke leaking from the barrel.

Kade nodded. "He tried hard enough." He turned and saw the slug hole in the wall behind him.

"Who is he, Kade?" She tore her eyes away from the body. "Who do you work for? He has all types of stuff in his cruiser. There are maps, memory crystals, tiny arrays, uniforms and..." She looked at the pistol she still held then dropped it from nerveless fingers.

"Maps?" Kade asked. Lana nodded in reply, staring at Londar again. "Is there a skyglass?"

She nodded again.

Leaving the pistol on the table, Kade collected his shirt and pulled it on awkwardly as he sidled past Lana and out through the door. His legs would barely hold him but he wanted to move, he wanted to do something or he would sit and do nothing more than breathe.

It was cold outside and long, wispy swirls of cloud followed the canal and clung to buildings. Londar's cruiser, a small single seater with a covered cargo area at the back, was parked under the shelter, as if he'd come to stay. Kade opened the rear hatch and stared. The cargo bay was filled almost to overflowing with a mixture of equipment and items. He might have stared all day but a drip of cold water on the back of his neck cleared his mind. He wiped away the drip as it started to descended, rubbed at his goose pimpled arms, then shuffled through the mess Lana had left behind when she found the pistol—uniforms, weapons, files and a dozen other things—before finally finding a crystal skyglass. He pulled it out and held it up to the pale, patchy sunlight to let it warm.

After a few seconds, spots of light appeared just below the surface and a few seconds after that, labels. Tribalin was a light blue color, indicating it was at high altitude, and close to the equator. It had almost caught Matharzo, little good that it would do. Heading north and almost touching as well, was a darker spot representing Beelamola. It was a huge farming skyland, almost fifteen kilometres across, which had been on the brink of bankruptcy for more than a decade.

A cruiser came around the corner of the house, hardly making a sound. Kade recovered from his surprise quickly enough to close the cargo door of Londar's cruiser and look something close to innocent. When he turned around, he saw that he needn't have bothered.

"Kade, how did you go?" Roke climbed out of the cruiser and stretched.

Kade tried to calm his breathing and stepped away from the cruiser shelter as another drip of water found its way onto his head. "That depends on what our goal exactly was," he said, shivering as the water ran across his scalp and down onto his neck.

"To locate the array."

Kade held up the skyglass. "Success then. It's on Beelamola." He pointed at the spot of light with a finger that shook slightly, then shrugged. "At least it was about an hour ago."

"And how do you know this?" Roke looked at the skyglass, a confused expression creasing his face. "And how, in the name of Thorn, did it get there?"

Kade tried to clear is head. "Come inside and I'll tell you."

He led the way up the stairs and through the door. Inside, Lana hadn't moved. She was still staring at the body, perhaps making sure it didn't get up and run away.

Kade knew how she felt but wasn't going to show his unease.

"Lana, what are you doing..." Roke froze as well. "There's a body on my mother's kitchen floor," he said after a moment.

Kade nodded and scratched his ear as he tried to think of something to say. "Yes. Do you like it?" He quite liked the idea of flippant humor. It made events seem less immediate, more unreal. It had worked before.

"No. What's it doing there?"

"Not a lot, really."

"He was going to shoot Kade," Lana said. "He had a gun..."

"You shot him?"

Kade interjected. "No, I did. He was—"

"Don't lie for me. I don't want..." She shook her head and glared at Kade. "Don't lie for me. Don't you dare..." But the anger leaked out of her as she turned back to look at the growing pool of blood. She chewed her thumbnail.

"Thorn, what a mess." Roke stood over the body and ran his fingers over his scalp tattals. "And I don't just mean the blood." He glanced at Lana. "Ahh, Kade, let's put him in the cellar for now—at least the blood will be easier to clean off the pavers—and then you can tell me what the hell is going on."

"We aren't going to report this?" Lana asked. "Detective, you can't mean that. A man was shot here. I killed him."

Roke looked at Lana again. "Let's just wait for now and give ourselves some time to think. We can still report it later, if we want."

"If we want to?"

"Let's just take a minute."

Kade grabbed Londar's legs and related the morning's adventures while he and Roke shuffled awkwardly through a low, narrow door near the fire and down to the cellar.

They were back up stairs, sitting on stools in the kitchen by the time Kade finished. Lana was leaning against the door, ready to escape.

Roke scratched at his head. "So what are you going to do?"

"I don't know. According to the skyglass, the array is about a hundred kilometres away and getting further away by the moment. I can't... jump." Kade didn't even want to think about that. He held up the skyglass.

Lana cleared her throat. "It looks like Beelamola is heading for Come-and-Go Archipelago." It was about to pass another skyland that seemed to be sitting stationary in the middle of nowhere but beyond that was a group of five skylands all moving together. She moved closer to read the labels. "What's Valakeen doing?"

"Valakeen gathers water from the ocean and purifies it to sell," Kade said. "I think. If it's not going anywhere, then it's probably about a hundred metres above sea level and will be there for a while."

"Right." Lana chewed on her thumb nail some more. "What of it?"

She looked at Kade then Roke and seemed to reach a decision. "If you take a plane and go there, then you can change planes and continue on."

Roke nodded slowly and checked the position of all the skylands. "Say, an hour until you can get a plane and leave Tribalin. Valakeen will be about two hundred kilometres away by then. That isn't a problem, but Beelamola will be another... I don't know... Two hundred kilometres beyond that and still moving. You'd struggle to make that second flight."

Kade nodded. "It would never work. What about a blimp?"

"Too slow, obviously."

Kade knew that already.

"So you just give up," Lana said. "You let the Green Sea Raiders have the array?"

"We don't know it's the Raiders. We don't even know if they exist." If Lemar was still in the Skyway Men... If everything Kade had been told before being exiled to Whiparill had been a lie...

"But what if they *do* have it? What if even half the stories about them are true? And now give them a weapon that can kill from 200 metres away?"

"I probably wouldn't even make it to Beelamola." Kade fiddled with the skyglass, as if tilting it to a difference angle might bring all the spots of light closer together. He wanted to get there. There were a lot of questions he wanted to ask Lemar, and then he wanted to wring his neck. Slowly.

"You've got to try," Lana said. She turned to Roke. "You must see that, Detective. Kade is just a criminal but you..." She stopped as if suddenly giving thought to the constable's role in all that had happened. "We can't leave a weapon like that in the hands of criminals."

"We can pass on a message," Roke replied, though he didn't sound convinced.

"How long until this message gets to Come and Go? A month? Two months? Like Kade said, these men were not amateurs. Even if we send a message by blimp, the men will be long gone and we'll never see the weapon again."

"It could take a few hours to find a pilot," Roke pointed out.

"I can fly," Lana said softly.

They turned to look her.

"You can fly?" Kade asked.

She nodded. "I was taking lessons because I was thinking about going into the spotter division of the constabulary. I have about twenty observed hours."

"Twenty *observed* hours?" Kade asked. She hadn't even flown on her own?

"No way," Roke said. "Not going to happen."

"I'm part of this too, Detective. I—"

"You don't know half of what's going on, Lana," Roke almost shouted. He calmed himself down. "Trust me, you should just—"

"I know Kade's a thief and a murderer."

Kade tried to laugh at the suggestion but Roke continued with the conversation as if he hadn't heard. "There is a whole story here that you don't know..." He trailed away into silence as her words finally sank in. He cleared his throat. "That's ridiculous."

Kade didn't say anything. He knew he'd sound about as convincing as Roke and not help at all.

"I don't know how it all fits together, but the robbery at CRG, the gunfight at Madam Larinal's and the break in at the morgue are all connected. And Kade is connected to them. In fact, he may well be in the Skyway Men."

"The Skyway Men? You're kidding," Roke said, though his heart wasn't in it.

"If I'm linked to robberies and murders, if I'm a Skyway Man, why do you want to help?"

"I know Detective Mirani. I trust him and like him, even though he's involved with all this as well. I know nothing about Bolkin at all, other than he has a terrible weapon... It isn't all that hard to choose sides."

Roke switched stools to sit beside her. "Lana, you don't want to do this. This could end your career with the constabulary. If anyone finds out..."

"I'm trying to recover stolen property." She didn't sound sure. It was as if she really did want to be talked out of it.

"Yes, but—"

"You want me to go back to the office and make some more coffee? Do some more filing? If my parent's have their way, and that quite often happens, then that will be all I ever do."

"But—"

"You need a pilot."

"Twenty observed hours?" Kade said. The idea of flying scared him enough as it was. "That isn't a pilot. Maybe a 'pi' but certainly not a 'lot'." He tried to laugh but it just sounded as if he was choking. Apparently humor didn't always help. Or maybe it actually had to be funny. He gripped the edge of the table, hoping *someone* would talk her out if it. And he hoped that they wouldn't talk her out of it.

"I can help."

"You helped a few minutes ago," Kade said. "There's no need to over do things."

"If I helped once, I can again. I'm already in this up to my neck."

Kade looked at the bloodstain on the floor. It could have been his. "That's right. Much deeper and you'll probably drown." Looking at her he knew she wouldn't be talked out of it. He sighed.

"I'd like everything I've done to mean something. If we stop now, it has all been pointless."

"If you're doing this you have to do it now." Roke sighed as well, shaking his head. He rose to his feet. "I can't believe I'm about to help you steal a plane."

Lana nodded. "Can I go home first? To get some things?"

"Everything we need will be around here somewhere."

"But—"

"There isn't enough time. You aren't trying to back out already are you?"

Lana swallowed and glanced towards the door. "No."

Valakeen

I

"It would be a lot easier if—"

Kade shook his. "Yes, Detective, we know. It would be a lot easier if it was dark."

Roke adjusted his mask. "Well, it would."

"Obviously, but we can't wait." Kade leaned against the wing, ducking slightly so he could look under the body of the biplane. It looked old enough to have been used by Gafol Martinol to tow the skyland up away from the world below. The Tribalin symbol on the side was all but invisible. The grey paintwork was scratched and stained and there were plenty of dents.

"It's all right for you; you went into your line of business knowing full well what the end result might be."

Kade laughed softly. "You obviously don't know as much about the Skyway Men as you should, Detective." He shook his head.

"You want me to feel sorry for you?"

"I want you to shut up." Kade shifted his grip on his pistol.

"I wish you'd both shut up," Lana said softly. She was wearing dark, borrowed clothes, a mask pulled down past her chin. "If we get caught..."

The worst of it was behind them anyway. Probably. They were over the fence and crouching in the dust near the end of a line of twin-engine biplanes, waiting for a guard with a dog to move back amongst the hangars half way down the length of the aerodrome. Kade rose to his feet when the man, about a hundred metres away, eventually disappeared from sight. He put the pistol in his pack and looked around.

"Any plane in particular, Lana?"

There was no answer. Kade looked around and saw Lana, staring at the spot where they'd last seen the guard and trying to chew her fingernail through her mask.

"Lana?"

She started. "Yes? What?"

"Which plane?"

"I don't know." She looked around as if she didn't want to get in any of them.

Kade was committed now and didn't want Lana backing out. "That weapon has a long range Lana. There'd be no fighting it. It'll kill you before you even know you're a target." Of course, if you were going to die that wasn't a bad way to go. A plane crash on the other hand... "But if you want to back out I'd understand." Kade was hoping she'd rise to the implied questioning of her courage.

She glared at him for a moment then stood up, dusting off her hands. "Most of the newer ones will need keys," she said, turning to the plane they had crouched near. She climbed up on the wing to look inside the cockpit.

"Well?" Kade climbed up with her to have a look himself. Only he didn't know where he was looking.

"It doesn't need a key." She chewed on her fingernail some more.

"Well..." Kade looked from Lana to Roke and back again. "Come on. Get in. It already has plenty of dents so a few more won't matter."

Lana lurched over the side into the rear of the two seats. After a moment of hesitation, she started going through pre-flight checks, flicking switches and examining crystal displays.

"Trouble," Roke whispered fiercely.

Kade crouched down behind the fuselage, cursing the fact that he'd been standing up in full sight in the first place. Lana tried to shrink. The guard was out in the open again and heading slowly towards them.

"How much time do you need?" Roke asked.

Lana had stopped working. She started again, shoulders hunched as she tried to stay out of sight. "A couple of minutes."

"Thorn." Roke examined their surroundings.

Kade followed his gaze. They were beside the end of the runway, about fifty metres from the end of the rectangular aerodrome complex. The high brick fence on the opposite side of the runway was also about fifty metres away.

"I'll draw him away," Roke said, pulling his mask on tighter as if every little bit of wind resistance might make the difference.

Before Kade could say anything, Roke was on his feet and dashing out from behind the plane. In a couple of seconds, he was on the macadam runway, head down and running hard.

The guard, a big man and well into middle age, finally reacted. He shouted and huffed out onto the runway, dog straining at the leash, at an angle that was never going to cut Roke off. The man seemed to realize this. He released the dog and it raced away, ears back, barking loudly. Roke looked back over his shoulder and ran harder.

The guard paused, turned around to wave his arms in a complicated signal to some unseen observer. When he started to jog after his dog, Kade stood up and started to climb into the plane's front seat.

"You need to turn the propellers," Lana said.

"What?"

"There's no automatic ignition arrays because of the weight. We have to spin the propellers by hand to get the engines started."

"Right." Kade dropped his pack into the foot well and climbed to the ground. "Are we ready?"

Lana was concentrating on the controls again, mumbling to herself, finger rubbing at her temple. "Ummm... Yes. I think so."

Kade made his way to the first propeller, set on the underside of the top wing, and waited for Lana's nod. Then he gripped the cool, smooth wood and flung it clockwise with all his might. The engine hummed and vibrated, then died. Lana did something and nodded again. This time, Kade jumped back as the engine caught and the propeller immediately picked up speed. He moved to the second one, on the other side.

On the far side of the aerodrome, Roke used a pile of bricks to scramble up the concrete fence. The dog was right behind him, lunging, snapping at his heels. Too late. Roke paused on top of the wall. He seemed to say something to the dog then waved both his arms in the air and pointed back towards the hangars.

Kade followed the gesture. A half dozen more guards were on the runway. Two were heading towards Roke, but the others had seen the activity around the plane and changed course. They were closing quickly.

"Thorn." Kade turned his attention to the propeller and flung it into motion. It caught the first time and he raced around to climb onto the wing. "Let's go, Lana."

"I have to—"

"No time."

"If I don't..." Lana looked up from what she was doing, stared for a moment, then got the plane moving.

They had bumped up onto the macadam before Kade worked out how to fasten his safety belt. He glanced over his shoulder and watched as Lana flicked her eyes over the instruments then back out at the runway. Her continued muttering didn't instill him with confidence. The guards were getting nearer. One of them crouched, raised a blunderbuss to his shoulder and fired. Kade ducked instinctively but had no idea where the shot went. Lana didn't even seem to notice.

"Come on, let's get out of here," Kade shouted.

"The engines aren't warm yet."

"I don't care."

"We could shatter something."

"They'll shatter our heads if we don't move."

"But..."

"If you don't get this plane moving, we'll either be dead or in prison." He twisted around in his seat. "Now go."

Lana looked out at the guards, gasped as another shot was fired, and increased the power to the engines. The plane picked up speed, shuddering and making all sorts of strange noises. A shot stuck the wing over Kade's head, making a dark hole in the grey timber. He hunched lower and scrabbled in his pack for his pistol, but by the time he looked up the guards were left behind and the end of the runway was approaching. The biplane lurched into the air, hit the ground, rose again. The wind increased. They were flying. Kade gave a 'whoop' of joy and looked back at Lana. She had removed her mask and was trying to pull on a leather cap and a pair of goggles. She was concentrating fiercely and didn't look as pleased.

"Twenty observed flying hours," Kade said to himself. "Thorn, what have I gotten myself into?"

When he was turning away, looking for something else to think about, he saw another plane coming out of the clouds, zeroing in from the right. He stared for a moment, then wiggled his arm out of the cockpit and pointed. He didn't know if Lana saw, but she swung the plane around towards the skyland's port side.

That was no better. There was another spotter plane, coming in from over the top of a huge factory complex.

Lana swore and Kade decided that was worse than the mumbling. After a few seconds they swung back towards the Administration Centre.

The skyland hardly seemed to move beneath them. Kade had to remind himself that the land itself was moving at about 80 kilometres an hour in the same direction as their own small speck of a plane.

The faint popping of gunfire carried on the wind. Another plane joined the chase. Lana dived low and they skimmed across the tops of the buildings, so close Kade thought he could hear the wind of their passage against the timber and stone. The plane wobbled and dipped down into a ball of cloud as they crossed into cooler air over a small water reservoir. Kade felt his stomach heave as Lana overcorrected and they climbed quickly for a few seconds. She was still swearing.

When he opened his eyes again, Kade could see five planes in the air around them. They may have been shooting; he didn't know. Lana was twisting one way and the other, trying to see every direction at once

"Why didn't we steal a plane with guns?" he shouted over the wind.

Lana didn't answer.

"We're going the wrong way," he shouted.

"Do you want to do this?"

Kade shut up and hung on as Lana stood them on a wing tip and weaved between two ancient smokestacks.

A plane was coming in at them broadside. It was just metres away. At the last moment, Kade heard the crack of gunfire and a scatter of pellets struck the side of the plane. Their attacker climbed quickly, passing just above them.

"Get us out of here!"

The Administration Centre was just ahead and Lana lifted the plane up and over the top in a lazy climb. Then, suddenly, she dipped a wing, turning left and racing down across the outside face, dropping into a cloudbank that was bunching up against Tribalin's relatively warm leading edge.

The wall, stark and grey, was right there. For a moment, Kade thought he could see the Captain's face on the Bridge, mouth wide with shock. There were high-ranking constables in offices with large windows, and government departments with desks lined up in neat rows. People stared and pointed until suddenly, the clouds thickened and nothing was visible at all. That wasn't a bad thing.

Then the plane lurched again and the wall of the Administration Centre loomed sickeningly close through a gap in the cloud. Lana twitched and the wing dipped. They dived harder and Kade, heart in his mouth, closed his eyes, waiting for the collision.

Kade's stomach lurch again as the plane leveled out.

"That was close," Lana said.

Kade didn't think he was supposed to hear. He opened his eyes and decided it was *still* close. The skyland's hull was just metres above his head.

When the circle of land had been torn free of the world below the outer surface had been sprayed with a dark, liquefied metal that held everything together when it hardened. Pipes and cables, wires and tree roots, had all been left where they were and could still be identified, though they too had been coated. In some places the metal had run and dripped before solidifying. Tribalin's story, past and present, was written across the rough, uneven surface of the hull.

Kade's knuckles were white on the top edge of the cockpit. He wanted the cloud to come back so he couldn't see but on the other hand he wanted Lana to be able to see... A big loop of pipe protruded further than all the others, missing the top wing by barely a metre.

Kade closed his eyes and hung on. He didn't know how long he stayed like that, teeth gritted against the wind, until Lana tapped him on the shoulder.

"What?" he asked, eyes still closed.

"I think we're in the clear." The relief was evident in her voice.

Kade checked and saw Tribalin, a huge bowl of buildings, slowly dropping behind, angling across their line of travel. There were planes buzzing about, but they weren't pursuing. He gave a shout of joy and pulled off his mask.

"That was easy," he said.

Lana shook her head. "Taking off and flying in open air are pretty easy. Landing is the hard bit."

"Excellent."

Kade's cheeks and lips were freezing in the thin air so he searched around near his feet he found a cap and goggles like Lana's. There was also a green scarf that he wrapped around his nose and mouth.

"I'm coming to get you, Lemar," Kade said quietly.

Valakeen was still a long way away, a tiny dark patch against the blue of the ocean. It grew steadily. And the whole world grew with it. The deep dark blue of the ocean was like a puddle spreading away from a leaking tap as they dropped towards it. Soon, it was too large to comprehend. It was mesmerizing. Everywhere Kade looked, there was only the ever-shifting water and he couldn't take his eyes off it. He didn't notice anything else until an hour and a half later when Valakeen intruded on his consciousness.

It was a couple of kilometres across and most of it was covered with water. The runway Lana was aiming for hung out over the edge into nothing. It was only ten metres wide and had water on either side. Possibly it had water beneath as well, like a knife laid over the edge of a saucepan. Half a dozen planes of various colors were lined up on huge timber raft halfway along the runway. They rose and fell slightly with the movement of the water. There was a floating village near that and, around the rocky curve of the Skyland's hull, a small gate-complex. The Administration Centre, a low hunched form, was located on a small spit of land a few hundred metres beyond.

Lana was muttering more than ever as she made fine adjustments to the plane. She was fighting a slight cross-wind, lining up the narrow strip of runway.

Kade hung on and closed his eyes.

The plane hit the runway with a hollow thump, bounced and hit again. Then it was rolling smoothly along the macadam and Kade loosened his grip. He took off his goggles and mask and wiped sweat and mist from his face.

Lana let out a sigh of relief but kept concentrating.

Eventually, the plane stopped at the end of the runway and while Lana tried to catch her breath, Kade climbed out with his pack. He wanted to just stay where he was, eyes closed, enjoying the feel of ground beneath his boots. But they didn't have time. It might already be too late. Nobody came to greet them. All remained quiet, apart from the constant sigh and slap of the water.

"Come on Lana. No time." He jogged back along the runway to where the biplanes waited.

Four of them were single seaters. Kade went to the first of the two seaters and looked inside. He immediately saw that a key was needed and went to the next. Same again. When he climbed back down to the ground, Lana was waiting for him.

"We have to find a key."

There was only one way to go. A pontoon-bridge led to the village further out in the lake. Kade slung the pack over his shoulder as he went. His hurried progress set the bridge to wobbling, sending waves towards the village. The constant motion made him nauseous before he got to the first small shack. It had a thatch roof and shuttered, unglazed windows that had been propped open to let in the breeze. Like many of the other structures, it had a mural painted on the wall.

There was nobody inside what turned out to be a small office. Kade took a few minutes to search for a key, but there was so much clutter he'd have been lucky to find anything useful at all. Lana stood in the door and watched.

"You could help," Kade said.

"I'm sore and tired," she said. "Just shut up and let me relax before I have to do it all again. Anyway, there's someone rowing a boat across the water."

II

Kade pushed out past her and continued away from the runway, stumbling noisily along the ever-moving path. Water splashed over his boots. A building nodded to him from either side, moving separately, upsetting his sense of balance even more.

He was more than happy to stop when three men came out of a small narrow alley between two buildings. They wore only breeches, cut off at the knees, and wide-brimmed hats. Their skin was as brown as old leather, tattals glistening wetly. The first man in line, oar clutched in his big hand, stopped short, surprised, and adjusted his hat while he regained his composure. The oar may have been for protection, but Kade doubted the stranger could confidently use it for anything besides rowing.

The other two men bunched up behind.

"What are you doing here?" the oldest asked. He had one eye close against the glare coming off the water. "All visitors should come directly to the Administration Centre."

"Hello," Kade replied, ignoring his tone. "I'm Kade. What's your name?"

The old man spent a moment deciding if he was going to answer. "I'm Goran."

"Nice to meet you, Goran. The thing is, we've just flown in and were wondering if we could swap our plane for one of yours. We're in a bit of a hurry, you see."

The man leaned sideways slightly so he could look at Lana and then past, as if he could see where the planes waited beside the runway.

"I doubt it very much," he said. He slipped past Kade and made his way easily along the bobbing sidewalk to a spot where he *could* see. "Looks like your plane was out of date about twenty years ago," he said with a sniff.

"It's very important," Lana said. "We—"

"We can sell you a plane for... forty thousand doms." That was about twice the going rate. "Or a new crystal battery for five hundred." That was expensive too and it would take half an hour for a qualified crystal mechanic to complete the installation. An hour for Kade.

"We don't have any doms." That wasn't true, but they certainly didn't have enough.

"Well then, I guess you're just going to have to wait until your battery recharges." Goran smiled and made his way back to his companions. "You'll have to wait out on the runway. Either that or make your way to the Administration centre for processing." He scratched his cheek. "I think it would be best for everyone if you waited in your plane."

"Best for you, you mean," Kade said.

"Those are your choices. And it's more choices than you should be getting." Goran spat into the water.

Kade sighed. "All right. We may have some money," he said, taking off his pack. He pulled his pistol and pointed it at the man. "How about you just get us a key and we'll be on our way."

None of the locals looked particularly worried, as if being held up was an every day occurrence. Goran shook his head. "That's a single barrel pistol. What do you do after you fire the first shot?"

"You'll be dead, so that's hardly your concern, now is it?" Kade heard a click behind him as Lana cocked another pistol. He smiled. "I'm sure I can handle whoever's left."

"Yes, but then you still won't have a key."

"Not everyone around here will be willing to die for a plane."

Goran shrugged. "There isn't anyone else here."

"I can't imagine there are too many places they can hide on a Skyland like this."

Goran shrugged.

"Look, it's just a plane, for Thorn's sake," Kade said, stepping forward.

"Yes, but it's *our* plane."

Kade stopped when he could push the end of the barrel against the other man's forehead. "Just get us the key." He imagined Beelamola getting farther away by the minute.

"No." Goran moved, quick for someone his age.

But Kade had seen the telltale shift of weight and was ready. He swayed to the side, letting the jab slide past his face and lashed out with the butt of his pistol. As Goran fell, unconscious, Kade was already spinning away from an attack by one of the other men. He stepped in and rammed the heel of his hand into the man's solar plexus. The man collapsed, gasping for breath.

"Don't," Lana said, the word hardly audible.

Kade glanced up and saw Lana staring at the final local, as if force of will, or hoping, would help keep him out of the fight. The man back away slightly, hands raised.

While the other man was still struggling to breathe Kade manhandled Goran off the side of the raft into the water, keeping hold of his arm.

"In ten seconds I turn him over so he's face down," Kade said. He started counting out loud and made it all the way to eight.

"All right." The healthy man held up a hand. "All right."

"Good." Kade took a deep breath. "What are your names?"

"I'm Sarat," the standing man said. "That's Hern." Hern was still lying on the ground, wheezing, eyes watering.

"Very well then, Sarat, you get in the water so Lana can keep an eye on you and you Goran. And Hern, you take me to the key."

Kade helped the man to his feet and followed as he slowly led the way into the village. There were more than thirty buildings. Some were two stories high with balconies overlooking the lake or the runway. Some were on their own rafts, ten metres or more in the clear. Others were clumped together as if seeking protection from all the open water. There were rooms that were open to the air and rafts that held nothing but drying racks. A small flotilla of boats bumped hulls and strained at their tie-ropes like skittish animals.

"How many people live here?" Kade asked.

Hern glanced back, wincing as he twisted. He rubbed at his chest. "There are about fifty of us all up," he replied after a moment. He turned between two small buildings that shared a raft. Tree trunks, vines and undergrowth were painted on both of the rough, dry timber walls; it was like walking along a narrow forest path.

"You're much friendlier than Goran. You don't mind us stealing a plane?"

Hern shrugged and regretted that too. He paused to catch his breath. "I'd rather you didn't, but there are thieves and there are thieves. You flew to Valakeen in a stolen Tribalin spotter, so you obviously aren't an amateur and it's doubtful you'd take no for an answer. At the same time, you were obviously reluctant to use violence. I wouldn't have pushed my luck."

"And yet you helped when he attacked."

"Goran can be bit stubborn at times but he's still my boss. There are some things you've got to do, I suppose."

Kade could only nod.

They crossed a long wobbling bridge towards another small group of buildings. Kade looked down into the water between the planks. "So all you do is mine water?"

"We make plenty of money from that, but we also do some fishing. We have species in the lake that you can't get anywhere else and we spend a lot of our time just fifty metres above sea level, so we lower a platform down to the water and use it as a bit of a wharf for fishing."

"You take fish from the planet?"

"Yes."

"But..."

"We've never seen any monsters. Maybe they only live on land." Hern opened a door between two painted columns and went into a small, low building.

It was dim inside but Kade could see a messy desk in one corner and some filing cabinets close by.

"We also grow some vegetables near the Administration Centre." Hern started to search amongst the clutter. "We get by." He said the last as if it was a joke and Kade wondered how often places like Tribalin ran out of water. "Here you go."

"That's a two seater?"

"Of course. The blue one, I think."

"Come on then."

Kade sent Lana to check the key while he watched the three men floating lazily in the water, as if that was how they spent most of their days. A couple of minutes later, he heard the first engine start. He watched through a gap in the buildings as Lana rushed towards the cockpit from one of the propellers. She climbed onto the wing and leaned in to do something to the controls, just managing to keep the engine from stalling. It hummed and purred while she went to work on the next.

Five minutes after that, she was taxiing slowly down the runway.

When the plane was halfway to the end, Kade decided it was time he left. He took a couple more steps. "Just remember," he said, "we *did* ask nicely. And it *is* very important. The Green Sea Raiders are..." *The Green Sea Raiders are a myth*, he thought. He shrugged, turned and ran. "Thank you," he shouted back over his shoulder.

By the time he reached the plane, Lana had already turned around and was starting to move slowly down the runway. As he climbed onto the wing and swung his leg into the cockpit, she pushed the throttle down and increased speed.

"I checked the skyglass," she shouted as Kade strapped himself in. "I don't know if we're going to make it."

Kade wanted to spin around, but was fumbling with the belt. "What? What do you mean?"

"The one thing in our favor is we're going against the wind. The skyland will be affected much more than we are."

"Maybe we shouldn't try then." Kade knew that leaving Tribalin in the first place had not been one of his better plans—and his standards were fairly low at the moment—but staying on Valakeen where they'd just threatened to kill people was even worse.

"You're kidding, right?" Lana obviously wasn't taking him seriously. The biplane left the ground and floated out into open air.

Kade scanned the sky as she turned the plane towards their destination but could see no sign of Beelamola. It could be hidden in cloud or... "Are there any back-up plans," he shouted.

"Yes. If we aren't going to make it we crash into the ocean."

Kade was starting to change his mind about flippant humor. "I don't like your plans."

"Plans aren't my job, they're yours. I'm just here to fly the plane. This is all your fault anyway."

"You volunteered, remember? I don't want to drown."

Lana shook her head. "Are you completely stupid? Do you really think we'd survive the landing?"

Kade tried to avoid looking down at the water. He continued to scan the horizon, straining against his safety belt.

Nothing. And nothing a few degrees above that either. He kept looking anyway, gripping the side of the cockpit until his fingers ached and he forced himself to relax.

An hour later, Beelamola was visible, a dot swimming amongst a drift of clouds. It still looked like it was a lifetime away. They had climbed a thousand metres and were staring the skyland in the eye, but had to claw for every tiny gain.

"Look up there," Kade said, hanging his arm out into the wind to point. There were a few wisps of cloud another thousand metres up that were hanging almost perfectly still. Lana didn't need any more urging. She pulled back on the yoke and headed for the layer of still air.

Time seemed to slow. And speed up. He held his breath. His heart raced. Days passed. Weeks. And all the while, they slowly caught up, a turtle chasing a tortoise.

Almost four hours after climbing above Beelamola, they passed over the edge of the skyland. Kade had never dreamed that a wilting, twiggy orchard could look so good. He tore off his mask and let out a shout of joy, but Lana's voice interrupted him.

"We aren't going to make it."

"What do you mean? We already have made it."

Even as he said it, the first engine cut out, muttering and whirring to a stop. A moment later, the second one followed suit. There was no airstrip in sight, but Lana dropped the nose of the plane, heading them towards the ground at a sharp angle as the skyland tried to race away from them.

"Hang on."

Kade couldn't hang on any tighter.

Lana pulled the plane out of the dive at the last moment.

The wheels touched down on a rough, unused rim of the skyland and snapped away completely. The plane crunched down and broke free onto a section of dirt road. It spun, bounced, clipped a rock and spun the other way. They came to rest in a gully, tilting to the side, dust swirling about them.

Farmers came running from among the fruit trees. Tools forgotten in their hands, they crowded around the plane.

"Are you all right?" an older man asked as he climbed up onto the wing to take a look for himself.

Kade coughed and wheezed, trying to undo the suddenly tight safety belt. He tried to spit dust as he breathed more in. His heart pounded in his chest. His head still seemed to be jangling around.

"Landing's the difficult part," he said eventually. He finally freed himself and stumbled to the ground. A quick look at the plane suggested taking off might be difficult as well.

Lana groaned and blinked away tears. "That went fairly well, considering."

Kade didn't know if she was acting, but she looked much calmer than he felt.

Beelamola

I

The Administration Complex and Flight Tower were both located in a three-storey building. There had been larger private houses on Tribalin. The ground floor seemed to be multi-purpose offices with a small meeting hall wedged into a corner. From all the evidence, it hadn't been used in a while. The windows were locked tight and dust coated everything. The five councilors had unstacked chairs to sit on but hadn't bothered unfolding a table. Four of them sat in a semi circle facing Kade and Lana. The final member of the group, a tall, gangly man with protruding ears, was in the corner trying to work out how to plug his wristal scanner into a socket in the wall.

The head of the council was a woman named Larci. She was about forty years old and looked like she had spent most of that time in the sun. "Now that all the excitement is over, there are obviously a few questions we have to ask."

"Right." Lana sounded confident.

"First of all, you flight sounds very impressive, but it also sounds dangerous. So why did you do it? Why are you here?"

Kade swallowed. "Ahh..." He almost jumped out of his seat when Lana took his hand.

"We're going to get married," she gushed.

Kade's mind went blank for a moment. "We are?" he said, turning to her. It was the worst thing he could've done but, by the time he realized, it was too late.

Lana was up to the challenge. "There's no need to act any more, Kade." She leaned her head against his shoulder. "They can't stop us now and I want everyone to know."

Kade still didn't know what to say.

"You're eloping?" Larci asked. "That's a lot of trouble to go to just to get married."

Lana shook her head. "Not really," she said. "My parents would *never* have allowed me to marry Kade. To them he's just a metal worker from Whiparill." She turned to look at Kade and smiled. "To me, he's... He's everything."

Larci nodded, but still didn't look certain.

"My parents are people who don't like being trifled with, Councilor. They were trying to frame Kade for theft and assault. And the man they want me to marry instead..." She leaned forward. "I don't think he has ever made any girl's heart flutter."

The man with the scanner finally worked it out. He strolled across the room trailing the filament cable behind him.

"This is Farno," Larci said. "He's the head of the constabulary and customs for Beelamola."

Kade looked the man up and down. He was still wearing the leather apron from his more regular job as a woodworker. Tools filled a big pocket at the front.

"If I could just see your wristals," he said. Apparently he did everything at a leisurely pace.

Kade and Lana both held out their arms and Farno waved the scanner over the wristals. He showed the results to Larci and the other councilors, switching between screens and pointing things out.

Larci raised her eyebrows. "Lana, your mother is Tribalin Secretary? And your father is Chief Engineer?"

Kade was glad nobody was looking at him. It took a moment to compose himself. Secretary? The second most powerful person on a skyland. And Chief Engineer?

Lana nodded. "They say I can do better than Kade, but they haven't even tried to get to know him."

"I see. Kade was only on Tribalin for a couple of days. Your parents may be concerned that you don't really know him either."

Kade waited with interest to hear Lana's answer to that one, but Farno got in first.

"I don't really think that's any of our concern. We should be concerned about the law, not social conventions."

Larci glowered at him.

"What about these things in your packs then?" One of the other councilors held up the packs that had been taken from Kade and Lana soon after they landed. She was a young woman, hardly more than a girl, and pulled the first thing out with her emotions passing clearly across her face. "A pistol?"

Kade opened his mouth to make up a story, but Lana beat him to it. "I'm a constable," she said. "My wristal should have told you that. That's my service pistol, and the one in the other pack. We didn't know where we'd be going."

All the lies were close to the truth. Kade was impressed, if still a little stunned.

Next was the crystal skyglass. It would cost more than a junior constable would make in a year.

Lana smiled. "All right, so maybe Kade is an accessory to a theft *now*, but he wasn't when my parents started all that nonsense."

"What?"

"I took that from my parents' house before I left. Think of it as their contribution to a nice little apartment somewhere."

"You stole this from your parents to sell?"

"That's right."

"And what did you sell to buy a plane?"

Finally, Lana's stories ground to a halt and Kade stepped into the breach, glad to be making a contribution. "Two cruisers and just about everything else I owned. We were hoping to sell the plane when we got to Come and Go, but I guess that isn't going to happen."

Larci looked at Farno and accepted the story with a small nod.

There wasn't anything else suspicious in the bag. A light array, a spyglass, some food and clothes.

Larci examined their small pile of possessions. "Juno, make a note of all this stuff."

The young woman nodded.

"Also, enter their story into the system for future reference. After that, I don't think we have much choice but to—"

The oldest of the Councilors interrupted. She was an old lady with a shock of white hair and had been looking bored up until that point. "I think we should talk about this and look at the choices before you decide there are no choices," she said.

"There is nothing to discuss, Tippi."

"There is always something to discuss."

Larci sighed as if she knew what the outcome of all the discussion was going to be. "Very well. You two, please wait outside."

It looked like Lana was ready to complain but Kade took her hand and led her out into the hallway. They sat on a hard wooden bench and listened to the indiscernible rumble of voices beyond the door.

"Do you think they'll throw us in prison?" She said it like an accusation, as if it was all Kade's fault, which it probably was. "My parents will kill me."

"We won't go to prison."

"Why not? Just because you've never been caught before—"

"I don't know what their reasoning will be, but Larci knew she was beaten the moment old Tippi spoke up."

"And how long before the truth catches up with us? My parent's will get me out of prison eventually, just so they can kill me, but they have to know where I am first."

"It will be a while before anyone knows anything, I imagine." Kade shrugged. Authorities tracked movements around the world by accumulating data from every skyland they docked with, then passing it on. As Kade and Lana had not legally left Tribalin the system would put up a flag as soon as it discovered they had entered Beelamola. "Months, at least. By the time Come and Go gets back to High Plain, Tribalin will be long gone."

"Maybe."

"I imagine Matharzo is still a higher priority than us."

"You don't know anything—"

The door opened a crack and Farno's head appeared. "Come on in."

Kade and Lana resumed their seats inside and waited to hear the verdict.

"Against my better judgment," Larci said, glancing sourly at her companions, "we will grant you legal entry, but there will be some community service involved."

Lana raised her eyebrows. "Community service?"

"Yes." She looked at Tippi. "It's jam making season and a couple of deaths have left us short staffed at the factory."

Kade cleared his throat. "Jam making? We don't know anything about—"

"It isn't hard. It will just be a couple of days."

Kade shrugged. "I guess we don't have much choice."

"No, you don't. You'll need to pay the Gate tax and we'll throw you out the gate as soon as we reach Come and Go."

"You don't know a man named Goran, do you?" Kade asked.

"Who?"

"Never mind."

The young woman, Juno, indicated the pistols, piled with everything else on the floor. "And we'll keep those."

Lana looked like she was going to complain, but Kade didn't want to push their luck. "Of course," he said. "And thank you."

The councilors chatted while Farno entered the details into the Beelamola system.

"I suppose this is the most excitement you've had around here for a while," Kade said while Farno worked on the scanner. He took out his purse and started counting money.

"You're right about that." Farno scratched his nose. "Can't remember any visitors for quite a while. Don't think there are many people in the hold either. It's a big skyland, Beelamola, but hardly anything ever happens. And that's the way we like it. No surprises, no trouble."

It was obviously a warning and Kade wondered if the laid-back constabulary chief might contain hidden depths. "We'll be sure to let your boredom continue unabated."

Farno finally finished his work. "That's fifty doms each for the gate tax."

Kade stopped counting and looked up. "Fifty each?"

"That's right."

"But we don't have that." He checked the coins in his hand. "That's the highest tax I've ever heard of." More than double, in fact.

"We don't much like strangers here."

"I've got..." Kade finished counting. "I've got eighty-five."

Farno pursed his lips.

"Will we get some compensation for the pistols?"

Farno shook his head.

"Would someone here buy the skyglass?" He didn't want to sell it but according to Lana's story they were going to anyway so if he didn't ask...

"Not much use for one, I wouldn't imagine."

Farno turned to where the others still chatted and called to Larci. The woman excused herself and came over.

"Seems they don't have enough money," Farno said.

"Don't they?" She sniffed, looking them up and down as if they had knocked on her door begging for scraps. "How much do they have?"

"We have eighty-five doms," Lana said. "Please let us stay."

It wasn't as if they could throw them over the edge, but they could hand them over to the High Council or the Wind Patrol in just a few days time.

Larci sniffed again, turning to look as Tippi joined them.

"The tax is fifty doms for individuals," the old lady said, "but only seventy five for married couples."

"You'd let us say we're married?"

"Not unless you *are* married," Larci said firmly.

"But..."

"I am willing to stretch things in some areas, but rules are rules. I will not let down the people who voted me in to office."

Typical small town official, Kade thought. The people who voted her into office probably didn't care one way or the other how much money was extorted from visitors. "Then what are you suggesting?"

Tippi pursed her lips, as if thinking. "I can conduct the ceremony for ten doms."

Kade was staring at the woman. "Umm..."

"Here?" Lana said. "Now?"

"What, you've suddenly got cold feet?"

"No." Lana rubbed at her tattal and glanced towards Farno. "But... I was hoping for something a little more... romantic."

Larci glanced at the fourth member of the council, a small man with a drooping moustache and buckteeth. "Romance doesn't often come into marriage," she said, turning back to Lana.

Kade collected his thoughts. It was like catching sparrows wearing a blindfold. He didn't want to get married. "But then we wouldn't have enough money to pay the gate tax at the next skyland."

"We're heading for Come And Go, so you can sell the skyglass there." Farno suggested.

"But not until after we get through the gate."

"Right." Larci gave the problem some thought.

"I can't go any cheaper with the ceremony," Tippi said. "It costs me ten doms just to submit the details to the High Council." She scratched her head. "We might be able to come up with some small payment for your work in the jam factory."

"Wait a minute," Larci said. "I don't know if—"

"You were taking advantage of the situation to get a couple of laborers. I think me keeping my license is just as important."

"So this is all about you keeping your celebrant's license?" Kade asked Tippi.

"I need to conduct a ceremony in the next month or so and there aren't any likely local options. All means the same thing to you in the end." She shrugged. "I was going to suggest it in a couple of days."

Kade turned to look at Lana. She was biting her lip. Kade sighed. "Well, I don't suppose we have much choice."

"That's the spirit," Farno said with a wry smile.

"Let's get this over with," Kade said.

Tippi looked in his direction.

"Like Lana said, this wasn't how we pictured it." Kade held up the money. "Who wants this?"

Farno took the money and pocketed it without even looking. "Congratulations you two, and good luck. Now, I really have to get back to work."

"Thank you," Lana said with a smile. Kade thought she was almost overdoing it. "Ahhh, Farno..."

"Yes?"

Lana looked around for a moment, then shook her head. "Nothing. Just, thank you."

Farno nodded and sauntered out the door. Tippi and Larci were talking quietly. Eventually the younger woman sighed and Kade knew she'd been badgered into changing her mind about something again.

"I've got some good news," Tippi said as Larci left the room.

"We don't have to go through with the wedding?"

"Don't get too carried away. You'll still be getting married, it just won't be until tomorrow afternoon."

"Oh, right."

But Lana gushed some more. "Oh, thank you. That will give me a chance to get cleaned up a bit. And maybe I can find a dress."

Tippi nodded. "I'm sure something can be arranged. Larci also agreed to let you off workfor the next three days as a bit of a honeymoon."

"And will our pay cover the cost of a hotel room?"

Tippi laughed. "There's nowhere to stay in Beelamola. No tavern or whatnot. You'll have to stay at my place. It isn't big, but you'll have your own room and it's the only place you can afford."

Lana glanced at Kade. "In that case, thank you very much."

"Think nothing of it." Tippi shrugged. "Since my husband died and young Farno got married and moved out I need the company." She led them outside and pointed directly away from the Administration Complex. "See the place right down the end of the street? The one with the blue roof and the roses? That's my place. But I have to get back to work now— jam doesn't make itself. I won't be home till dusk, so you'll have to amuse yourself until then." She smiled a sly smile. "I'm sure you can think of something to do."

Kade and Lana looked at each other for a moment.

"Thank you," Lana said, clearing her throat. "We'll see you at dusk then."

Tippi nodded, "Enjoy your afternoon," and started to chuckle as she walked slowly away.

Kade and Lana stood on the steps in silence. Kade gazed at the blue-roofed house for a moment.

"Let's go for a walk," Lana suggested.

"Yes. Good idea." Dusk probably wasn't much more than an hour away but Kade knew, with Tippi's suggestive remarks, hanging around at the house would make things even more awkward than usual.

They went the same way as the old woman, walking along the ancient cobbles of the narrow street. Tippi's house was not the only one with a blue roof, but other colors were just as popular. Red and yellow, green and brown. The buildings they protected were a standard white weatherboard with glazed windows and stone chimneys. They crowded close to the street but had room between for yards and gardens.

"This is nice," Kade said after a long silence. "Not what I expected with all the stories about Beelamola."

It was said the skyland had been one payment ahead of the creditors for the better part of twenty years.

Lana grunted. "Maybe we can settle down here after we get married."

Kade sighed.

There weren't many people about. A woman working at a washtub under a sloping roof that protruded from the side of her house. She watched them pass, nodding a greeting. Further down, a man was shelling peas on his steps, his hands working quickly while he leaned back against the wall with his eyes closed. And across the other side of the street, two women were swinging a shutter back and forth, examining the hinges critically.

It seemed like a typical small town. Things might not happen today, but they'd happen eventually, and just in time. If someone couldn't do it on their own, then help would be available. Life just rolled along without any major deviations or impediments.

"It does almost feel like home," Kade said softly, stopping to stare at a sheep that was watching him through a picket fence. After a moment the animal shuffled backwards, on the edge of panic as sheep seemed to be most of the time.

They soon came to a huge, lowset building that could only be the jam-making factory. Through wide, smoky windows they could make out about a dozen people, no more than blurred patches of color. What they were doing was anyone's guess. To the left, was another building. It was half the size of the factory, though still large by most standards, and made from timber. A rough stone chimney belched smoke into the sky and a soft glow emanated from the large open door.

Kade stared.

"What is it?" Lana asked, eyeing the building as if she expected a horde of black-clad criminals to burst forth at any moment.

Kade stalked down the street and arrived at the open door just in time to see the smith take up a pair of tongs and pull a glowing rod of iron from the furnace.

"Hello," Kade said, pausing by the door.

The smith turned to look at him and nodded a greeting. "You must be Kade. And Lana."

Lana suddenly switched on, smiling and nodding. "You know our names?"

"I'm sure everyone knows your names by now. Talk of the town." The piece of metal was starting to cool. He put it back amongst the coals. "I'm Gript."

Kade hurried forward to pump the bellows. He kept the rhythm slow and steady. "What are you making, Gript?"

"An idea I've had for a while. An engine. We don't have any crystal makers here so if something breaks down... I do my best but it would be nice to have another option."

As he continued to pump, Kade glanced at a large, solid construct in an open space on the other side of the workshop. It was about a metre to a side and made from a vast range of different parts. It reminded Kade of an array—a very advanced array—except it was made from metal. The smith had it bolted to a block of wood.

"So you aren't using any crystals at all? How does it work?"

The smith grunted. "At the moment, it doesn't."

"Well, how is it supposed to work?"

"Well, hot air expands, right. But what would happen if you heated air in a rigid, sealed container?"

"The container would eventually explode, I suppose."

"Right. That's a lot of energy. So, instead of letting it explode, I'm letting the air out through a valve. And I'm using the air to... do things. You know. Turn a wheel or lift a lever or something similar."

Kade gave a nod. "It could work."

"That's what I thought. The trouble is, the air just rushes out when I open the valve and..."

"And you're left with no air for next time."

"Right."

Gript pulled the rod from the coals again and started to shape it with hammer and anvil. Several minutes later he was done. He broke off the worked tip of the rod and dipped it in a bucket of water, sending off a drift of steam.

Kade laughed.

"What?"

"Steam. Fit your container with an inlet pipe and connect it to a water tank. You heat the water, it turns to steam and drives your... whatever it is that it drives. And you can just keep letting more water in as you go."

Gript smiled. "It just might work. Won't be a simple as you make it sound, of course."

"Of course, nothing ever is."

"Like all Kade's plans," Lana said.

Kade smiled and she ignored him.

When he next looked around, darkness was creeping into the building and Lana had gone. She might have left five minutes after he and Gript started talking for all he knew.

II

"You were looking for Farno earlier, Lana?"

Lana cleared her throat. "Yes, I was." She shrugged. "It's just... Well, Kade was talking to Gript so I thought I'd talk to Farno about constabulary stuff as well."

"He was out at the apple orchard trying to fix a water wheel."

"Oh right."

Kade watched Lana carefully. She was obviously nervous about a lie, but it wasn't possible to pick it out amongst all the other lies.

"I'll catch up with him some time."

Tippi nodded. "He's usually around somewhere. He can't go far. And you found the smithy, Kade?" she said, scraping the last of the thick stew aimlessly around her plate. "Metal workers always seem to find each other, as if playing with all that metal has made them magnetic or something."

"I haven't been off Whiparill in years, so it was nice to talk to someone different."

"Teach you a few tricks, did he? Gript has been in that place almost every day for as long as I can remember; we've been trying to find him a wife for years."

Kade glanced at Lana but ignored the comment about wives. "He does know his stuff."

"There are some advantages to living somewhere like Beelamola," Tippi said. "Nobody rushing around ruling every minute of your life. And it's cheaper."

Breathing in the fresh air, Kade turned to look out over the view. Tippi's dining table was on a small deck outside her kitchen. It was at the top of a steep slope with seemingly the whole of the skyland spread out below. He decided there were probably quite a few advantages. Grain and vegetable fields filled about a quarter of the area, mainly in a wedge on the port side of the skyland. The rest was orchards. In the relative darkness it was easy to forget the poor quality of the crops.

Tippi collected the plates and stacked them at the end of the table. "Are you going to stick with being a blacksmith, Kade?" she asked. "Blacksmiths will never be short of work. Them and crystal engineers. But engineers are a shifty lot, I reckon. Who can argue with anything they say?" She gave an emphatic nod. "Smithing is a good honest way to make a living."

Kade stared out at the moon-washed landscape. "I don't know what I'm going to do."

"I suppose it all depends where you end up," Tippi said. She took up the plates, gesturing Lana back into her seat when she made to rise. "I can handle these, love."

"Are you sure? I don't mind."

"You're getting married tomorrow." She headed for the kitchen, leaving Kade and Lana sitting in the soft glow of the single crystal lamp.

"What *are* we going to do?" Lana asked softly.

"What?"

"Bolkin is probably in the hold. Or Lemar, or whatever his name is. Are we going to see if we can find him?"

"No." Kade sat back in his chair. He could hear Tippi in the kitchen washing the dishes. "Firstly, if we ask to have a look in the hold then your very thin story about us eloping will fall apart on the spot."

"We could say we are looking for someone to sell the skyglass to."

Kade shook his head. "Secondly, I don't imagine Lemar will be so careless two times in a row."

"So we just sit here?"

"If the thieves are still here then they'll be here when we reach Come and Go Archipelago."

"Well, what if I talk to Farno and tell him what's going on?"

"You should have thought of that before you went and said we were eloping. When you admit to one lie people generally don't trust you after that."

"But he could check the facts."

Kade laughed. "Yes, he could eventually find out that we stole a plane to get away from Tribalin very soon after a major crime spree. By the time we get locked up, the array will be long gone." Kade turned to look at her. "Is that what you were going to do if you found Farno this afternoon?"

Lana examined her fingers. "No."

Kade couldn't work out if she was lying or not.

"If we told him, then we wouldn't have to get married tomorrow."

"I'm not looking forward to that either, Lana, but it's far better than prison."

They sat for a while longer, Kade staring out at the night, Lana running her fingers over the whorls and patterns on the table.

Eventually, Lana started to say something, but Tippi emerged from the kitchen once more. "I've had a long day," the old woman said. "I'll show you where your room is, then I'll have to leave you to amuse yourselves."

"Of course," Lana said, rising to her feet. "We don't want to keep you up. We've had a long day ourselves."

"I imagine so." Tippi led the way inside, through the kitchen and into the small sitting room. "Bathroom is that way," she said, pointing to a door on the right. "Towels and what not are under the sink and that's your room there." A second door was slightly ajar and spilling a wedge of light out onto the timber floor. "I've got to get up early so I'll be turning in." She went through the one remaining door and closed it behind her.

When Kade looked at Lana she shrugged and headed for the bedroom. She opened the door to reveal a double bed but not much else.

"I'm going to have a shower," he said collecting the clothes from his pack and quickly heading the other way.

Ten minutes later, feeling almost like a new person, Kade pulled on some clean underwear and breeches. He hung the shirt over his shoulder, grabbed his dirty things and stepped out into the sitting room. Lana was waiting for him. He stopped and stared as she crossed to stand in front of him.

"My turn."

"What? Oh, Right." He stepped out of her way and crossed to the bedroom without looking back.

The room was barely large enough to contain the bed. Kade sat on the edge, knees almost brushing the wall. He looked around then removed his breeches and climbed under the covers. The sheets were rough woven but clean and cool. They felt like heaven against his skin. He tried to work out how long it had been since he'd slept in a proper bed and discovered it was nowhere near as long as he had thought.

Lana returned not long later. She stopped in the door, toweling her still wet hair.

"Sorry," Kade said. "I would have slept on the floor, but there's no room."

She didn't reply.

Kade smoothed the covers. "Which side do you want? If you prefer I could..."

"Whatever."

"Right. Good. Well, if you change your mind just say?"

"Thorn, it doesn't matter."

Kade nodded. "Right." He rolled over and didn't even notice when Lana climbed into the bed beside him.

III

Kade stood by the dining table, trying to stretch his back. The bed had been the softest he ever slept in and the pillows all but useless. While he rolled his shoulders and flexed his neck, he looked out over the skyland. The crops and the orchards created a patchwork of brown and yellows. People were already out working. A handful picked fruit. Another couple drove machinery around a fallow field, throwing up a storm of dust in the cool morning air. A few kilometres away stood a steep-sided, rocky hill. It was higher than anything else and would have uninterrupted views of Beelamola.

"Come on," Lana said, emerging from the house. She wore a straw hat and had one of the packs slung over her shoulder.

"Where are we going?"

"The Tor." She pointed at the hill Kade had just been examining and, stepping off the patio, started down the hill. She slipped and slid, setting off small landslides. "Tippi has insisted. I think they're planning something."

He looked over his shoulder, in the general direction of the smithy, but followed over the edge.

"It's strange how two such similar places can be so different," Kade said when he reached the bottom of the slope.

Lana looked back at him, but only briefly. "What?"

"Whiparill is a bit smaller than here, but it's all farmland too. But it's green. There aren't enough workers to keep up. Here..."

"Not everyone uses money and fame as a way of keeping score."

They found a narrow path that skirted along the edge of a peach grove then dipped beneath the trees, heading in generally the direction they were after.

"What do you mean?"

"Work twelve hour days and be rich or work six hour days and live comfortably." She shrugged. "Everyone knows Beelamola is almost bankrupt and has been for years. But the people don't seem to be starving. Tippi took us in quick enough, fed us, offered us some clean clothes. They aren't broke. So maybe they don't want to be rich."

Kade shook his head. "Or maybe they are just lazy. Or bad farmers. Or..."

Lana shook her head and walked on in silence.

"You could have warned me about the eloping plan," Kade said eventually.

"Should I have passed you a note? Maybe used semaphore?"

They left the peaches behind, crossed a stone lined canal and entered an apple orchard.

"Why didn't you tell me who your parents are?"

"It's none of your business, really."

"Yes, but—"

"I don't know anything about your parents either. Does it matter? What difference does it make?"

"None." And it didn't. "Except we *are* getting married later."

"Don't even joke about that, Kade."

"You think ignoring it will make it go away? Surely you should be back at Tippi's place trying on dresses. The Lana who was in that council hall yesterday would be."

"This might be easy for you, Kade, you chose a life of lies, but..." Lana stopped abruptly and sat down on a rock beside the path. She buried her head in her hands. "I was going to wear my mother's wedding dress. It's been handed down for five generations." She drew in a deep shuddering breath. "Your parents may not care who you marry but—"

"My parents?" Kade laughed humorlessly. "You really want to know about my parents? They sold me to the Skyway Men when I was five years old, Lana. They got a hundred doms and shoved me in the back of a lorry with a dozen other kids. Let's see if we can work out exactly how much they cared, shall we?"

Lana looked up, wiping her eyes. "They sold you?"

"Don't talk to me about the choices I've made. Don't tell me..." Kade suddenly deflated as if the last few days had finally drained all the energy from his body. He sat on a rock on the other side of the path. "I lived in a Skyway Men boarding school from then until I was sixteen."

It was the first time he'd ever talked about it. Other Skyway Men already knew how it was and generally weren't the type of people who wanted to talk about their problems. Not the ones who made it through training anyway. And everyone else? Tell anyone else and chances were you'd die a slower, more painful death than they did, but only just.

"The only parents I ever really knew were my teachers, and they weren't very nice." *And Lemar.* Or perhaps he was an older brother, always looking out for him. Well, almost always.

"Oh."

"I suppose some of them were as nice as their jobs allowed, but they weren't training tour guides." The dark, dusty halls of Girendault didn't really come with a lot of nice memories. "It was dawn to dusk every day and often beyond. Martial arts, weapons, climbing, lock picking, chemistry... A dozen other things. About one in ten completes the training."

"What happens to the rest?"

"There wasn't any particular spot for us to throw the bodies over the edge of the skyland, just where ever was closest." He sighed.

She stared at him for a moment. "Oh."

"It wasn't the place to make friends." *Friends only let you down. They walk out on you when you need them most.* Kade stood up. "Come on. If we are going to make it to the top of the hill we have to get a move on."

Ten metres up the path, Kade looked back. Lana was still staring at him. A moment later she rose to her feet and hurried to catch up. She didn't say anything else for a long time.

There was a low stone fence where the orchards ended and the hill made its final climb upwards. Kade looked each way but there was no evidence of a path leading towards the top so he climbed the fence and offered his hand to help Lana over as well.

"Should we leave the path?" But she handed him the pack and clambered over on her own.

The way quickly became very steep and rocky. Half the time Kade, pack on his back, was using his hands to help as he scrambled over boulders or up long, dusty rockslides.

He stopped at the top of a low cliff and looked back. Lana had fallen behind.

"Do you need a hand?"

She looked up, took off her hat and wiped sweat from her forehead. "No, thank you." But when she reached the base of the cliff she stopped to sit on a rock and look up. Her face was flushed. Sweat was dripping from her nose.

Kade shook his head and crouched down to help. Lana stood up, hesitated, then reached out to take his hand.

Half an hour later Kade pulled himself over the lip of one last boulder and found himself at the top of the Tor. He was sweating, and his clean clothes were no longer clean, but he felt good. Lana was already leaning against the rail of small platform, looking out over the skyland. Taking a deep breath he went to stand by her side.

"There's no views like this on Tribalin," Lana said, half to herself. She shaded her eyes against the sun.

Kade nodded. "You're right. But there are no views here like the ones on Tribalin."

"You'd rather look at all the dirty walls and streets than at this?"

Kade looked at the trees and crops, the colors that seemed so much more vibrant than anything on Tribalin, even if they were just different shades of brown. He made his way to the other side of the platform and examined the village. It was just two score buildings occupying a low, flat hill at the base of the Flight Tower. It looked like Whiparill. It looked like home.

But as often as not, Whiparill had frustrated him. He'd regularly found himself bored and gone to pace the streets and the fields as if he might walk far enough to escape. And every time he'd made his way back to the smithy, to his workshop, to the people, and sunk down as if into a comfortable old chair.

"All I'm saying is that there is good and bad in every view, if you choose to see it."

A thin stream of smoke rose above the smithy, shredding in the wind like a dream.

Lana cleared her throat. "Do you want some breakfast?"

Kade looked back at her. She made her way to a small table near the far edge of the platform and started pulling food and drinks from the pack. She moved with crisp economy and seemed to put everything in a particular place. She looked up and saw him watching silently.

"Tippi packed it for us," Lana said, looking embarrassed. "I'm not sure if it's going to be added to our bill."

"Do you think we can add another bed to the bill?" Kade's back was still aching.

"It would be slightly suspicious if we asked for another bed, Kade." Lana removed her borrowed hat, revealing the butterfly tattal at her temple. The swelling was finally starting to go down.

"I want a different bed, not an extra one. How could I not want to sleep with my wonderful wife tonight?"

Lana sat down at the table and started to eat. She said nothing as she stared out at the day.

"That was a good piece of flying yesterday," Kade said to fill the silence.

"I just did what I had to do."

"You didn't *have* to do anything. You could've stayed at home."

"No, I couldn't. If the array really does what you say it does, I didn't have a choice."

Kade shrugged. "Either way, it was pretty impressive."

"Thank you. So, they didn't teach you to fly?"

"Not everyone. That's a specialist thing. I never wanted to fly anyway, because it's always scared me a bit."

"It doesn't show."

"A lot of things don't." Kade turned to look at his food. He could feel her watching.

IV

Kade and Lana waited a short distance away as Tippi made her final preparations. The dining table had been removed and some potted plants had been arranged on the deck. With the view beyond, it actually didn't look too bad.

Other people started to arrive as the old lady fussed. In just a couple of minutes the remainder of the council and about twenty others had gathered nearby. Kade recognized some of the women. There'd been a line of them outside Tippi's door from early in the afternoon, each with offerings of clothes or flowers, jewelry or expertise.

Kade didn't know about anything else, but they'd done an amazing job with Lana on such short notice. Her dress was a strapless thing, very pale blue. Tight across her breasts and hips it flared slightly at the knees and had a short train behind. Her hair was piled high on her head with flowers and beads braided into it. Her only other adornment was a necklace with a sapphire pendant.

She turned to look at him. "What?"

"We don't have to do this," Kade said, quickly looking away. "They hand us over to High Council, we tell them what's going on…"

She shook her head. "They'd have to do a thousand checks before they did anything and we don't have time for that. If we don't get lucky as soon as we step through onto the Archipelago we may not get another chance."

"Right."

"We don't have any choice. We can't let anyone have that weapon."

There was a determination in her that Kade wasn't going to argue with. He nodded, "Right."

Gript came hurrying around the side of the house. The blacksmith was still doing up the buttons on what was probably his one and only set of good clothes. And apparently he was the only thing delaying the ceremony. As soon as she saw him, Tippi waved Kade and Lana over.

"So, we're getting married?" Kade asked.

Lana nodded.

"You might want to try smiling then."

She applied a thin smile and smoothed her borrowed dress.

Kade grabbed her hand as she started to walk away. "You look great," he said.

She smoothed the dress again. "It could've been worse. I was lucky to even find something that fits properly."

"Well, if your mother's wedding dress looks any better than this it would've left me a blubbering mess."

"Thank you." She gave a real smile then, and she was more beautiful than ever.

Kade loosened his shoulders and offered her his arm. *It definitely could have been worse*, he thought as they walked forward together.

The preliminaries passed in a blur for Kade. The little he did tune in for was all fairly standard anyway. He absently held Lana's hand, not exactly sure who was shaking, and stared past Tippi, watching a pair of birds dart about in the nearest of the fruit trees down below. It wasn't until the old woman asked who would stand witness that he really took notice.

Kade wasn't surprised when Juno stepped up to stand beside Lana. They were about the same age and the Councilor had helped with dress fittings and makeup. But he stared stupidly for a moment when Gript took up position as his witness.

"What are you doing here?" he whispered.

The blacksmith shrugged. "Somebody has to, and that idea with the steam... I think it'll work. I did some tests and—" He cut off quickly, dipping his head and blushing when he saw Tippi glaring at him. Kade knew he was going to have to get involved in the ceremony soon so he tried to concentrate as well.

"Nobody here really knows Kade or Lana," Tippi said, "but they have chosen to be married here in Beelamola, so they are a part of our family. And we should all be happy that they are happy. It is obvious in the way they look at each other, as if words are not necessary. I don't know how long they've known each other and I don't know where they've come from in their lives, but I think they will always have the same story from now on."

Tippi looked down at her notes. "Now is usually the time when the bride and groom say a few words but with the short notice and all I—"

Lana cleared her throat. "I would like to say something."

Nothing Lana did surprised Kade any more. He realized she was turning towards him and he spun in her direction as well. When she looked up from his shoes a few seconds later there were tears in her eyes. "There are some things you can never plan for," she said softly. "Sometimes, someone arrives in your life and changes everything, they sweep you up and carry you along, showing you a world and a life you never knew existed. Kade did that for me and I know I will never be the person I was before. He gave me the courage to find my true self and..."

She floundered over an ending, obviously trying to avoid the word love or anything like it. But she was crying openly now and Kade decided that was probably good enough. Nobody else needed to know the real reason behind the tears. He leaned in and kissed her cheek. But the natural progression was for him to make a reply. He cleared his throat.

"I suppose it's my turn now," he said. The audience gave a polite laugh. He cleared his throat again. "Lana says I changed her life but I think it is the other way around. The day before I met her I was living a quiet life. I am just a metal worker and she is... I never thought I needed anyone, but she has proven me wrong." Kade realized his speech was going the same way as Lana's had. It was honest and evasive, giving the people of Beelamola what they expected to hear without actually lying. Most of his life had been a lie— Kade suddenly wondered why he was avoiding a simple lie now. "Her love has lifted me up," he said, "and I only hope that I can do half as much for her."

They stood for a moment, not moving, before Kade gave Lana's hands a light squeeze. She blinked and he pulled her gently forward so she could kiss his cheek.

"Right," Tippi said.

Kade turned to see that the old woman was crying as well.

"Have you brought the bracelets, Gript?"

"Of course."

This was news to Kade as well.

The blacksmith turned to Kade and Lana as he took the bracelets from his pocket. "I know it's traditional for the two of you to get these for each other but..." He shrugged, looking slightly embarrassed. "I wanted to do this for you, just as a temporary thing until you can both get the ones you really want."

How appropriate, Kade thought, glancing at Lana.

Five minutes later they were officially married. He didn't know if there was some type of get out clause for people who need to go undercover to find stolen weapons. Probably not.

Kade looked at the sandwich. "Jam," he said. "You've got to be kidding."

"If you don't like it you don't have to eat it."

"I've seen enough jam to last me a lifetime. Just the smell of it..."

Lana took a bite of her own sandwich without complaint but didn't look all that keen either. "It's only our first day. Do you think we'll get used to it?"

Kade shook his head. "There will come a time when we don't notice the smell at all, that's when it will hurt the most."

She took another bite and chewed silently.

The wall that had been between them had come down on their walk to the Tor, but the space it had occupied was still there. Kade didn't know if it would ever go away. He was still a criminal and a murderer. Lana knew it and might never be able to accept it, even knowing the reasons.

Kade sighed and examined the wedding bracelet Gript had made. It was beautiful. Made from brass, it had patterns that matched his tattals and fitted snugly around his wrist. It must have taken hours to make and apparently Gript had still found the time to make another bracelet for Lana and do some tests on the steam engine idea. The man had been working at his craft for years, but still loved what he was doing and was trying to improve. Kade realized that he'd never felt that way with the Skyway Men. He'd been good at it and gotten enjoyment from that, but not from the job itself.

Metalworking had always been something to do while he waited, but it suddenly seemed a worthwhile occupation. He had received his Journeyman tattals not long ago and the next strata, though a long way away, was something he wanted to work towards.

To do that, he had to make it through this one last job alive. That seemed a long way away as well.

He ate some more sandwich. "They don't seem particularly ruthless, do they?" he said after a moment.

"What? Who?"

"The Green Sea Raiders, or whoever they are."

"There were dead people everywhere back on Tribalin."

"As far as I can tell, they only actually killed two people and that was because I turned up when I wasn't supposed to. They didn't even kill me."

"Your point?"

Kade shrugged. "I'm not sure that I have a point at this stage. But it *is* something to think about."

Minimbuk

I

Once the winches had fired and started reeling Beelamola towards the Come And Go Archipelago, Kade turned to examine the activity in the Local Yard. He stood on the top of a lorry, searching amongst the faces for any sign of Lemar. He wasn't there, just a bunch of tired, disconsolate looking farmers with some produce that looked much the same.

"Can you see anything?" Lana asked.

"Plenty," Kade replied, "but nothing that helps." He did notice Farno crossing the Yard towards them. The lean man had left his scanner back near the gate with two part-time deputies, waiting for anyone who came through from the Archipelago.

Kade climbed down.

"We'll be sorry to see you go," Farno said as he reached them.

"We enjoyed our time here too, thanks, Farno," Lana said.

Kade knew what was coming.

"Gript says you've been a great help over in the smithy. He caught up on his backlog and still got to fiddle with that contraption of his." He smiled. "And my mother enjoyed your company. You could always stay on."

Kade shook his head. "Not now. But maybe we'll come back."

Farno gave a nod, as if it was all decided. "I hope you find what you're looking for," he said. And with that, he returned to his post by the gate.

"He knows something's going on," Lana said, holding onto her hat as the wind whipped up.

"So, I assume he came to that conclusion by himself then?"

Lana stared at him for a moment then quickly looked away. "I never really had the chance. He was always busy or..." She shrugged.

"Don't worry about it. I don't think there was much he could have done anyway, even if he had believed you. Our eloping story wasn't all that believable, but the truth is hardly any better."

"But if they knew we were lying why didn't they arrest us?"

"Larci was going to, because that's what her precious rules suggested, but maybe they all just like the excuse to pass trouble on to someone else." Kade shrugged. "Maybe they like us."

"Well, maybe they like *me*," Lana said.

Lana picked up the pack, but Kade took it off her and slung it over his shoulder. Farno had kept the pistols but they still had all the other equipment they'd taken on to Beelamola. Their supply of clothes had also significantly increased.

The two guards, one on either side of the gate, smiled and nodded as they passed through onto the bridge. Kade remembered them, vaguely, from the wedding celebrations. Probably in a few hours they'd be back to working in the grind house or picking fruit.

More than a dozen men and women lined the wall on the other side of the bridge. They stared stonily at the growing line of people as if it was the most important task in the world. Their grey uniforms, double-breasted with elbow length sleeves and big collars, were pristine. Blunderbusses were held at precise angles.

Kade stood next to Lana and tried to look innocent. He felt that everyone was watching him.

"Why are you visiting Minimbuk?" the customs officer asked when Kade and Lana reached the front of the queue. She looked as if he'd rather be anywhere else.

"Just visiting, ma'am," Kade said, clearing his throat.

"We are not," Lana gushed by his side.

Kade sighed.

"You aren't?" The officer suddenly looked suspicious, as if Lana was about to admit to being assassins. Her hand went to her wide belt as if readying to draw the ceremonial dagger she wore there.

Lana slipped her arm through Kade's and slapped him playfully on the wrist. "We've just gotten married," she explained.

"This is your honeymoon?" the officer asked, the suspicion turning to a smile.

Lana leaned forward conspiratorially. "My parents don't approve of Kade because he's a metal worker from Whiparill, so we're looking for somewhere to start our new life."

"Not Beelamola?"

"Have you seen the place?" Lana whispered.

"I've heard."

"Everyone has. So definitely *not* Beelamola."

"Well, I'm not sure if Minimbuk is looking for couples at the moment. You can go to Admin and check."

"Thank you. We will."

"Now, let's get you on your way, shall we. Wristals, please."

Kade held out his arm to be scanned and watched as Lana did the same.

"Neither of you have been here before?"

"No ma'am," Lana said. "I only left Tribalin for the first time recently. It's very exciting."

"I'm sure. Do you have money?"

"About fifty doms," Kade said. With the tax to come out of that, it wasn't much.

Lana spoke up again. "And we have some things to sell." She pointed to the pack, leaning forward again. "I suppose if we were being totally honest, we would have to admit that we are carrying stolen goods, but they're things my parents haven't seen in years. Let alone used."

The customs officer patted down Lana, looking for concealed items, and a man came forward to do the same to Kade. When they were done they looked inside the pack.

"Your parents aren't going to miss the skyglass?" The customs officer raised a carefully shaped eyebrow.

Lana giggled realistically in response and held up her thumb and forefinger just a few centimetres apart. "Well, maybe a little bit. But they still got out of it cheaply, I think. They tried to have Kade arrested."

The woman checked her scanner screen. "Your mother is Secretary of Tribalin? And your father is the Chief Engineer?"

Lana nodded. "They can afford to lose one little skyglass."

The man who had searched Kade grunted and smiled. The woman shook her head. "I suppose they can. Serves them right for forcing you to this, really."

"That's what I told Kade."

"But now they really do have a reason to hate me," Kade said. "Not only have I stolen their daughter, I've also stolen a skyglass."

"I'm sure they'll forgive you if grandchildren arrive," the male officer said. "I know my wife's parents suddenly liked me a whole lot more."

"We can only hope."

"Right. Taxes please. Jasparac and Galiloop are docked at the moment and we'll be arriving at High Peak in a week."

Lana smiled and gripped Kade's arm tighter. "Thank you." She kissed the female customs officer on the cheek.

Kade shrugged apologetically and rolled his eyes.

The man shook his head and clapped Kade on the back. "Good luck."

"Thanks." Kade took up the pack and, with his arm still linked with Lana's, moved out of the Local Yard and into a small square.

It was a busy place. There was a market over one side and some type of sport being played on a grass area closer to hand. A group of boys were kicking a ball quietly amongst themselves. Every now and then, one of them would pick it up and, for a short while, the game would move into a different phase. Kade laughed a short, humorless laugh.

"What's so funny," Lana asked.

"It's just this game the boys are playing. I have no idea of the rules but they seem to change all the time, one game becoming another."

Lana turned her attention to the game for a moment, nodding slowly. "Sometimes that's when games are the most fun, or interesting at least, when you just jump in and play and see what happens."

"It can also end with someone getting hurt."

"Maybe." Lana, arm still linked with Kade's, stopped suddenly, nearly pulling him off his feet. "Let's sit here for a while."

"Why?" But when he sat by her side on a low stone wall that divided a café from the square, Kade could see the slow stream of people exiting the Beelamola Local Yard, and he could also see into the Crossing Yard. "Oh."

But if that was the best plan they could come up with they were in trouble. They could sit there all day and see nothing and they both knew it. Even if Lemar and his friend were still on Beelamola and going to Minimbuk, there was no saying they would do it immediately. The Come and Go Archipelago was still a week out from High Peak so if that was their destination they may well stay where they were for a while yet.

"What do they do on Minimbuk anyway?" Lana asked absently, as if merely saying something to fill the lull in conversation.

"Cruisers, I think. They make cruisers and lorries and scooters and... planes maybe. I don't know."

"Oh, of course. That's where I've seen the name." She leaned to the right, trying to see around two women who were blocking her view of the Crossing Yard.

The styles of clothing worn by the local civilians didn't deviate much from the standard set by the officials and guards at the customs station. The one concession to fashion seemed to be brightly colored belts and collars in a variety of hues. Perhaps one or two in ten were dressed in what Kade considered to be more normal clothes.

"It feels like we're chasing a ghost," Kade said. It felt like they were chasing the past. He didn't really want to catch it. "It's like..."

Kade didn't finished. A man had sat down on the wall, a couple of metres away. Tattals covered his head like a lace helmet. The man didn't say or do anything suspicious, just sat and stared at the crowd, but Kade watched him uneasily.

He only looked away when he saw two people openly wearing swords and pistols. It took a moment to realize they were constables. They were hardly distinguishably from the mob.

"There he is." Lana grabbed his arm.

"What?" But he looked around and saw Lemar exiting the Crossing Yard. He was dressed in the local fashion—grey suit with a wide red belt and green collar. He stood outside the gate for a moment, looking around as if he expected to see someone he knew.

Kade didn't even think to turn away. He sat and stared. It was ridiculous. The odds of finding the thief again were... The odds of it really being Lemar, after all this time...

The man started to walk away and Kade allowed Lana to draw him to his feet. "Come on." They were going to stand out, dressed as they were, but that couldn't be helped.

The city was clean, but far from attractive. Buildings were huge blocks of concrete, sharp edged and imposing. They sat shoulder to shoulder with small windows overlooking the streets. The place had a military feel. There were no open spaces, no trees to break the monotony. Residents walked or drove as if the life had been drained from them. Their facades were as bare as those of the buildings.

Lemar wasn't hard to follow. The crowd ebbed and flowed between them, but he didn't double back or check behind. He walked along the street like he didn't have a care in the world. He nodded silent greetings to other pedestrians and even stopped to hold a door for a woman with a child in one arm and a parcel in the other.

"So do we want to catch him? Or do we just want to get the cell?"

Lemar was wearing a pack but it didn't look all that big. "We need to secure him, at least until we know for sure that all the stuff stolen from CRG is in the pack. If Lemar doesn't have the cell or the files we'll need to ask him where they are."

"Right. That shouldn't be too hard."

Kade laughed and shook his head. "Right, because he's an amateur and we won't arouse any suspicion when we kidnap him."

"Well..."

Lemar stopped at the next corner and looked around. Kade's heart pounded, but he didn't want to draw attention to himself by suddenly turning away or changing direction. He slowed down, then stopped to look in the front window of a store. Lana stopped with him. There were still people in the way and if Lemar wasn't really expecting to see either Kade or Lana then he may not really look.

After a moment Lemar turned on his heel and started walking again, around the corner and out of sight. Kade breathed a sigh of relief and set off quickly. Lana rushed to keep up. Around in the next street, their quarry hadn't gone far.

II

"When do we get him?" Lana whispered.

"When we find somewhere a bit quieter than a main street."

"Right."

They followed again past tall, square shops that looked like they'd come off a production line. Each angle was perfect, each window aligned exactly, each door clipped open with a small metal bracket of half moon design. Where Tribalin was a city of smudges and smears, shadows and grime, Minimbuk left you with the cold antiseptic feeling of having just been washed. With their harsh clothing the people fitted in perfectly.

A minute later, Kade turned to look as someone fell into step beside him.

"Hello," the stranger said.

Kade had an uneasy feeling. "Hello."

The stranger noticed. "Just stay calm. Wif sent me."

Kade slowed his pace as he looked around. There would be other men close by and none of them would be particularly friendly.

"My name is Cillun. Come with me. Both of you."

"We're busy," Lana said uncertainly. She looked at Lemar as the man continued to make his way down the street. Soon he would be gone from sight.

"Did anyone ask you, Lana?" Cillun motioned them the other direction. "Come on; Wif doesn't like to be kept waiting."

Kade shook his head when Lana started to complain again. Refusing would probably buy them a few minutes at most.

Cillun, hand in pocket, walked by Kade's shoulder. They returned to the street they'd been following previously. Not long after, they climbed a low hill. From the top, they could see to the other side of the skyland. It was barely a kilometre across. There were factories towards the aft, a dozen huge buildings that seemed to take up acres of land on their own. Raised roads led out from there, long curves of concrete and macadam held above the city on thick, frieze carved legs. The roads led to parking areas close to the Yards where hundreds of vehicles waited to be shifted to other skylands.

"Amazing, isn't it," Cillun said, sounding honestly proud, as if he'd played a major part in the city's construction. "Fifty years ago, Minimbuk's main revenue came from a tanning factory and meat production. There was a population of about a thousand and I think nine hundred and ninety nine of those people wanted to leave. The place stank—literally and figuratively. The noise was constant and the air was poisoned. Now..." He waved his arm expansively. A long line of brand new scooters exited a factory and raced along one of the raised roads towards a parking lot. Behind them came the biggest omnibus Kade had ever seen. It was large enough to carry all the drivers back in one trip with room to spare.

Cillun motioned them onwards.

Street blended into street, building into building. Grey blended into grey. All around, pedestrians and vehicles moved with humorless focus. Silicates in the cobbles sparkled in the sunlight but didn't add much to the scene.

Kade's mind swirled. He came up with and rejected a dozen plans before they came to a building that sat in the shadow of the Administration Complex. It looked much the same as all the other buildings. He checked the doorframe as Cillun found the right key; there was no code-mark. The military feel continued inside. A wide hall with polished concrete floors led from one side of the building to the other. Numbered doors, evenly spaced, led off either side, offering no hint as to what was beyond.

"Lovely," Lana muttered. "They traded one kind of stink for another, apparently."

Kade didn't say anything. He followed their guide as he led them through one of the grey doors. This too, was unmarked by the usual Skyway Man code. Beyond was an apartment.

"If you just want to wait in there," Cillun said, opening the first of three doors that lined one wall of a long sitting room. "Mister Plist will be with you in a moment."

Lana took a seat in one of two chairs in the middle of the room while Kade looked around. The room was only small, with the desk jammed into the back corner with a row of shelves beside. There was a wall to ceiling tapestry in the other corner and a glass fronted cabinet beside the door filled with artifacts similar to those in Madam Larinal's office.

"I thought we were going to talk to Wif."

"Wif is just a code. It means 'someone more important than you'. Which, right now, is just about everyone."

He shifted from foot to foot for a moment then moved to sit down as well, putting his pack on his lap. He fiddled with the buckle, opened the bag and looked inside. There wasn't much in there that was interesting.

On the desk was a wooden cell. It had a grille carved on the front, a switch and push button on the side. Kade leaned forward and picked it up, turning it about in his hands. Madam Larinal had one just the same. He was about to try the switch when there was a sound from the back of the room.

In a moment of panic, Kade shoved the cell into his pack as a small, almost dwarvish man, stepped through a door behind the tapestry and marched across to sit at the desk. He scratched at his beard, adjusted his spectacles and leaned back, putting his feet on a partially opened drawer.

"Well, well, well, Kade Traskel. You have been busy, haven't you?"

"I... Well..."

"You made a hell of a mess on Tribalin." He didn't seem particularly worried. "Which shouldn't really surprise anyone."

"It wasn't *my* fault," Kade said softly, feeling like he was back in a classroom on Girindult.

"It wasn't your fault?" Mister Plist shook his head and looked over the top of his spectacles. "Maybe it wasn't, but you're certainly stuck in the middle of whatever's going on. Who else are we supposed to blame?" Plist took down his feet and leaned forward. "Why don't you tell me what happened. From the beginning."

How did Mister Plist know any of that information? It should've been impossible for any message to arrive quicker than Kade had. He tried to think, tried to gather all the dangling ends of the situation and tie them together in some kind of neat bow.

"Well?" Plist said.

"Well..."

Plist sighed and sat back. "You really are starting to—"

"Sorry, Mister Plist. I'm just very tired," Kade said. "We've been going non stop for a while now. Ummm, here's what happened." He told the story from the start, sticking mostly to the truth. He left out Leni Miklor and Londar

Oludis and Lana became a crooked constable who helped him raid the morgue. He also didn't let on about what the stolen cell actually did. "Bolkin lost us under the city. After that Lana and I decided it was time to get out so we stole a plane," Kade concluded. "And here we are."

"Here you are, indeed." Plist sighed and sat back. "That's quite a story. But surprisingly it generally matches the other information we received. Though you *have* supplied some details that we weren't aware of."

Kade felt a little bit sick. "Oh." *How could they possibly know anything? Did Londar submit an initial report? But how could* anyone *have read the report, let alone someone on a different skyland?*

"Such as?"

"Well, we didn't know who was involved, but we— not us here," he waved a hand, "other people— did some checks and your name popped up. You know what the Council thinks of co-incidences." Plist smiled. "You have certainly left a big mess for everyone to clean up. Tough job for a new Operations Manager."

Kade played with the buckle on his pack. "Things started happening and I just had to keep up."

"All right. I can see that. You needed to get off Tribalin because you were the only loose end there. But you landed safely on Valakeen. Why didn't you stay there? Why did you feel the need to undertake a very risky flight to Beelamola?"

"I... That is, we..."

"Have you ever been to Valakeen?" Lana asked.

"No," Plist replied, giving a short, sharp shake of his head.

"It's impossible to hide there," Lana continued. "There's maybe a dozen buildings and a hundred square metres of land on the whole place and it wasn't going to be moving for a few more weeks." She licked her lips and glanced towards Kade. He wanted to encourage her, but didn't dare. By the look on her face she knew just how much danger they were in. "We killed constables escaping from Tribalin. We shot down a spotter plane. We were sitting ducks if we stayed on Valakeen."

"I see. I see, I see, I see." Plist sat up straight and clapped his hands on his knees. "I see. You did well then. You really did."

Kade glanced at Lana but didn't say anything. Plist was glossing over more than Kade had himself. He wasn't worried about any of the important details. Where was the cell now? Who had it? What did it do? Did he already know those things? Londar and Kiri had both insisted that there was no job, but Plist was suggesting otherwise.

"So," Plist continued, "I guess we just put that one down to experience and carry on. Not the best of results. Obviously. But we can't do anything about it now. The Council will have to be informed that you are now here with us, of course... So, if you just step back out into the living room, Cillun will find you a place to rest while we work things out."

Kade stayed where he was. It was all too neat and if he said nothing Plist would know he was suspicious.

"Thank you," Lana said quietly. She didn't seem very keen to stand up.

The moment was gone, so Kade *did* stand up and held out his hand to the other man. "Thank you for your understanding, Mister Plist. I just want to prove to the Council that I'm ready for active duty again. I want to get of Whiparill. I can clean up the mess."

Plist smiled and stood up as well. "We'll see."

Kade nodded and when the other man leaned forward to take his hand he lashed out. He struck Plist in the throat, a swift, solid blow with the edge of his hand.

Plist's eyes went wide. He raised his hands as he struggled for breath. He tried to say something, but nothing more than a gurgle emerged. A moment later he slumped forward onto the desk and Kade reached out to stop him falling to the floor.

Lana was staring.

"He'll probably live," Kade said. He didn't know if that was actually true. He'd used the attack previously but didn't know if anyone had recovered. If he disliked someone enough to hit them in the throat their continued health was not going to be high on his list of priorities. "Come on."

The door behind the tapestry led to a sparsely furnished bedroom in an adjoining apartment. There was nobody there. There was nobody in the sitting room beyond that either.

Kade took a deep, relieved breath but quickly went into the hall. Still nobody. Even the street out the front was quiet, just a cruiser parked out the front of Plist's apartment building.

"What now?" Lana asked.

"That," Kade said, pointing. "It's probably for us anyway. Come on."

When they reached the cruiser there was no key but Kade ripped away a panel and examined the ignition array. While he worked Lana spun about in her seat, opened the luggage compartment at the back and searched through the contents.

"Don't worry about feeling guilty," she said. "There are maps and a few cells and all sorts of useful stuff back here. I don't think there's much doubt who this belongs to."

"Normal people can't keep useful stuff in their cruiser?" Kade asked.

"Well, yes, but I also found this." Lana held up a piece of lead shot. "It was loose down the bottom."

"Good. Not that I was going to bother feeling all that guilty anyway." He sat back as the cruiser kicked into life.

"Well done. Couldn't you have done that with the plane on Valakeen?"

Kade swore. "Maybe. Damn. Who thinks of hotwiring a plane, though? Anyway, this is all going pretty well, considering."

But just then Cillun and another man stepped out of the apartment building Kade and Lana had exited earlier. Kade slammed the cruiser into gear and accelerated onto the street.

Kade looked back. Cillun reached for a pistol, but the other man stopped him.

"What are we going to do?" Lana asked as she looked back as well.

"We're going to get off this skyland."

"Yes, but—"

"How did they know what happened? Nobody could have gotten to Minimbuk quicker than we did." Kade wanted to race through the streets to the Local Yard, but forced himself to move with the flow of traffic, stopping at intersections and constantly checking over his shoulder.

"They must have been watching us," Lana said, checking around as well. "Maybe Londar had someone waiting outside, where we couldn't see."

"That's all very well, but how did the message get here? They couldn't have used the beamers." He took a deep breath and wiped sweat from his forehead with his sleeve and took a few more random corners.

Kade couldn't work it out. Lemar had once been a Skyway Man, but now? And the codes and the door marks? The communications systems? All of that could have changed, or been adjusted to suite the admittedly unusual circumstances. He wasn't sure about anything.

"Plist didn't mention Londar at all."

"One minute you're complaining that they know too much and the next that they don't know enough?"

"Well..." Kade didn't know what to think. He didn't *want* to think. So instead, he concentrated on driving.

Eventually, he found a main road and headed towards the port side of the skyland, racing along with a knot of traffic. He looked suspiciously at the driver of every vehicle that went by, wondering how long it would be before someone found them.

Galiloop

I

By the time they stopped just down the street from the Minimbuk customs station, Kade's nerves were on edge and he was expecting to be killed at any moment.

"What do we do now?" Lana asked.

Kade looked around. "We get out and walk," he said. "We go through customs and see what happens." But that meant giving up their one admittedly-slim chance of finding Lemar.

Lana knew it as well. "So we quit? After everything we've done?"

"I don't see that we have any choice. As it is, changing skylands may not save us."

"There may be another option," Lana said. She started to climb out of the cruiser. "Come on. Let's go."

Kade almost didn't see the woman walking quickly towards them. She didn't look towards the cruiser, though it was right in front of her, as she reached under her pleated jacket and...

Kade grunted, "Hold on," and jammed his foot onto the accelerator. Lana squealed, half in her seat and half out, as he wrenched the wheel sideways, knocking over a pedestrian and surging forward. They scraped along the side of a lorry. And then it was too late to stop. They'd drawn attention of the officials and they couldn't turn back.

Kade swore and sliced the cruiser between two customs officers and through onto the bridge. A blunderbuss fired. People screamed. Kade wipe sweat from his eyes and concentrated on driving.

They slowed as they crossed the covered bridge. Out the other side, Kade looked around for more trouble. He couldn't see anything, but that didn't mean much. There were only two people waiting to go through customs.

"What are you doing?" Lana whispered.

A mountain peak was visible beyond the walls. The lower sections were wrapped in thin tendrils of cloud. There was a sprinkle of lights that could just be seen.

Kade waved to the customs officer as they approached.

"What's the commotion back there?" the man asked, motioning back the way they'd come.

He'd find out for himself, soon enough. Kade could hear a group of men entering the bridge at a run from the other side. Lana turned to look. He hoped she was hanging on.

"Not sure," he replied. He accelerated at the last moment, darting between the men and away.

More shouts. More gun blasts. Kade ducked his head as lead shot thumped into the side of the cruiser and cracked the windscreen.

He felt a punch in his back as another shot hit home but managed to keep his concentration. "Thorn."

Up onto the footpath and through a café. Diners scattered, shouting and cursing. Back down onto the roadway, past a light post and out into the clear.

"They're chasing us," Lana said.

"What?"

"Two cruisers."

"Damn."

Galiloop was a mid-sized skyland, two kilometres across, with a population of about three thousand people. Once, it had made a fortune from crystal mines, but now the mountain peak that had been torn free of the earth was riddled with long, snaking holes and not much else. They struggled along on the remnants of a small marble quarry that supplied the best tiles and building blocks in the world.

The town clung to the skirts of the mountain and stretched out to either side like wings, leaving the front and back of the skyland clear for the farming of some basic crops. There was obviously not enough of the famed marbel to go aroundbecause the buildings were made from rough-cut, dull stone. They hunched beside the streets like blind beggars. Windows stared blankly.

Kade took streets at random, sweeping around corners as fast as he dared, scraping paint from the cruiser on buildings, startling pedestrians, climbing the hill. The road was rough, ancient cobbles that had sunken and twisted or gone missing completely. Kade clamped his jaw against the rattling and glanced at Lana's hands. One gripped the edge of the seat, the other a pole by her side.

"Watch it!"

Kade wove around a fruit seller's rickety wooden barrow on not much more than instinct.

They were in a small square where the last dregs of a market were slowly winding down. A clock tower, stark and black against the clouds, pealed the noon chorus.

He was having trouble staying focused. "Can you see them?"

"No. I don't think so."

He slowed the cruiser in the middle of the street and leaned forward on the steering wheel.

Another gun shot. Swearing, Kade accelerated and the cruiser lurched forward again. A group of children scattered. A merchant shouted abuse as they upset a pyramid of clay jars.

Racing along more narrow streets dark with years. Down an alley that was barely wide enough, rubbish swirling in their wake. Across a small green tablecloth of a park. A storm of pigeons burst into the air.

"Are they still there?" Kade said through gritted teeth. He wasn't sure if Lana would be able to hear him. The pain in his back was like fire.

Through an industrial area, eerily quiet, then back among houses. Finally, he pulled up under the skeletal branches of a tree standing in the middle of a square.

"I don't think you should..." Lana noticed the blood on the back of his shirt and gasped. "Are you all right?"

Kade coughed. "It hurts a bit."

Lana bit her lip for a moment then climbed from the cruiser, ran around to the driver's side and pushed Kade across to where she'd been sitting. He closed his eyes as they started to move once more.

Lana was looking at him so he gave her a small smile.

"You're awake," she said.

Kade gave a nod. When he started to sit up, she moved quickly to help him.

"How do you feel?"

"Fine." His back still ached, but he suspected that would be the case for a good while yet.

She seemed to realize what he was thinking, which wouldn't have been much of a guess. "I took five pellets out of your back." She pointed to a pile of lead balls on a stone close to his side. "None of them were very deep but... Well, I'm not a doctor."

"I'm sure you did great." He flexed his arm and winced. "See, it's fine."

She smiled at him for a moment.

"How long has it been?"

"We got here yesterday. They're searching for us."

'Here' appeared to be a small, triangular space formed by two leaning boulders. One end was filled with a pile of smaller rocks, the other with a tangle of trees and greenery that had obviously been upset recently. "Where are we?"

"On the back side of the mountain, about half way up in a wild, rough area. I hid you here then dumped the cruiser in the town. I bought some pain-killers..." She held a small jar of tablets out to him.

"Nobody saw you come here?"

Lana shrugged. "Maybe. Probably not though. We're still alone, after all."

"I don't imagine that will last much longer. Galiloop isn't that big."

"I know. So I've been having a bit of a look around. There's an aerodrome but they only have three planes and a serious if bored-looking guard. The Crossing Yards are only tiny and there seems to be three guards all the time."

"What about secret passages?" Kade said with a slight smile.

She smiled back, though her heart didn't appear to be in it. "Yes, there's lots. I bought a map from a tourist shop."

"Excellent." Kade leaned back against the boulder and tried to think. "How long until we reach High Peak?"

"Four days."

"Well, I think we should go to the hold tonight, anyway."

"Umm... All right. Great."

Kade could see she wanted to know the plan but wasn't going to ask. For a moment, he thought of telling her. "I think I'll get some more sleep before that," he said eventually. He probably needed more than sleep but that couldn't be helped. He wondered if he'd be able to move by morning.

He watched Lana battling with herself as he lay back down and saw the moment when she gave up. "What are we going to do?" she asked.

"You'll see."

"I just think—"

"Don't you trust your husband?"

She sighed and stretched out. She pushed her back against the stone wall but that still left her almost touching his side in the narrow space. "I'm never going to hear the end of that, am I?" she muttered. "If we really were married I'd just nag you until you told me."

"Yes dear."

They both laughed for a moment.

"I do trust you." It was a reluctant admission.

They were the last words Kade heard before he fell asleep.

Kade woke in the middle of the night with Lana curled up beside him, head resting on his shoulder. The weight added to his pain but he stayed where he was, not moving.

There had been women back on Whiparill—younger women, older women—but they all moved on eventually, knowing that he had shut a large part of himself away. Lana didn't know a great deal about who he was, but she knew a lot more than anyone had for a long time. She didn't particularly like him, but she was still there.

Kade laughed, wondering if he knew himself any more.

He pushed the hair away from Lana's eyes and drifted back to sleep with a thousand silver butterflies fluttering through his dreams.

II

Kade shifted his pack to ease the ache in his back. The painkillers were doing their work, but in a little while that might cause as many problems as it solved.

"How do you do it, Kade?"

He looked back. Lana was hardly visible in the low-hanging cloud, an indistinct blur that could have been anyone. "Do what?"

"This life of crime."

Kade laughed, thinking that perhaps his situation was not much different to hers. "A few days ago I was a metal worker." And a couple of days ago she'd been a constable, probably heading for a great career because of her parents' prominent positions on Tribalin. Now, she was a fugitive and just one eager, observant constable away from death.

"Still," Lana said, "it all seems to be so easy."

Kade thought of all the people he had killed. The old man at the laboratory, Tilli at Madam Larinal's house. It had been easy once, but not any more. He cleared his throat. "These last few days I haven't had any choice, just like you. If we don't work out what's going on we'll die. Or lots of other people will. So we do what needs to be done. I've had training in this, remember? What we should be asking is why you seem to be doing so well."

They continued across the field in silence. A spotter plane passed high overhead, the whirring of its crystal engines all that gave it away in the clouds. Kade ducked down amongst the crop anyway and the plane continued on its way, neither slowing nor turning.

"Where are we going?" Lana asked quietly when they were walking once more. She adjusted her own pack, taken from the cruiser before she dumped it. Kade didn't even know what it contained.

"We're going to the Crossing Yard. I told you." He smiled but kept his eyes forward. Their destination was one of the aft Crossing Yards. There were no skylands docked there but there would still be guards to make sure everyone stayed where they were supposed to. Minimbuk was away to their left.

"Yes, but..."

They saw nobody for the next half an hour as they continued through fields and over fences. The clouds stayed with them. This was a double-edged sword that hid them from view but also hid their destination. Kade navigated by guesswork alone, letting the flow of the landscape direct him.

Finally, they climbed a fence and, when they stepped out from the thick tangle of a windbreak, the high stone walls of the Crossing Yard and its twinned Local Yard became visible, bulky and black in the whiteness. There was one finger of tower on the inland side of the yards and Kade assumed that it divided the gates. It was where the guards would be. There was a small village as well, just a dozen houses clumped around the base of the tower, huddling together for warmth. A light burned in one of the windows but there was no movement.

They were little more than a hundred metres away.

"Let's go back to the fence," Kade said. He pushed back through the windbreak and followed the fence towards the edge of the skyland. Soon they came to another fence that met the first at right angles and divided the fields from a thick stand of trees. Kade angled through the woodlands until the trees and ground both ended and he was looking out at clouds and sky.

"They'll see us if we try to climb the wall, Kade," Lana said, almost whispering directly into his ear. "The cloud won't hide us enough."

"They'll see us before we get to the wall. These trees will stop a fair way short." Kade whispered as well. He didn't know if the sound would travel very far, but it felt like it would. The night was silent, expectant.

"Then what are we going to do?"

Kade stayed back from the empty sky and moved slowly towards the yards. Eventually, as he predicted, the trees ended leaving fifty metres of open ground. There were probably trip wires that set off bells as well, specifically for nights like this. Where the open ground started there was also a wall running along the very edge of the skyland, hanging its toes over the drop off into the nothing.

"Feeling fit?" Kade asked.

"Yes. Well, no. I could do with a bit more sleep."

Kade flexed his shoulder, wincing. "Couldn't we all."

"Are you going to tell me what we are doing?"

"We are going to climb into the Crossing Yard."

"But I just said... You just said that..."

"I didn't say we were climbing *up*."

Keeping to the trees, Kade finally made his way to the edge of the skyland and carefully leaned out to look.

Lana seemed to realize what he was talking about. Her eyes narrowed. "You're kidding?" she whispered fiercely, looking back over her shoulder as if she had spoken too loudly and expected a dozen guards to charge at them.

"I don't think it'll be all that hard, actually. I looked when we flew under Tribalin. There's all sorts of pipes and stuff."

"For one thing, Tribalin is a city, Kade. They need all those pipes, while this place..." She looked around as if trying to find a nice way to describe Galiloop. "And secondly... And secondly, you must be crazy."

Kade hadn't considered the first point of Lana's argument. The second had crossed his mind more than once in the past few days. "Do you have a better idea?"

"We could..." She chewed on her fingernail. "We could go to the constables and tell them what's happening."

"Do you really think that will work?"

Lana gave a quick nod.

"I'm not so sure. We made an awful racket when we arrived. They wouldn't just be able to ignore all that." He shook his head as he gave it some thought. "It might work, but... Let's save it as a last resort." Kade had another look over the edge of the skyland. "You don't have a rope in that pack, do you?"

"I'm not giving it to you. I still think we should go to the constables. Or the Wind Patrol, even. They'd help."

"How about you give me the rope then go do that. If they look too closely at my history it won't matter at all what you tell them. That will be the last resort."

Kade flexed his shoulder again, adjusting his pack. The skyglass and light array seemed to be dead weight, but he wasn't willing to get rid of them. He took another pain killing tablet and sat down with his feet dangling over the edge of the skyland. Despite Lana's concerns, there were plenty of things to hold on to. The wind tugged at him. It wasn't much more than a breeze, but in his mind it was a gale trying to tear him free. Of all the bad plans he'd had, this was the worst. He started to lower himself over.

"All right. Hold on." Lana pulled her pack open and took a look inside.

"What else is in there?"

"I've got two pistols, some shot and powder, the rope, one of those funny, wooden-box arrays—I think it's got a bullet hole in it—and somebody's lunch."

"Lunch? What is it?"

She gave him a look. "It's a squashed sandwich. Looks like ham. I wouldn't be eating it now if I were you."

"Well, I would've eaten it yesterday if you'd told me."

"I wouldn't have eaten it then, either."

"Then why do you still have it?"

Kade caught the rope when Lana threw it to him and fastened one end around a protruding pipe and the other around his waist. He tested the knots, then took a deep breath.

"You're going over the edge of the skyland, Kade. It feels strange. It feels as if we are defying Thorn or something."

"You never told me you believed in Thorn."

"I don't."

Kade sighed and looked over the edge again. It was crazy to climb down there, in the dark with a couple of thousand metres of nothing below. His mouth was suddenly dry, his hands shaking. Crazy. He started to climb down before Lana could see.

He used bolts and pipes and other random pieces that were all coated in the same dark metal. There were metallic tree roots and jutting rocks, bars, wire and things unknown. Past the lower corner he found a solid perch and rummaged through his pack. When he first pulled out the light, it didn't seem to reveal much at all except the yawning chasm of nothingness below.

Kade held on tighter and tried to concentrate. There were plenty of things to hold on to. The leftovers of the skyland's previous life continued as far as he could see.

Reigning in his attention as it started to wander again, Kade left the light hanging on a hook of wire and climbed back up.

"It shouldn't be a problem," he said when he was sitting on solid ground once more. He tried to calm his heart. "Just like climbing on play equipment in the park."

"My parents never let me do that."

"Well, I didn't do a lot of it either, but you get the idea."

Lana nodded.

"Good. Come on then." Kade untied the rope from his waist and gave it to her. "You go first."

"I'm not going first."

"All right, I'll go first."

"No. Wait." Lana got down on her hands and knees and crawled to the edge for look. "How high up are we?"

"Does it really matter?"

"Yes."

"Twenty metres will kill you as much as three thousand, Lana." Kade sighed. "We can't stay here." He looked over the side, imagining the world below. He decided he didn't want to climb either, but it was the only choice.

"Very well, but I don't know if..."

"There's no room for doubts, Lana. I'm going."

"Me first," she said after a moment's hesitation. Her voice sounded sure, her eyes told a different story. Thinking of the fall, Kade wondered if his arguments had been a little too convincing.

Lana held up her arms so Kade could tie the rope around her waist then barely hesitated as she started to climb. But it seemed to take forever for her to make her way down the side of the skyland. She went one slow step at a time, but Kade was amazed she was doing it at all. She continued to surprise him. She continued to push him further without even realizing.

Lana's voice eventually floated up to him, barely audible. "I've gone under the edge."

"I'm going to drop the other end of the rope down," he shouted back. "Get ready for that, then make yourself comfortable."

After he'd untied the rope and watched it slither over the edge into the darkness Kade took a deep breath, worked his shoulder again, and went over as well. In a few minutes, he was sitting in a loop of pipe by her side. It wasn't all that thick but seemed as solid as the skyland itself. Only the wind offered any suggestion of movement at all.

"That was easy, wasn't it?"

She nodded. "I don't know if I can do it for another hour or something though." It was obvious she was making a big effort to not look down. Kade knew how she felt. He kept his eyes on her.

"Where's the rope?"

"It's where you left it." She kept both hands locked around a coated tap fitting and looked like she might never let go.

Kade shook his head and tried to smile. "Huh."

"What?"

He reached over, took the rope and, holding on with the crook of his elbow, started to reel it in. "I was just wondering why there was a tap down here."

"What?"

"You're hanging onto a tap. Maybe if we turn it off we can cut of the whole skyland's water supply and they'll never be able to get it back."

Lana closed her eyes and didn't reply.

Kade tied the other and of the rope around his own waist.

"Don't do that," Lana said when she saw what he was doing. "I'll just drag you down with me."

"I wasn't intending to catch you."

"Oh."

"I'm not going to let you fall though." He showed her how to tie a strong knot around a pipe without using an end of the rope then got her to do one herself. At first she tried to do it one-handed, but it wasn't going to work. Kade watched her shaking fingers and said nothing. He let her come to the conclusion on her own then work up the courage to do something to solve the problem.

Eventually, she locked her leg around one pipe and her elbow around another and set to work, biting her tongue in concentration.

"Do it again. Just pull this bit to release it."

He watched her tie the knot again and then again, testing it each time.

"All right. Once more, right up near your end of the rope this time."

When it was done he gave her a smile. "Now, you sit here for a while, then follow the rope to my position when I call. Should be easy."

"No problem at all." She was clinging to the tap again, eyes closed.

Finally, she looked down and Kade watched as her knuckles turned white.

He followed her gaze for a moment then cleared his throat as he tried to concentrate. "Should be easy," he said again.

Taking the light, he set off, looking for a quick, easy route through the jungle of clutter. That would've been an easier task if his light reached further. It was a poor tool to use against the vastness of the night. It moved constantly— hooked on the skyland, on his belt, in his hand. Shadows stretched and receded, swayed and danced, offered handholds where there were none and hid others in a jumble of uncertainty.

Kade was forced to backtrack along the rope several times when he came to a dead end. Finally, he reached the end of the line. After resting for a moment, he hooked up the light, tied the rope to a pipe and called to Lana.

Waiting was worse than the effort of blazing the trail. There was nothing to distract him. The wind and the cold, the fall and the dancing light worked on Kade's nerves, making him doubt the world and his place in it. He tried to concentrate on Lana's tortuous journey along the dull white trail of the rope.

When Lana caught up, Kade gave her a smile. She didn't smile back. Her hands were shaking so hard she could barely hold on.

"Do you want to go first, or shall I go again?" he asked.

"I don't know if I can go on." She shook her head, swallowed. "No, you go first."

It was probably better that way anyway. Short blocks of work and rest would be easier. There would be less time to get cramps. Less time to think. He untied the knot and tied another at Lana's end of the rope. "See you soon."

And he set off again.

He calculated that the rope was ten metres long. It had taken about twenty minutes for both he and Lana to travel that distance. Fifty metres to the Crossing Yard, in a straight line. Allowing for a slowing pace and some rest breaks... Kade decided the entire journey would take about two and a half hours. It would possibly be light by that stage, depending on the altitude. "Don't tell Lana," he muttered as he stepped onto a huge, protruding bolt and swung around to the next handhold.

"Did you say something?"

"No. Stay there a while yet." He guessed she wasn't about to argue.

A few minutes later he found a comfortable seat, tied the rope off and called Lana. While she fumbled after him, hardly visible in the darkness, Kade worked at his shoulders. The trouble was, it didn't make his back feel any better. The drugs still blocked most of the pain of his injuries, but he was now aching all over. All he wanted was have a proper rest. He reeled in the slack of the rope and tied another knot.

"How are you doing?" Kade asked when Lana caught up. He tried to keep his voice light.

"It's so cold." She held on with one hand and stuffed the other in a pocket.

"I know. And that ham sandwich is sounding better by the moment."

"I threw it out before."

He wrapped his hand around hers for a moment. "You're doing great."

"Thanks. Doesn't feel like it."

"You're here, aren't you?"

Another nod.

"All right then. Here we go again, I guess."

He changed the knots and started searching for the next path.

When Lana caught up the next time, Kade switched the knots immediately. "Let's get this over with," he said. His whole back seemed to be numb. His hands were freezing. His thoughts wandered dangerously unless he made an effort to concentrate. The world below called to him incessantly.

He squirmed through a loop of tree root, taking skin away from his elbow, shimmied along a pipe, then walked along a thick wire mesh that protruded from the side of the metal-coated foundations of a long-buried building.

He was standing at the corner of the wall, breathing heavily, when the prong of wire supporting him snapped with an audible *ping*. His heart raced and he gave an involuntary shout of fear. He swung from one hand, fingers stuck in a narrow fissure in the concrete, and watched as the light fell away from him. It twisted and tumbled, quickly growing fainter. Before it had disappeared completely, Kade felt his shoulder cramping. He cursed, eyes watering, as a spasm passed through him. He let go and followed the light as the siren song of gravity finally claimed him.

Moments later the rope brought him to a sudden stop. Breath rushed from his lungs. A lance of pain ripped through his shoulder. Darkness.

III

Kade swung gently back and forth. The wind pushed him in lazy circles three metres below the skyland. He was freezing. The rope was cutting in under his arms as his weight tried to pull him down through the loop.

"Kade? Kade, can you hear me?"

"Yes. I'm all right." He wasn't all right, but admitting to that just then wouldn't achieve anything.

"Why didn't you answer?"

"How long has it been?" He reached up to grab the rope, partly to ease the pressure, partly to hide the shaking of his hands. Nobody could see him anyway.

"I heard you shout and the rope... It was a couple of minutes ago."

"Is that all?"

"Yes." She said it as if she was offended by his suggestion that it wasn't very long at all.

"I just slipped then passed out for a minute. I'm fine. Can you help pull me up? I don't know if I can climb."

"I'll try."

Kade tried to help as Lana pulled the rope back through the twisting route he had followed but any movement made him think he'd been shot again, this time with a cannonball.

It was almost ten minutes before Kade could reach up, gritting his teeth against the pain, and grab onto a piece of pipe. He pulled himself up carefully and hooked his foot through a tree root.

"Are you holding on tight?" Lana called.

Kade nodded, then realized she wouldn't be able to see. "Yes." As tight as he was going to be, anyway.

A few minutes later, he opened his eyes and saw Lana nearby, tying a knot and looking worried.

"Are you all right?"

"Not really."

Lana twisted around, balancing precariously with a foot wedged under an angled rock as she leaned back.

"You're bleeding," she said. Then she pulled at the bandages. "I think the wounds might be infected. We need..."

She didn't finish the sentence because whatever they needed probably wouldn't be in either of the packs.

"We need to get to the Crossing Yard," Kade said softly. "It's probably only twenty metres away."

"Twenty metres may take an hour."

"Well, should we just stay here until help arrives?"

"Don't be like that."

"We don't have a lot of choices here, Lana." A shudder passed through him.

"We could just head straight for the side." There was a hint of pleading in her voice.

Kade gave a grunt of laughter that hurt his shoulder. Their twisting, convoluted journey had only taken them a few metres from the edge of the skyland, but it wasn't an option. "You're forgetting about the wall that lines the edge here. Easier to continue under here than try to climb that."

"Oh."

"Let's just keep going. We really don't have any choices."

"All right. But I'll come with you to help."

"And what if I fall?"

She glanced down. "Well, I don't know if I could pull you up again anyway."

"Thanks. This is all very encouraging."

"Just remember to point your toes when you hit the water."

"We're probably over land by now."

Lana smiled wearily. "Well, you can still point your toes if you like."

"Maybe I can take out a shirt from my pack and hold it over my head like Lemar did." Kade sighed and looked around. "I went along the side of that thing last time," he said. It was barely visible in the darkness. It seemed a lot less solid than it had before. "There seemed to be some options after that."

"All right. I'll go and have a look."

Lana swung past and Kade followed slowly, back complaining at every slight movement.

Beyond the concrete wall they moved from rock to pipe, from tree root to strange remnants of machinery, from long buried civilization to ancient metal-covered nature. Kade hardly noticed any of the details. He gritted his teeth and moved mechanically, hand and foot, snatching a moment's rest when he could, concentrating on Lana's back, watching the muscles move under the thin, sweat-soaked material of her blouse. Lana talked continually, encouraging him, joking, urging him on. He wanted to tell her to shut up, that it wasn't necessary, but he didn't have the energy. And perhaps it *was* necessary.

Maybe she didn't do it for *him*. Maybe it was the best way she could think to distract herself.

After an hour, after five minutes, Kade noticed that the day was growing around them. He twisted carefully around and watched as morning started its march over the horizon. And if that surprised him, he was absolutely shocked when he saw that they were near the side of the skyland.

"We need to go to the Crossing Yard, Lana," he said.

"Where do you think I'm taking us?" Her face and hands were black with dirt and grime. Her eyes were as dead and blank—numbed by fear and exhaustion—as the back of a skyland's winch mechanism. Panic, barely held in check, was waiting for release. "Don't lecture me. I know where we're going."

"Sorry, I..."

She reigned herself in. "Let's just see if we can get up there without being seen."

There was a still a good deal of time before dawn would reach the Skyland; the sun was barely over the rim of the world below.

They cambered around the bottom corner and up the side. Just below the drop off, Lana paused, and Kade had no choice but to do the same. He hung on grimly. Sweat rolled down across his face despite the cool, stiff breeze.

After a moment Lana was up over the edge. She whispered for him to hurry up, but he didn't have the energy. His shoulder felt like it would never move again. The muscles were knotted and cramped. His hands ached.

"Come on, Kade. The guards can't see us here, but once we move off the dock and into the Crossing Yard..." She looked over her shoulder. "We may need all the darkness we can get."

Kade didn't have the energy to say he couldn't do it. He just shook his head mutely and stayed where he was. But he still had the rope tied underneath his arms, and so did Lana. She leaned back, wedged her feet against a slight protrusion of rock, and started to haul him up.

"What are you doing?" Kade's voice was a barely audible croak.

The drop into nothing still pulled at him, the world called, but apparently Lana was stronger. She continued to reel him in and Kade had to either help or suffer as he arms jerked and twisted with each tug of the rope. Finally, he slipped over the edge and lay panting in the dust.

Lana slumped over him for a moment, then climbed slowly to her feet. "No time to rest."

Kade was going to stay where he was. He didn't intend to move for a very long time, but once again, Lana gave him no choice. She grabbed his hand and started to pull him up.

"Leave me alone."

"No. I'm not going to be stuck on this place by myself, a criminal, with no idea of how... of... Of anything at all."

Kade sighed and managed to stand. Lana took his pack and started towards the gate into the Crossing Yard. They paused to examine the guards on the tower. The three appeared alert, but they were all facing the other way; the walls were high and were fitted with alarms, so the guards' main concern was watching the gates.

"Come on," Lana whispered, grabbing Kade's arm and pulling him forward once more.

Kade follow silently as Lana crossed the large open space towards the corner of the hold. There was no permanent settlement here as there was in Tribalin's hold, but nearly a score of people were clustered around one fire and half that number around another. A line of crystal lorries stood nearby with a few smaller cruisers.

Lana headed for the largest group and Kade stumbled into the warm circle of light at her heels.

"Is anyone a medic?" she asked. Nobody answered. "Does anyone know anything at all about healing?"

A man in a slightly tattered Spokesman's uniform cleared his throat but, before he could say anything, an old man nodded. "A bit," he said in a thickly accented drawl. "A bit."

Kade stood swaying on the spot.

"Can you help us?"

He shrugged. "Perhaps." He stayed where he was for a moment as if it were a matter that deserved some consideration, then slowly rose to his feet. He spat onto the cobbled floor and motioned for them to follow. "My name is Hooder, but my friends call me Hoo."

Kade had to be dragged along by Lana. He hardly knew what was going on. His head was swimming and he wasn't sure if he could feel any of his upper body.

Hooder stopped at the fourth lorry in line. It was so overloaded that when he pulled a box down from the back he almost brought the entire load tumbling to the ground. "Take a seat on this," he said putting the box on the ground. He stared at the load as if that would be enough to keep it in place. "Now, what's the problem, exactly?"

Lana removed Kade's shirt and unwrapped the bandages.

"Well, well, well," Hooder said softly. "What have we here?"

Kade didn't say anything and could imagine Lana desperately trying to come up with a likely story. She still didn't know when to stay quiet.

"It's... We were..."

Hooder nodded. "I heard some sort of commotion in the Local Yard yesterday when I was coming through to the hold," he said, still looking at the wounds. "Shots were fired and all sorts of ruckus."

"We weren't—"

Hooder rose to his feet and looked at Lana. "I'm not suggesting anything, young lady. I'm just making conversation." He went to the cabin of the lorry and returned a moment later with a first-aid kit.

"Thank you," Lana said when he set to work.

Kade watched her hands. She held the blood soaked bandages as if they would try to escape if she loosened her grip for a moment.

"Think nothing of it. Driving this lorry, I see the customs people every other day and nine times out of ten they overreact. They're probably paid to; it keeps everyone on their toes. Doesn't mean we all have to like it."

Kade almost cried out in pain when Hooder dabbed something on his back. He closed his eyes and gritted his teeth.

"A bit of an infection, I think. Nothing too serious though, by the looks." He sat and looked for a moment. "Could do with a couple of stitches, too." He looked from Lana to Kade and back again. "Don't suppose there's any chance of visiting a doctor in the next day or so." Hooder sighed when Lana shook her head, then rummaged in his kit to find a needle and thread.

For a while, Hooder whistled as he worked. Then he talked. "Happy to say I'm almost home. I'm from High Peak. Just a few days to go. I have to drop off this load, then I get a holiday. As long as I like. Course, my wife will want me gone again after a couple of days and I doubt I'll be in the mood to disagree." He laughed as he told a story about his last holiday.

Kade almost laughed as well.

Kade let Hooder check his wounds regularly and the old man continued to show absolutely no interest in how he came to have them. He just examined the stitches and dabbed on some 'magic cream'. Kade suspected the magic involved nothing more than antibiotics and some type of alcohol; the smell was almost enough to get him drunk. Whatever it was though, it did the job. The day before the Archipelago was due to dock at High Peak, Kade felt he was almost back to normal.

"Thank you, Hooder," Kade said after the evening examination.

The old man looked at him silently for a moment then around at the other people who shared the hold's main fire. "That sounds a bit final," he said eventually.

Kade nodded. "I really think we have to be moving on."

Lana looked surprised. He hadn't said anything to her yet.

"Fair enough. Good luck with everything."

A couple of others offered farewells. One woman crossed from the shadows on the far side to embrace Lana.

"I suspect we'll need all the luck we can get," Kade said. "You don't happen to have a light we can buy, do you?" He searched through his pack for his purse. "We can't pay a lot."

Hooder handed Kade the light he'd been using to do the check up. "You can have that for nothing."

Lana shook her head. "We couldn't—"

"It's got a few hours left in it, at most. I'm surprised it's lasted this long."

"If you're sure."

"Of course." He leaned forward and gave Lana a kiss on her cheek. "You two be careful."

"Thanks everyone." Kade handed Lana her pack and shook Hooder's hand. "Maybe we'll see you around some time."

A few of them laughed.

"Of course. Now, you'd better get going before you run out of darkness."

Kade nodded and started to walk away. Lana fell in beside.

"Where are we going?"

Kade smiled at her. "Are you feeling fit?"

She looked at him, eyes narrowing. "No way," she said. "I'm not doing that again."

"According to the records, we aren't in the Crossing System, we're still on Minimbuk. So, we really have to get back there without going thorugh any of the gates. I don't want to spend the rest of my life wandering these passages. Anyway, you've had practice now. This time will be easy."

Jasparac

I

When he climbed back up round the edge of Minimbuk and shimmied under a chain wire fence, Kade found himself in an overgrown area behind a warehouse. There were piles of scrap and a rusting water tank in the narrow space and the distinct, heavy odor of something dead.

He stood up, stretched the bottom of the fence upwards and called Lana through.

"See, I told you it wouldn't be so bad." They had crossed from Galiloop back to Minimbuk via the Crossing Yards, then gone to a vacant dock on the far side of the skyland to climb over the edge.

Kade didn't think the journey had been anywhere near as bad as last time but wasn't sure Lana agreed. She glared at him. "If you ask me to do that again, when you get close to the edge I'm going to push you over."

"Yes, dear."

She gave him a slight, tired smile and shook her head. "I wouldn't test me if I were you; I'm not sure I'm joking." She sat down on an upturned crate. "How do you feel?"

"I feel fine." He'd told her a dozen times already. Four days of rest and the 'magic cream' had done a remarkable job. He almost felt as good as new. "We should take off these bandages before we go through customs. They'd be a bit suspicious, I think."

He took off his shirt and started to work. "How about you? How do you feel?"

Lana nodded. "Now that the ground is *beneath* me, I feel fine. But seriously, I'm not doing that again."

"Hopefully we never have to consider it. Now come on, lets get to Jasparac before the yards start to get busy."

Kade scanned each shadow they passed and almost flinched at every sound though they were probably safer now than they had been for quite some time. Plist, if he was still alive, and his followers knew they had gone through to Galiloop. Seeing they had exited illegally the chances of them coming back unnoticed were slim.

There were twice as many guards around the dock than there had been last time. And the customs officer seemed on edge, as if they had been blamed for the last indiscretion.

As soon as he got close to the customs station Kade zeroed in on the youngest person of the eight there and held out his wristal to be scanned.

"Kade Traskel?" the man asked when the information come up on his screen. He smiled at Lana as he scanned her wristal as well. "And Lana Grindelia?" According to the badge pinned to his shirt his name was Darius Habbon. "You've been on Minimbuk for only a few days? What was the purpose of your visit?"

"We've just gotten married," Kade replied. The story was starting to feel normal now and it had a nice effect on the customs officer's smile. "We're traveling around for a while to see where we want to settle down."

"Why not Minimbuk?"

Kade shrugged. "We haven't ruled it out yet. It seems like a nice place but we just want to look at some other places as well." The questions were unusual for exiting a skyland so Kade felt he had to make a comment. "What's all the extra security for?"

Habbon grunted. "There was an illegal exit a few days ago. Suddenly there's a whole filing cabinet full of new procedures." He looked across at his superior as if he thought he might have said too much and turned his attention back to his scanner. "It doesn't mention a hotel on your records. Where did you stay while you were here?"

"We stayed with some friends," Kade said, waiting for the next inevitable question.

"Their name?"

"Surname of Plist." As soon as he said it he knew it was a bad idea. At the very least, Plist had been taken to hospital. That would be in the records somewhere and might well arouse suspicion. He kept talking while he tried to think. "I'm not sure of their address. They picked us up from the dock when we arrived, so it never really came up."

"Here it is." Habbon examine the information that came up on his scanner. "Vernor Plist, Factory Street."

Lana seemed to realize the danger as well. "We had some other friends on Beelamola," she said. The customs officer looked up from his button pressing and was hooked by her rueful smile. "They wanted us to stay there. They offered us jobs and everything, but who would want to live there?"

Habbon gave a grunt of laughter and clicked a button as more information came through.

Lana shook her head and gave a sigh. "Do you know they don't even have full time customs officials on Beelamola?" She laid her hand on the man's arm. "*They're* just amateurs."

Habbon smiled at Lana and straightened his collar. He cleared his throat.

"Do you want to search our packs and stuff?" Kade asked before Habbon could gather his thoughts.

Lana had repacked the packs at some stage. Hers had the skyglass and some food. Kade's had pain-killers and a first-aid kit and the spare clothes. The small wooden array he'd accidentally stolen from Plist's office was there as well. They'd dumped the weapons in the hold and everything else should get passed with the usual story if necessary.

"Yes. Of course." Habbon cleared the information off his scanner and Kade silently sighed with relief.

They handed over their packs to be searched.

"What's that?" the customs officer asked when he found the array.

"I'm not really sure," Kade said truthfully. There was a bullet hole in the side of it now, but Habbon didn't really look.

"We'll have to search you." He eyed Lana up and down, perhaps wondering if he could do the search himself. But he called over a female assistant.

Kade allowed himself to be frisked as well, wincing when the man patted his back. The bandages would have been noticeable underneath his shirt but blood would be worse if the stitches didn't hold.

"All right, you're both free to go."

"Thank you."

Kade and Lana walked across the bridge to Jasparac, trying not to rush. On the far side the uniforms might have been different—long, heavy green robes with dark stripes—but the searching looks and serious questioning were exactly the same. Kade no longer had anything to hide but his heart still pounded as he answered the questions and allowed his wristal to be scanned.

"Enjoy your stay on Jasparac," the customs officer said, slipping the scanner into a pocket. She pushed the voluminous sleeves of her robe up her skinny arms and assisted with the pat down. "Be warned, the constables are on alert at the moment so I wouldn't even haggle too hard with the merchants." The woman smiled. "They might just act first and ask questions later."

Kade nodded and smiled back. "We'll keep that in mind."

Lana sighed once they were halfway across the square outside the local yard. He shoulders slumped slightly as the tension drained away. "What now?" she asked.

"It would be good if we could bandage my back again," Kade said, "just in case."

"Then what?"

"Some different clothes maybe. We stand out like this." Most of the people he could see were wearing the heavy robes. Some had hoods, some had no sleeves, some were cut off to knee length. They were all different colors. "Or maybe not." It seemed unlikely they were any good for doing much more than walking. "Why can't everyone just wear sensible clothes?"

"These people are probably wondering the same about everyone else."

"They wore sensible clothes on Beelamola."

"They're farmers."

"Exactly." Kade sighed. "Come on. Let's find a place where we can have some privacy."

They found a secluded corner of a park and Lana restrapped Kade's torso.

"Now what?" Lana asked again when she was done. Her hand lingered on Kade's back for a moment.

"Let's find the Skyway Men and see what they know."

"Why would they know anything? Neither Kiri or Londar knew anything."

"They'll probably have a link into Jasparac's system. We can find out where Lemar is."

"Is that really likely?"

"I don't know. I don't know anything at all about Jasparac. And seeing the Raiders don't actually exist I'm not really sure what else to do." Maybe it was the Skyway Men after all, or a small faction, using the Raiders as cover as they had once done. He looked around. "I don't know what else we can do, other than wander randomly and hope we run into Lemar."

Lana cleared her throat. "There is the other option."

She sighed when Kade shook his head.

"If this isn't the last resort, then what is? Any new crazy plan you have now isn't going to work unless all the skylands align and four leaf clovers start growing out your ears and, on top of that, we have a whole heap of random luck."

"I don't care, Lana. I'm not going to the constables. I want to find this weapon, but I'm not going to jail."

"Very well, let's try your way." She sighed.

"I wasn't asking for your permission."

Lana stared at him, but said nothing more.

II

They spent hours wandering quiet residential streets, with tall, narrow wooden buildings on each side. They were all bright, wild colors, as if fighting the drab of Minimbuk.

Swirling patterns moved dreamily through the pavers on the footpaths. Gardens and parks seemed to occupy every second corner. The busier commercial areas looked much the same, only with larger buildings. As they went, Kade looked at doorways and windows, examined bulletin boards for coded messages. Lana's silence became more and more pointed. Nearing lunchtime, ready to give up, Kade finally found what he was after. He sat down on a low stone wall to think for a moment.

"Have we reached the last resort yet?" Lana asked as she sat down by his side.

Kade shook his head. "See that mark." He pointed though he knew she wouldn't see it. They'd walked down this street earlier and he'd missed it himself. The complex rune was carved into the doorframe of a crystal workshop, disguised amongst the whorls of the grain. "It signifies someone who isn't a member of the Skyway Men but works for them."

"I don't get the whole code marks on the door thing."

"What do you mean? They're there so Skyway Men can find the right buildings."

"I realize that. But how many Skyway Men would be on Jasparac?"

Kade shrugged. "Twenty, maybe."

"So surely they could just be told where to take their light array if it gets broken. Or where they'll get a bargain on cruisers, or what ever. Putting marks on the door that anyone can see doesn't seem very smart."

"They're for Skyway Men that come from somewhere else." But that didn't happen all that often, and not without the locals knowing about it.

Lana didn't look convinced either. "To me it just feels a lot like boys playing at being spies."

"It isn't like that at all." But he wondered if maybe it was. "For one thing there are a lot of women as well." *Nice. That showed her.*

"If you say so." She shrugged. "So, now we wait here until a Skyway Man turns up?"

"No, we go to them." He opened his pack and took out the small wooden cell with the bullet hole in the side. "I'll take this in to be repaired and, if I'm right, then we'll be on our way."

"If you're right?"

"I have no idea what this is, but I reckon it's unusual enough to get the attention of an expert. The crystal engineer will know the Skyway Men will be interested."

"You spend a lot of time coming up with these plans, do you?"

But Kade was already striding across the street and into the shop.

A woman behind the counter looked up. "Hello. How can I help you?"

"I have an array I want repaired."

When Kade handed the box over the woman pushed her spectacles up on her nose and spun the box one way and the other to look, as if the cell itself would tell her anything. She paused when she came to the side with the bullet hole. "What's this from?"

He paused for a moment, as if inventing the story on the spot. "My son was playing with a drill." It wasn't much of a story, but that was the point. "Can you fix it?"

The woman sniffed again, and continued her inspection. After a moment she released the catch, opened the top of the box and pulled the array free of the wooden housing. She paused and looked up. As Kade had hoped, she was immediately much more interested than she had been. Her fingers were trembling slightly. "This is the power." The crystal cube she pointed at had a chunk missing from the corner. "Needs to be replaced." She removed the piece in question, disconnecting it with an audible click. "And this here..." She pulled another part clear as well. It was a disc about the size of a dom coin. She cleared her throat. "Well, I don't know what it is but you need one of them as well." The second piece was shot through with cracks and fissures.

"How much?"

She gave it some thought. "Fifty doms."

Kade almost choked. "Fifty? Are you crazy?" He thought he was a better actor than she.

The woman shrugged. "The power crystal isn't a standard size. I'll have to make it special. And I don't even know if the other bit is a uniform shape; this side looks like it might be slightly concave. I'll need to have a look with a spectograph."

Kade sighed "How long then?"

"Come back at noon tomorrow."

"All right. Do I get a receipt?" Kade walked out onto the street.

Lana was where he had left her but was finishing off a sweet pie and watching the crowd. "Well?" She licked her fingers and stood up as he arrived.

"Now we wait."

"Oh. Do you think they're watching us now?" she asked in a whisper. "I think that man near the corner was watching me earlier."

Kade looked at the stranger, in his early twenties, and laughed. "He probably thought *you* were watching *him* earlier. And he probably liked the idea."

There was activity in the crystal maker's shop. The owner banged closed the shutters on the front window, then stepped out onto the path and started to lock the door.

"You ready?" Kade asked.

"Ummm... Yes."

"Good. See that woman there? Follow her. I'll follow you. And please be subtle about it. No ducking into doorways or slinking along in shadows, all right."

"What?"

The woman was starting to walk away. "Follow that woman." Kade pushed Lana to her feet. She stumbled for a couple of steps, looked back, then started to follow. Kade, in turn, followed Lana, hoping he could stay far enough behind to remain unnoticed.

The small, spaced out procession wound through the crowded streets as Kade continued ruminating on the possible dangers. Cruisers, scooters and lorries nudged slowly along, crystal engines setting up a background hum. Everyone waved as they passed or smiled and nodded. The buildings jostled close together like a friendly crowd come to watch a parade.

Little more than five minutes later the crystal maker had led them away from the main streets and into a quieter neighborhood. There were apartment blocks and even freestanding houses looking out over small dooryards. The buildings were older here but no duller.

Kade rounded a corner and nearly ran into Lana. She was standing in the doorway to a little bakery, munching on a pastry as she looked down the street.

"Stop for a snack, did you?" He had to admit, he was a bit hungry too.

Lana tore off half the pastry and gave it to Kade. She used her own piece to gesture down the street. "She went in that building down there. The one with the red door."

It was four storeys high with a small balcony poking out over the street on each of the upper levels.

"Are you sure she didn't come back out while you were inside ordering lunch?"

"It's hardly lunch. And no, I could see the door the whole time."

Kade took a bite of the hardly-lunch. It was very good. "That isn't the point," he said between mouthfuls.

Lana shrugged. "So, I assume that's the Skyway Men headquarters."

Kade finished the pastry and licked his fingers. "I doubt it's the actual headquarters. It will be some type of drop point."

"But you're going to go in there and shoot someone or something?"

Kade looked around to make sure nobody was close by. "As soon as you hand over whatever gun you've been hiding."

"Huh."

It wasn't long before the crystal maker emerged from the red door and hurried in their direction. Kade pulled Lana into the bakery and passed a couple of minutes by scanning the shelves and buying another pastry—a glazed twist with custard and apple.

"She didn't have the box," Lana said.

"Just wait a minute." Kade took a bite of his food. "Do you want some of this? I think yours was better but it's still pretty good."

Lana tore off an end.

A couple of minutes later, two men emerged from the building. One of them carried the wooden cell. They looked both ways and hurried past the bakery. Kade followed, staying as far back as possible, strolling along with Lana on his arm. Thankfully, they didn't have to go far; the men ducked inside another apartment building a few streets away.

"Now where are we?"

"That first place would just be a drop point, as I said. This will be something more. And that array must be important for them to basically come straight here without spending half an hour wandering around to lose people."

"Maybe this isn't anywhere at all. Maybe they are just trying to lose us."

Kade shook his head. "I don't think so. See the mark on the door for one thing."

She squinted at the wood and nodded, though Kade doubted she could see anything at all out of the ordinary. That was the point.

"Come on. We have to find somewhere to stay for the night. We have an appointment to keep tomorrow."

"We aren't going to go to the crystal maker's are we?"

"Of course not. That would be stupid."

III

Just down the street there was a small hotel, with a café on the ground level and a garden on the roof. The receptionist was a grumpy old lady but the price was reasonable.

"Just the one night then?"

"Yes thanks. At the moment."

The woman handed him some keys. "All right then." As if they had offended her. "Shared bathrooms at either end of both floors. Out by Ten Bell." She wiped her nose on her robe's baggy sleeve.

"Thanks."

The room was only small with a double bed against one wall, a wardrobe and small table opposite. There were towels and soap on the table.

"Lovely," Lana said, wiping dust from the windowsill above the bed.

"Well, it's better than the cave."

"I quite liked the cave, thank you. The view was great, once you fought your way past the bushes."

"Come to think of it," Kade responded, "it wasn't even a cave. It was just a gap in some rocks."

"If you don't like my cave, then next time I'll leave you in the cruiser and you can find your own." She smiled then sat on the bed and looked around. "So is it safe to go out, do you think, or do we have to stay here?"

"I think I'd go crazy here. Let's go down and have something to eat."

The café on the ground floor was still busy with the last of the lunch customers. An old couple sat in a corner, heads close. A woman read a newspaper at another table, hot drink bleeding its life into the air in a thin line of steam. A small group laughing loudly.

Kade and Lana found a table and ordered meals and drinks. Kade stared silently out at the street while he waited.

"So, did your parents really sell you?" Lana said quietly after the waitress set their meals on the table.

Kade nodded. "It could have been worse, I suppose. I might have been left on the street. I was given food and shelter and schooling."

"And you were trained to kill people and break into houses and—"

"I've never broken into a house in my life. Wait, I actually broke into Kiri's house the other day. But before that it was only businesses."

"Well, that's so much better then. Why are you defending them?"

"I'm not..." But he was, he realized.

"If the Skyway Men hadn't been willing to buy you, your parents may not have abandoned you at all."

"It could have been worse." Kade started in on his food.

"Sorry." Lana started to eat as well.

When the meal was done they wandered fifty metres down the street.

"I don't think you're a bad person, Kade."

Kade grunted.

"I didn't realize how the Skyway Men worked. I guess you didn't really have a lot of choice."

"No, I didn't."

"But you have a choice now and look what you're doing."

"I don't really have a choice now either," Kade said. "They're just different choices I don't have."

"You could go to the constables. How could that be any worse than spending the rest of your life running from the Skyway Men?"

"Would you stop talking about that?" Kade lowered his voice and looked away. "You go if that's what you want. I'll see my crazy plans through on my own." He wondered if the only reason he kept going was to see if he could— like a kid jumping over a storm water drain even though ther was a perfectly good bridge right there. Even though you knew you probably *couldn't* make it and were going to end up hurt. Or maybe he was just too scared to stop. Maybe he wasn't really ready to admit he was a metal worker from Whiparill. Was he chasing Lemar or was he chasing the past?

"Did you really want to be a constable?" Kade asked after several minutes of silence.

"Of course. What do you mean?"

He shrugged. "My parents chose my profession for me. I thought yours might have done the same for you, though obviously in slightly less drastic ways."

"My parents didn't want me to join. They wanted me in a safe career in Administration or something similar."

"So you rebelled."

"And then some. They think I'll grow out of it. Or they'll just get me promoted so quickly that I'll be in a cozy desk job by the time I'm thirty."

Kade laughed. "I wish them luck."

Returning to the hotel late in the afternoon they found a small pile of books in the foyer and took a couple upstairs to while away some time as evening darkness gathered outside the window.

Some time later, Kade was sitting on one of the chairs, feet on the table, reading about local history. He could feel Lana's frustration growing. After an hour, he laid his book down just as she threw hers on the bed.

"This is ridiculous," Lana said. "It feels like we've been going non-stop for the past few days and now we're sitting around doing nothing."

"We sat around doing nothing in the cave and on Beelamola."

"Yes, but that was different. This just feels so... normal. It's like we're some old married couple." She held up a hand. "Don't say anything."

Kade gave a small smile but avoided any mention of marriage. He looked around the room. "Normal is good," he said softly.

"Pardon?"

"Nothing. I'm going to have a shower."

"That sounds like a good idea." She threw him a towel and beat him to the door.

Both bathrooms were free and when Kade emerged a while later he felt better than he had in days. Towel in one hand, bandage in the other, he returned to the room. Lana was already waiting, sitting at the head of the bed, pillows behind her back.

"You look a bit more relaxed," Kade said.

"I feel much better, thank you." Her hair was still wet as well. It clung to the side of her face, hiding her butterfly tattal. "Do you want that bandage back on?"

"I suppose so." He threw it to her and sat on the edge of the bed, carefully taking off his shirt as she crawled down to meet him.

"They seem to be healing well," Lana said, gently touching a wound.

"They feel all right, and I haven't taken any drugs for ages."

"Good." She poked at another of the wounds. "I think you'll be left with some scars though."

Kade laughed. "Good. I'd hate to get shot and have nothing to show for it. How would I impress the women then?"

"You think women are impressed by that sort of thing?"

For a moment, Kade said nothing. Then he turned slightly, looking at her over his shoulder. "I don't know, *are* you?" He could feel her hand, warm against his skin.

Her hand lingered for a moment before she pulled it away. "Not really," she said. "I'm impressed by men who are smart enough to avoid getting shot."

"Oh," Kade smiled and looked away quickly. "You're one of *those* types."

Lana poked her tongue out at him, collected the bandage and set to work.

IV

Just before noon, three men emerged from the Skyway Men building, looked each way along the street, then hurried towards the crystal maker's workshop. Lana went to step out of the store where she and Kade waited, pretending to browse at carved alabaster figurines, but Kade held her back.

"Wait. Watch the door of that next unit block along."

A couple of minutes later, three men stepped from this second door and hurried away.

"Who were they?"

"Skyway Men. They'll own all the apartments on a certain floor in both those buildings. They'll have been joined to make one large facility. Come on."

"But what if there are still more? Surely there are if the place is so large."

Kade shrugged. "Most won't be hanging around there in the middle of the day."

"So, what you're saying is you don't know but don't want me to worry?"

"That's right."

"Well, don't try to talk me out of coming."

Kade laughed as Lana took his hand and moved quickly down the street.

Inside the first building they found a small foyer with a stairway as the only access apart form the door they had used.

"Probably the second floor," Kade said, starting to climb.

Lana didn't question him. She followed close behind.

On the first floor Kade stopped to look for a moment but an old lady with a shopping basket over her arm emerged from the closer of two doors, erasing any questions he had. At the top of the next flight of stairs he stopped again. Skyway Men liked to use the second floor because, if they watched the main entrances to the building, they would have a warning if serious trouble was approaching but were not so far above the ground as to make escape a serious task.

"Pick a door," he said to Lana. But he made his way to the second without waiting for her to reply. It really wouldn't make any difference. "Are you ready?"

Too bad if she wasn't. Kade knocked.

"Maybe there's a secret knock," Lana suggested after a few seconds of silence. She jumped when the lock clicked and the door swung open. A tall, slender woman was revealed. She had a touch of grey in her hair and a wary look in her eyes.

"Can I help you?"

"I think we have the wrong place," Lana said.

Kade punched the woman in the stomach. She staggered back and Kade went after her, punching her again and sweeping her legs out from under her. A blow to the back of her neck knocked her unconscious. Her red robe lay on the floor around her like a spill of blood.

They were in a small, well furnished sitting room with a kitchen, dirty plates on the sink, off to one side. Sunlight slanted in through a window, throwing a bright stripe across the floor and wall.

Kade looked back at Lana. "Well, close the door."

Lana snapped her mouth shut and stepped inside, shutting the door behind her. "What are you doing?" she whispered fiercely. "It's just some lady. You'll..."

Kade ignored her, crossing the room to the single door on the far side. He glanced back then carefully opened the door, peeking through the gap.

The room on the other side took up most of the floor. There were five doors, one to each of the apartments that concealed the place and another through a wall towards the rear of the building. It looked a bit like the constabulary offices in Tribalin with rows of desks, filing cabinets and maps on the walls.

One man at a desk. More than he had hoped for, fewer than he had expected.

He took a deep breath. "Wait a few seconds then follow me," he said quietly then opened the door completely and walked in like he was supposed to be there. The man looked up immediately.

"Who are you?" He rose to his feet. "Where's Tilda?"

"I'm Kade," Kade said, wishing he knew the current codes. "They sent me over from Minimbuk to see if you know anything about that illegal crossing the other day." He kept walking forward.

"That hasn't got anything to do with us. Whoever it was went to Galiloop."

"I know, but it may have been one of us."

"I don't—"

When Lana entered the room the Skyway Man glanced in her direction. While he was distracted Kade hit him in the face. Elbow to the side of the head. A knee to the face as he went down. It was over in a second. Kade tried to shake feeling back into his hand.

Lana was standing just inside the door, staring.

"Just some lady?" Kade said.

"All right. What do we do now, then?"

Kade shrugged. "Let's see if we can find anything interesting."

"Like what?"

"Like that, if nothing else." The wooden box they'd taken to the crystal maker was on a shelf, the bullet hole staring like a dark eye. And in the back corner was a desk with a scanner and hardwired LCD screen. "I'll check the system, you look for any reference to the Green Sea Raiders or Bolkin or Lemar Navid. Any mention of the weapon array. Come on. We probably have about half an hour or something."

"Probably?"

"Sorry. We have twenty-two minutes and thirteen seconds." He shook his head. "The Skyway Men aren't a bus service, Lana. They don't do things to exact timetables. Just look around and see what you can find."

First, Kade went to the table to collect the box. The thing, or similar ones, had haunted him since Tribalin. He wasn't going to leave it behind. Then he went to the scanner and set to work. It had been years since he navigated through the system but he soon found the entry and exit details that had been collated from all around the world and passed on every time Jasparac docked. His and Lana's names would soon create an alarm when the algorithms decided that they couldn't have entered Beelamola when they had never left Tribalin. But that could be months away yet. Anything could happen before then.

He soon found what he was after. "Bolkin left Minimbuk earlier today."

"Are you sure?"

Kade turn to look at Lana. She had paused for a moment in her search of the room's main desk.

"Sorry. Where did he go?"

"High Peak, which is the obvious choice, I suppose. Why would he go to all the trouble to get onto Come and Go so quickly unless he was going to High Peak?"

"Has he booked in to accommodation?"

Kade shook his head. "He only passed through customs a couple of hours ago."

"So, unless we can come back in later this afternoon that isn't a lot of help."

"Well, we can go to High Peak," Kade said.

"And hope we just bump into him?"

"It happened at Minimbuk."

"Yes, but..." Lana cocked her head to the side.

Kade heard it too. The sound of multiple sets of feet, of talking, coming from one of the entrance apartments. And just a few seconds after that, sounds from the other side as well as the second team returned.

"Tilda," one of them called. Obviously they'd seen the unconscious woman.

"Thorn." Kade looked around, scanning the room, as if there might be an option he'd missed. There wasn't. "This way." He grabbed Lana's arm and pulled her towards the fifth door in the room's narrow side.

The smaller room beyond was full of equipment with unmade beds crammed into two corners. There were two windows. The closest of which opened easily enough.

People entered the room they'd just left.

Kade looked out the window. There was a tree partially blocking the view, but the building backed directly onto a small park. People were sitting on the grass under trees and on benches beside the gravel paths. They would probably be seen, but it was better than getting caught inside. "Come on," he whispered motioning Lana over.

She looked out the window. "What are you—?"

Kade opened a wooden box under the window and pulled out a rope ladder. It was already attached to a ring screwed into the wall. He threw it over the sill and pushed Lana after it almost before it had slapped noisily against the wall.

"Go."

She went out awkwardly and Kade was right behind her. The ladder swayed dangerously, knocking toes and knuckles against the wall. Blood flowed. They had clattered half way down when a cry erupted from the park behind them.

"Thieves. Thieves!"

Kade hit the ground a moment after Lana and looked up just as a Skyway Man stuck his head from the window above. Kade waved to him and smiled but a second later four men burst from the back door of the apartment building and he felt like an idiot.

"Run," he shouted, but Lana was already half way across the park and he struggled to catch up.

Out of the park, across a street. Breath coming in ragged gasps. Kade looked back over his shoulder. They were close. Too close. Just there. Turn at the first corner, around a gaily painted picket fence, and at the one after that. Their pursuers were just ten metres behind now and gaining. Apparently the robes didn't hamper them much at all.

Lana was slowing.

Down the street, a woman stood in the dooryard of a terrace house, looking at a bunch of keys. As they approached she opened the door and stepped through. Kade grabbed Lana's arm, and shoved her through the gate, along the path and through the door just a moment before it closed again. He slammed the door with a solid thud.

"Who are you?" the woman shouted, cringing back against the wall. "Get out of here. I don't have any money."

Kade ignored her, clicking the lock closed and slipping the bolt. The Skyway Men started pounding on the door as he headed quickly down the hallway. Through the back door was a courtyard with a small, bright garden, a rubbish bin and damp washing on a sagging line.

V

Out the gate, mind racing, heart racing, Kade looked each way along the alley. They could be trapped in there, but there were gates along either side. He crossed to the other side and opened a gate. Beyond was another courtyard. Lana started towards the door into the building but Kade grabbed her arm, spun her around and pulled her back into the shadows behind the gate. She struggled for a moment and he wrapped his arm around her waist and put his hand over her mouth.

The Skyway Men rushed out into the alley where they'd been a moment earlier.

"This way," someone said, and the gate started to open with a squeak of complaint.

Kade held his breath and felt Lana doing the same. He released her mouth but kept her pressed tight against his chest. The Skyway Man's shoulder was visible through the crack between the gate and the wall.

"Wait."

"What?"

"It's too obvious. It's a false trail. You go that way and check the gates. We'll go this way."

Kade stayed where he was, listening carefully.

"How long do we wait?" Lana whispered, breath warm on his neck.

"I don't know." He released her and she stepped away slightly, tilting her head to look up at him.

"And what do we do next?"

"Let's just get away from here first." Kade nudged past her, out of the corner, and carefully poked his head out into the alley.

"After that... Who knows? We're starting to run out of options." He stepped out into the open and Lana followed.

"We could..."

Kade saw her gaze shift and reacted before she could utter a warning. He moved to the left, dropping, taking Lana with him.

The sound of a gunshot.

He landed awkwardly, felt his shoulder dislocate. A starburst of pain. The air rushed from his lungs. He gasped and came to rest by the wall. He struggled to get to his feet, but his arms wouldn't support him. Darkness swept over him in waves. Slumping to the ground he watched as one of the pursuers stepped out into the alley and smiled.

"Not quite as smart as you thought," he said, coming slowly forward. He glanced at Lana where she crouched nearby. He saw the fear on her face, and decided she wasn't a threat.

That was a mistake. As he came closer, slowly reloading his pistol, Kade could see the tension building in Lana's arms, in her legs, in her eyes, as she tried to hold still until the right moment.

The man smiled some more. "But then if you had any brains at all you wouldn't pick a fight with the Skyway Men, now would you." He shook his head. "I don't know who you are but..." There was a noise behind him and he turned. Kade looked as well and saw the other two Skyway Men entering the alley.

And at that moment, Lana surged to her feet. She covered the two steps before the man could react. Her shoulder hit him under the rib cage, lifting him from his feet. He grunted with the impact. So did Lana. But when the man tumbled to the ground she was on him. A kick in the ribs. A kick to the side of the head. A boot crunching down onto his throat. He didn't move.

The other two Skyway Men raced forward, guns raised. Kade could hear Lana crying as she searched frantically for the fallen gun. She darted across, scooped it up and spun. But she didn't fire. She waited. Hand steady, tears streaming from her eyes. And while she waited, she edged towards her fallen opponent.

The others had slowed, but kept coming.

Kade could see Lana's tension rising. Her jaw was clenched, eyes staring.

"Not yet," Kade croaked. "Not yet."

But she fired, and Kade sighed. It was too far. Too far...

But one of the men clutched at his chest, blood streaming between his fingers. And even as his companion stopped to look, as dumbfounded as Kade, Lana was reloading, taking powder and balls from the fallen man by her side. Finally, the wounded man fell to his knees and flopped face first onto the ground. His companion recovered. He turned to look at Lana, saw her reloading, and ran forward. He pointed his gun, shouted wordlessly as Lana rammed the ball home. He fired.

Kade flinched, instinctively. So did Lana, but a moment later she raised her pistol, steadied, fired.

The Skyway Man fell to the ground, tumbling into an untidy heap just metres away.

"Nice shot," Kade said. He tried to breathe. His shoulder screamed at him, his head swam.

"Throw down your weapon," someone shouted. "Throw down your weapon or we *will* shoot."

Kade turned slowly, painfully, to look behind him. Five constables were lined up across the end of the alley. Three were kneeling with muskets nestled into their shoulders.

"Throw down your weapon."

Kade heard Lana's pistol clatter to the ground and two of the constables hurried closer, sticking to he edges of the alley to avoid their companions' field of fire.

"Last resort, Kade," Lana said softly. Then, louder: "I'm an officer of the Wind Patrol. Code, Whisper Alongo. Registration KB1980."

"You are not."

"Just do your job," Lana replied wearily.

"I failed," Kade said to himself. In the last few days he'd failed as a bad guy and as a good guy. He'd come with in few metres of success on Minimbuk but in the end had not been good enough. He clung to the thought and it sank with him into the depths of unconsciousness.

High Peak:
Wind Patrol

I

Kade lay where he was for a long time and stared at the ceiling. It was painted with a soft light that rippled with the breeze. The bed was soft beneath him, the sheets crisp and clean.

Eventually he moved to look at more of the room. Shards of pain poked his back and chest and he gasped. He closed his eyes for a moment and concentrated on breathing before taking a more careful look around.

The light was coming through an open door that led out onto a small balcony. Filmy curtains danced in the opening. There was another door, opposite, but it was closed. Nearby, Lana was slumped on a chair, eyes closed, mouth slightly open. A book on her lap was just a twitch away from falling.

"Where are we?" Kade asked, his voice barely more than a croak.

Lana stirred, waking fully when the book clattered to the floor. "What?" She rubbed at her face and pushed hair away from her eyes. "You're awake."

"Where are we?"

"We're in the Wind Patrol headquarters in High Peak."

"Where?"

"You really should get some more sleep."

But he was already drifting away, watching the light on the ceiling, hand gently touching the bandages that swathed his body.

She was still there, or there again, slumped on the chair like a rag doll. She stirred without his prompting this time as if she could sense the shift in his breathing.

"How are you feeling?" She moved her chair to the side of the bed, scraping it across the polished stone floor.

"Good." Kade sat up slowly, leaning back against the bed head. "Surprisingly good." And he did. There was a general numbness to his back and chest, but it was a marked improvement on the pain of last time. "How long has it been?"

"Two days since we were in the alley. The doctors say you should recover completely."

Kade nodded slowly, remembering the scraps of their last conversation. "And these doctors work for the Wind Patrol?"

Lana winced. "Yes."

"And you're an undercover officer?"

She winced again. "Yes."

"Did Roke know?"

"No."

Kade nodded, closed his eyes for a moment. "So... Why? Why everything?"

Lana sighed and sat back in the chair. She rubbed at the butterfly on her temple. "When I first started following you I didn't know what was going on. I knew Roker had connections to the Skyway Men. I knew there were a whole lot of strange things going on. And I knew that you happened to turn up about the same time. I pointed all that out to my superiors. They couldn't spare anyone for what might just have been a co-incidence so they told me to see what I could find out."

"But why the whole charade of following Lemar? You had all those resources and..."

"There was no way anyone could have followed him quicker than we did. The stuff we did..." She smiled. "Nobody else would've done anything like that. And once we were moving I didn't really have a chance to contact anyone anyway."

"Not if you were going to keep your cover."

"That's right. I did talk to Farno on Beelamola. He went and had a look in the hold but couldn't find anything, apparently. I asked him to send a message when we reached the archipelago but couldn't really wait around to see the results. And seeing I've spent the whole time since my induction sitting behind a desk on Tribalin..."

"You've never been in the field?"

Lana shook her head. "I've done all the training, of course, but never actually used it. I kept track of records. Followed paper trails."

Kade was impressed. "It doesn't show. To jump in the deep end like that and still be on your feet now... I mean, I'm a professional and look at me."

"You used to be a professional, Kade. That was ten years ago. For a metal worker, you did pretty well."

Kade nodded. "Maybe." He stared at his hands. They were definitely the hands of a metal worker. "It didn't do us any good though, did it? We followed Lemar all this way but he could be anywhere by now. That weapon could be anywhere."

Lana nodded. "They've done some checking, but other than confirming that Merick Bolkin, Lemar Navid— whoever—entered High Peak, they don't know anything at all."

"So, we failed completely. I'm going to end up in jail for nothing."

"My superiors haven't given up and you shouldn't either."

"That's comforting."

They sat in silence until Lana suddenly rose to her feet. "I've got something for you," she said. "A present."

"Is it a pardon?"

She collected her pack from the floor by the door and pulled forth the small array with the bullet hole in the side.

"I took this down to the Patrol's crystal shop and got them to replace the broken parts."

"Why?"

She shrugged and turned to examine her fingers. "It's a present. A thank you present."

"Thanking me for what?"

"For getting me out of the office in Tribalin. For... I don't know. For everything."

Kade picked up the array and turned it over in his hands. "Why are your superiors letting you give me thank you present?"

She looked away for a moment. "The present isn't from them. There's a trainee in the workshop who did a favor for me."

"He probably thinks you owe him one back now."

She shrugged again. "It's not my fault if he somehow got that impression."

Kade smiled and shook his head. He ran his fingers across the surface of the box and poked his little finger into the bullet hole. "What does it do?"

"No idea. Well, I'd better let you get some more sleep. People will probably want to talk to you soon. They like reports around here and take every opportunity to make someone give one. I suppose that's better than having to write it all out."

"I suppose." Kade was exhausted, but didn't want her to leave. She paused in the doorway for a moment, as if she wanted to say something, but slipped silently out.

Kade flicked the switch on the cell and tried the button. He tried both actions in different combinations but nothing seemed to happen. He wasn't sure if he really wanted the array; it just seemed like a reminder of the array he *didn't* have.

II

The three men and two women looked very serious. Three of them wore dark military uniforms though it wasn't obvious if any of them had seen active service. An old man, half asleep, was in a crisp, expensive suit. The final man, short and muscular, was dressed casually.

"I am Commander Karis Haverik," the older of the two women said, straightening her uniform as if to be sure Kade had noticed it. "I am in charge of the High Peak unit of the Wind Patrol." She indicated the man at the end of the line. "That is Warker Wint, the overall head of the Patrol."

Kade nodded to them both. The other three were introduced as well.

"We will be asking you some questions today," Commander Haverik said. "Your full co-operation would be appreciated."

He nodded again.

"You currently use the name Kade Traskel? Is that correct?"

Kade looked from one person to the next and didn't say anything.

The Commander sighed and leafed through a few sheets of paper. "The last known activity undertaken by Arik Woolloon is more than ten years ago."

Kade gave a slight nod when she looked up.

"We are not here today to investigate any past crimes. As for more recent crimes..."

"Your co-operation now will certainly help you in that regard," Wint added in a rasping voice. He had slate grey hair and one drooping eyelid. Perhaps he looked half asleep all the time.

Danil Barro shifted slightly in his chair. The uniforms sat awkwardly on the others, but his casual clothing did nothing to hide his military background. "We are aware that situations can change," he said. "Sometimes everyone has to forget the past, or forget what they think they know, if they are going to reach the best outcome."

Kade looked Barro up and down. Short and solid with a spider's web of tattles on his head, the man had the stillness of a hawk in the moments before flight. "You work in the field?" Kade asked.

Barro nodded. "I'm Head of Operations."

Haverik cleared her throat, intent on drawing herself back into the centre of the conversation. "You thought the Skyway Men had recalled you?"

"That's right."

"But now you aren't so sure?"

"No. The Green Sea Raiders, or a group using that name to their advantage for this whole operation, were setting me up. I was supposed to get caught before I even made it to the laboratory, thereby pointing any investigation towards the Skyway Men."

"Right."

One of the other men leaned forward. Kade tried to remember his name. "You have no actual confirmation of these suspicions though?" Valal Corri. He was tall and thin and had a nose sharp enough to cut cheese. He had the look of a bureaucrat.

Commander Haverik gave him a glare and he settled back in his seat.

"No," Kade answered, "but there certainly seem to be two groups involved. Either that or nobody is talking to anyone else. And I can tell you how to find some of the people on Minimbuk."

Haverik checked her notes again. "Back at the start of all this you were sent to steal the Triba-light?"

Kade shrugged. "No. I was sent to a tavern with a general idea of the mission and the constables were informed I'd be there. It was just luck that I wasn't picked up."

"But *they* were after the 'light?"

"What they were after or what they now have, I couldn't tell you for sure."

"And you were following a man called Merik Bolkin?"

"There were two of them at the start. But yes, one of them was using the name Bolkin, though that isn't his real name. You could ask Lana all of this."

"We have. We just want to make sure."

The other woman, Lushel Sait, spoke for the first time. Apparently she hadn't noticed the look the Commander had given Corri a few moments earlier. "Do you have any idea where Bolkin might be now?"

Haverik gave her an exasperated look but turned to Kade for the answer.

"He entered High Peak the day Lana and I were caught. But I assume you already know that and have been looking for him."

"He hasn't been scanned since he came through customs," Haverik said. "There isn't a lot we can do."

"Well, I think that will be all for now," Warker Wint said, rising carefully to his feet. "If we have any further questions we will return."

"I'm sure you will."

"Thank you for your time, Kade."

"As if I had any choice."

Commander Haverik led the small procession from the room. A moment after the door closed it locked with a solid clunk. They knew who he had been. They knew what he had done recently... Kade looked at the locked door and tried to calm his breathing.

"Are you sure?"

"Of course I'm sure."

"Does it work?"

"I don't think so."

"All right. All right. Wait a moment..."

Kade hovered between waking and sleep, reveling for a moment in the silence as it settled into the half perceived room around him. When the voices started again, cold and distant, he half sat up and peered around the dim room.

"You'll have to go and get it."

There was nobody there. Even Lana had vacated her chair. Still half asleep, he tried to locate the origin of the voices.

"What? It—"

"Even if it doesn't work now, they might be able to fix it. You'll have to get rid of him as well. He could know anything."

Suddenly fully awake, Kade looked at the wooden box on the table beside the bed.

"He doesn't know anything."

"That's what he told you? Well, that's all right then."

They were talking about him, whoever they were. Kade was sure of it.

"I can't just... I'm not a killer. Since when have—"

"Look, this comes from Reven."

"What does Lemar say?"

"Just get it done. Delegate if you like, I don't care. If you can get the girl while you're at it... Hold on again..."

There was another pause.

"You can also let Valal and Amiska know that they're coming home. They're to meet us at the Trough at midnight."

"And me?"

"Soon, Karis. Everyone will be coming home soon enough."

Kade stared at the box for a long time after it fell silent, waiting to see if anything else would happen. In the end, he decided the details didn't matter all that much. All he needed to worry about was that someone was going to try to kill him. He assumed it was a person anyway. Karis Haverick? The head of the High Peak Wind Patrol? That seemed unlikely but no more unlikely than anything else he could come up with.

He didn't know what time it was. Night, that much was obvious. There seemed to be a bit of noise drifting in through the window so perhaps it wasn't *too* late. Or perhaps his room looked out over an all-night market. He didn't know much at all, apparently.

Kade had swung his bare legs off the bed and was vaguely looking around for some clothes when the lock on the door clicked and the door started to swing open.

"Thorn." He got to his feet, looking for a weapon. The only thing available was the chair by the door or the wooden cell by the bed. By then it was already too late.

III

He was standing by the bed—wearing nothing more than underwear and bandages—and looking lost, when Lana uncovered a muffled lamp and let the door swing shut behind. "Are you all right?"

Kade breathed a sigh and slumped back down. "What time is it?" He rubbed at his scalp.

"About Fourteen Bells. Why?"

"Someone's coming here."

"Right."

"To kill me. And you too, if possible."

Lana looked dubious. "How do you know this? The guard told me nobody had entered the room since I left for dinner a couple of hours ago."

"The box. It talks."

Lana raised her eyebrows.

"It's... I don't know. Maybe if two people have the things they can talk to each other or something."

"That's ridiculous."

"So's a light that can kill a man from hundreds of metres away."

"Yes, but... This is crazy. You really think—"

A muffled thud from the hallway stopped her mid sentence.

"What was that?"

Kade was already silently signaling her into the corner that, in a moment, would be behind the door. She snapped her mouth shut and did as she was told. He laid back down.

It was almost a minute before anything else happened. Then the door swung silently open. In walked tall, gangly Valal Corri.

Kade lay still in bed, watching through half open eyes. He almost laughed. Corri looked even more like an office clerk than he had earlier in the day. But Kade was stuck in the bed— why had he laid back down?— and the man carried a dagger along his wrist. There was also the bulge of a pistol at his waistband. It was no laughing matter.

Corri started to creep forward.

"I'd go for the gun if I was you," Kade said softly. "Using that knife will require a bit more courage than you possess."

"You're awake?"

"Yes. And I intend to stay that way for a while yet."

"I know you don't have any weapons. And even if you have recovered completely I don't imagine you getting to me before I can kill you."

"You're probably right."

At that moment, Lana grabbed the man around the neck with one arm, his knife hand with the other.

"Lana you should have..." But it was too late.

Corri fought back instinctively. Twisting and squirming violently, he broke free.

"Give it up," Lana said. Kade could see the fear in her eyes. His own heart was racing. His hands were slick with sweat. He wanted to get up and help, but didn't think he'd make it in time. He pushed away the sheet and blanket anyway.

Corri lunged forward with the knife and Lana swayed aside, letting the attack slide by. She counter-punched. Once in the ribs, once jamming a fistful of knuckles into the sensitive spot where the shoulder joined the arm. The dagger tumbled to the floor, clattering on the smooth stone.

Lana froze for a moment as Corri tried to pull the pistol free of his pants. It stuck, catching on the gathered material.

Kade took two steps towards the end of the bed. Lana dived towards the knife. She came to her knees with it in her hand. But Corri finally had his pistol out and was bringing it to bear. He was smiling though fear filled his eyes.

Kade froze. He wouldn't make it. Lana wouldn't make it.

The moment slowed. Stretched. Expanded. Stopped.

Kade breathed.

Lana launched herself forward as Corri pulled the trigger.

Kade shouted wordlessly.

Nothing happened. Corri pulled the trigger again but the pistol was only half cocked. He looked surprised when Lana plunged the dagger into his chest. She stepped away.

The pistol dropped from Corri's hand and he stared at the hilt of the dagger. He tried to say something but only managed to gurgle as he fell backwards. He was dead a moment later.

Lana stared at the dagger and the spreading bloodstain.

"You knew it was half-cocked, right?" Kade asked.

"Of course. Do you think I'm crazy?" She had a wild look in her eyes that suggested she might well be.

"You'll never be afraid to shoot someone again, will you? It's much easier than stabbing them."

She shook her head, still staring. "I think I must be the only person who's known you more than a few hours and didn't end up dead." She spent a few seconds just breathing and seemed to enjoy the experience.

"You've been cut," Kade said, pointing to a patch of blood growing on her own sleeve.

"What?" Lana pulled at the damaged material of her blouse to look beneath. "Ouch." She quickly sat down.

"And the day isn't over yet."

"What?"

"This guy was supposed to meet someone at 'the trough'. They were leaving at midnight, apparently."

"What? Who was leaving? Where were they going?" Lana shook her head. "And how do you know?"

"I told you. The box talks."

"Right." She looked around. "We have to tell somebody."

"We can't."

"Why not?"

"Because Commander Haverik is involved." *Maybe.*

"No, she isn't. She's—"

"Don't tell me. Tell the box." Kade looked at the cell by his bed.

Lana sighed. "So, what do we do then?"

"We get out of here before someone comes in and finds us with a body."

"But he came here."

"If the boss is involved, who knows who else is?" Kade started going through the chest of drawers by the bed. He found his clothes and pulled them on. "What's over the balcony?"

Gathering herself, Lana went to check, flinging the curtains aside and opening the door violently. "I'll make it. Not sure about you."

"What are you suggesting?"

"I'm suggesting you're injured."

"I've been worse."

"Yes. Yesterday."

"Those doctors did a good job." And it was true. He felt better than he'd felt since... Since he'd been shot. Grabbing the array, he went out onto the balcony with her. "Thorn." It was going to hurt.

Below was nothing but rough, jagged cliff and grey cloud. To the right, the cliff the Wind Patrol stronghold occupied ended about twenty metres away. The other direction, the bulk of High Peak loomed out of the darkness. Fifty metres away the clean white stone of the Wind Patrol balconies were replaced by flimsy wooden affairs or simple shuttered windows.

"Can we just go through the halls?" Lana asked, watching his face.

"You tell me."

She thought for a moment, then shook her head. "Possibly but... We have to go up four levels, past a few dozen offices and some sleeping quarters. Then past the guards on the main door."

"Come on then. Where's your pack?"

She went inside and returned a moment later. While Kade was placing the array inside he had another thought. "The pistol."

Lana sighed and, flinging the curtain aside, went inside once more. When she came back she gave two pistols and some ammunition bags to Kade. She had another pistol in her belt and was tucking the dagger, still smeared with blood, into her boot.

"The guard had some weapons too," she explained. Then she took the pack back and gestured over the rail. "You first?"

"I guess so."

Wincing, Kade tucked the pistols into his belt then flexed his shoulders and swung his leg over the rail. He examined the stone wall for his next foot hold and started to move slowly out onto the cliff. He tried to calm his racing heart and didn't look down; he wasn't afraid of heights but there was a point where 'height' became something else entirely.

IV

It seemed to take forever. His back and shoulder ached from his wounds. His fingers ached from gripping the cold stone. His toes ached from being jammed into his boots. He kept his eyes on the stone and his mind on the careful placement of each hand and foot.

Five minutes after he started out, Kade stopped to rest on a ledge about as wide as his hand. The wind gusted and shifted, one moment trying to tear him free of the wall and throw him down into the clouds, the next pushing him against the stone.

"Are you all right?"

Kade opened his eyes. Lana was right next to him, so close their shoulders were almost touching, but she had to shout to be heard over the wind. There was fear in her eyes, and she was making an obvious effort to not look down, but what Kade saw most clearly was concern.

He nodded slightly. "I'm fine. Just a bit sore and sorry."

"Good. Keep going. Let's get off this cliff."

"What's the matter with it?" Kade asked, trying to smile. "I get you this lovely cliff for a present and you don't appreciate it at all."

"Yes, you're right. Some men give their wives rings. I get a cliff. I should be grateful."

"Well, you must admit, the stone is pretty impressive."

She smiled and shook her head. "That's terrible. Come on, let's get going." She gave him a nudge.

He felt better, like he was ready to go again. Working his shoulder gently, Kade drew in a deep breath and looked at

224

how far they still had to go. The wind plucked at him again, tugging his clothes, humming across the face of the cliff. He stretched his foot out to a protruding rock, found a new hand hold, and shifted his weight.

It was another five minutes before Kade made it to the first window. The shutters were latched but still came open easily enough when he tugged; it was not a route that most thieves would be willing to take. The wind slammed it back against the stone. The sound seemed like an explosion to Kade but it was probably hardly audible just a few metres away.

He clung to the stone as he examined the window sill. Another sound drifted to him on the wind. He would have ignored it but Lana touched his arm.

"What?"

She pointed back the way they'd come. Kade swore. Someone was on the balcony, looking at the rail and the cliff as if trying to convince himself it really was possible to climb. In the end the man turned to look at Kade and Lana before racing back inside.

Kade swore again and turned to the open window. He clambered headfirst over the sill, slithered down over a bench and onto a cool tile floor. Lana came through in a much more nimble fashion and crouched by his side.

"Are you all right?" she whispered.

"No."

"What's wrong?"

Kade sighed and sat up. "Besides the usual? Nothing really." His hands were numb with the cold. His shoulder ached. But it was nothing half an hour in front of a warm fire wouldn't fix.

"Oh, right. Hurry up then. We don't have very long."

Kade nodded and clambered to his feet. He had a quick look around but couldn't see much in the near-complete darkness. The murky grey light coming through the window revealed a kitchen bench, strip of brown tiles and a brown wall.

Lana took his hand and led him across the room, away from the light. "The exit should be this way."

They found a solid wooden door, slipped the bolt and went out into a wide, well-lit public hall. Nobody else was there. Kade only realized he'd been holding his breath when he leaned against the wall and filled his lungs.

He'd only been at it for a second when the sound of footsteps roused him. "Thorn."

Lana didn't wait to reply. She ran and Kade followed as she led a winding course through the passages. Down stairs, along cold, quiet passages. He didn't know if she was trying to confuse their pursuers or if she was simply lost. He suspected the latter, seeing she'd been in High Peak for only a few days. He almost made a joke but managed to remain silent. Eventually they found a door that led out into the night.

The city of High Peak, one of the largest in the world—land-locked or flying—was spread out below them. It filled a bowl shaped valley with high, jagged hills all around. To the right, High Peak Mountain seemed to block out half the sky. Snow on its upper slopes reflected the lights from the city in an eerie glow. There was almost no wind at all. It seemed positively warm.

"I think we've lost them for now," Kade said, leaning against the wall again. He decided he felt better than he had in a long time. The Wind Patrol doctors had done a good job and the run had loosened tired, cramped muscles.

"We'd better not just hang around here near the door though," Lana pointed out. "Let's go find this trough of yours."

Too late. A man and a woman burst through the door. They paused to look around and were obviously surprised to find their prey right there.

Kade pushed away from the wall, kicked at the woman, missed as she stumbled back. She recovered quickly and advanced. Kade blocked a kick, punched, then spun and slammed his elbow into her stomach. She went down, gasping for breath, and he finished her off.

"We didn't kill the guard," Lana said.

Her opponent didn't seem inclined to listen. As he turned, Kade saw the man dart forward to attack. Lana turned the blow aside. Countered. Then danced away. She was reluctant to engage with any real conviction.

"Valal Corri came to kill us. We were defending ourselves."

The man attacked again and Lana danced away. Kade sighed. The way the two of them were going, they'd be there all night. So he walked in behind the man and hit him on the back of the neck.

"You didn't kill him, did you?" Lana said, checking both Wind Patrol agents to make sure they were breathing. "Come on then. Let's find this trough and finish this."

"So how are we supposed to find it? At this time of night?" Kade felt like pointing out all the faults in her plan. Seeing she was only here because of him and it was really his plan anyway, he held his tongue and collected a pistol, shot and powder off each of the Wind Patrollers. He gave them to Lana to put in the pack, made sure the ones he already had were still secure in the band of his breeches, then headed towards a low murmur of sound that indicated the presence of people.

High Peak:
Green Sea Raiders

I

Despite the hour, the entertainment district they found a few minutes later was bubbling with activity. Cafes spilled out onto the streets, rumbles of sound emerged from taverns. Couples and groups chatted and laughed and sipped their drinks. Or they wandered to and fro between the still-open shops, or drove by in their cruisers at a leisurely pace. Every time someone looked their way Kade's heart raced as he decided if he would fight or run. And, every time, the strangers went about their business so Kade could breathe again.

"At least we don't look completely out of place here," Kade noted.

A man in baggy purple pantaloons went by but there did not seem to be any dominant fashion. Regular breeches and blouses were as common as Jasparac's flamboyant robes and Minimbuk's stern suits or a dozen other styles.

Kade tried to catch his breath. "What do we do now?"

Lana shrugged, then stepped up to the next person who walked by. "Hi. How are you?"

The woman looked at her suspiciously.

"We're looking for a 'trough'? Do you know where we might find one of those?"

The woman shook her head and continued on her way.

"That's your plan?" Kade asked.

"There can't be too many troughs around here," Lana explained. "It's not as if there are animals roaming the streets everywhere."

"Right. Of course you're right." Kade motioned her back to the street. "There's only one trough in the entire city and the next person who walks past is sure to know where it is."

He sat down in the deep gutter and looked around.

Unlike the people, the city was as one. The uniformity of Minimbuk was crass and ugly but this was a thing of beauty as the grey stone buildings seemed to have grown from the very mountain. Most were two storeys and flowed one into the other, along curving streets, up and down gentle slopes towards the steeper walls of the valley. The lower floors were larger than those above, leaving room on top for balconies. Gardens flowed over the rails and down towards the streets, softening sharp edges and adding splashes of color. The roofs were sharply peaked as if, in other seasons, heavy snow was a common occurrence. For now, all was grey and dry.

"Excuse me," Lana snagged a large man with tattals all the way up his arm. "We're looking for a 'trough'. Do you know where that—"

The man laughed. "There's only one trough around here, love. That's *The Drinking Trough*." He pointed the way he was heading. "Follow this street until you come to Falling Way. Turn left. That will take you up over the hills and all the way down to the Weir. *The Drinking Trough* is about three buildings back from the park." He nodded amiably and carried on.

Kade sighed as Lana turned to look at him. He tried to head her off. "Yes. All right. You were right, I was wrong. I admit it. Well done. Now can we go and put and end to this?"

But it didn't help. "*The Drinking Trough*," she said. "A tavern, I imagine." She smiled. "We follow this street here, make one turn, follow that street and there we are. *The Drinking Trough*."

Kade was about to add to the banter but spotted a pair of men moving slowly down the street. They were still fifty metres away but there was no mistaking the fact that they weren't just out for a night on the town. He turned casually away from them, took Lana's hand and started walking. Lana knew better than to look around. She linked her arm through his as though they were any couple out for a stroll.

A few of blocks further on they turned away from the street they were on to circle around a group of four men who stood too straight and watched the passers by a little too intently. For a while, Kade thought they were being followed but the woman went into a shop and didn't come back out.

By the time they made it to Falling Way, a wide boulevard with a line of stone artworks down the middle, Kade's nerves were on edge.

If anything it was even busier here, which was a double edged sword; they were harder to spot, but so were those trying to find them. Lana paused to look around. Kade surveyed their surroundings as well but took her arm to keep her moving. "There will be time for sight seeing if we get out of this alive. Come on."

They hurried along until Kade saw a cab. "Do you have any doms?" He was hailing before Lana had finished nodding. "How much to get us to the end of Falling Way?" he asked, reluctant to give out their actual destination.

The driver shrugged. "About ten doms."

Lana was checking her purse. She nodded and they climbed onto the front facing seats on the back of the cab.

From where they were, the street climbed quickly, and the houses grew larger as the views improved. Then finally they topped the edge of the valley and could see down the side of the mountain. The driver kept talking as if nothing had changed but all Kade could do was stare.

Below, the city continued for more than a kilometre, clinging to the side of the mountain like chocolate sauce on a scoop of ice-cream. It ended at what appeared to be a haphazard wall of piled stone. It was hard to tell from the distance, but Kade thought the Weir had to be at least thirty metres high and the same wide. A road ran along the top, hidden behind a smaller wall, and a small contingent of men walked a slow patrol.

Kade had heard of the Weir, everyone had, but to see it was something else.

"What sort of creatures must be down there for us to need a wall like this?" Lana muttered.

The Weir had been there for as long as anyone could remember. History books spoke of men guarding the ramparts for twenty thousand years. The wall kept away the Wilders, which had forced men into the skies in the first place, though they had long since forgotten what the creatures were actually like.

Ten minutes later the driver pulled over where a pedestrian mall started a hundred metres from the Weir. Just a little bit further down was a tavern with a sign above the door showing a few pigs clustered around a trough. Light and noise spilled out onto the street. A dozen people sat at small tables on a wide, low porch, looking as if they'd been there a while and intended to be there the rest of the night.

Kade had a look around while Lana paid. The building seemed to butt up against a warehouse at the back. Probably no exit there. Deli on one side, haberdashery on the other. Just the two doors at the front then.

"Are we going in?" Lana asked.

"No." Kade sat down on a fixed chair outside a closed café. Further up the hill was relatively quiet but the mall was still busy. Trees, statues and decorative artworks were visible amidst little knots of people. Trickles of people wandered between. "If we go in there and they see us then all our options disappear."

"But if they don't see us..."

"They could be sitting in the tap room, watching the door to see when their friends arrive." He continued to shift and move his shoulder. Out of the freezing cold and resting, it was starting to feel better. "Lemar will recognize either of us in an instant."

"But nobody else would."

Kade sighed. It was still more than half an hour till midnight, so he tried to make himself comfortable.

"How can you just wait so calmly?"

"You get used to it. It's nice sometimes just to be." He gave a rueful laugh. "I've spent most of the last ten years waiting, one way or the other."

Lana moved to stand behind him and pushed his hand away from his shoulder. Her long, strong fingers started to work at the muscles and Kade groaned with pleasure. Five times, Lana paused in her ministrations and Kade almost jumped to his feet as one of the doors of the tavern swung open. Five times, they were disappointed when one group or another of varying inebriation stumbled out onto the wide porch before parting ways down on the street.

II

The tide of noise surged as the door opened again and this time Kade immediately knew something was different. The first men to emerge were quiet and sober. They carried packs, slung over their shoulders or hanging negligently in their hands. Five of them first, stepping out amongst the relative quiet of the porch, looking around, walking the rest of the way down to the worn cobbles of the mall. Then came another two, glancing around. One was Lemar Nevid, cool and confident. He looked good. He looked much happier than he had ten years ago. But that probably wouldn't be hard. He and the other man carried a long black box that might have been used to hide the body of a small child.

"There he is," whispered Lana.

Kade glanced her way. "They've put the cluster together."

"Do you think? Why would they do that?"

He shrugged. "To make sure it works. To make sure they don't have to go back and get something else." He stood up. "Or maybe they think they might need it in the next little while."

"What do we do now?"

That was a good question.

"Let's just follow and see what comes up. There are too many of them."

"Right."

A final three men exited the tavern and Lemar gave a quiet order. The group headed down the hill. No matter how casually they dressed, no matter how slowly they tried to move, it was obvious that this was a group of men with a purpose.

Kade and Lana made their way down the mall behind them, making their way closer to the looming bulk of the Weir. From this close it seemed even larger than the mountain blocking the sky to the west. They moved slowly, arms linked, a couple out for a late night stroll. They kept their heads down and close together and stuck close to the buildings where awnings occasionally threw shadows to hide them, if only for a moment.

"Where are they going, do you think?" Lana asked.

"How would I know? I know less about this place than you do."

"Right. Well, I don't know that there's anything significant down here. They certainly can't actually *go* anywhere."

"Well, they seem to disagree."

Less than fifty metres later the mall ended at a narrow park that tickled the toes of the Weir. Their quarry turned right and continued along a cross-street. Their pace was steadily increasing.

"What now?" whispered Lana, her breath warm on Kade's ear. "They'll get suspicious if we stick behind them."

"Probably not. There are only two choices at the corner." Kade paused as a voice from nearby surprised him.

"*Lemar, can you hear me?*" A pause. "*Lemar?*"

He recognized the hollow, scratched sound of the voice. "That's it," he said. "That's the array."

"What?"

Starting to walk again, Kade took off his pack and pulled the small array from inside.

"I don't hear anything."

"Wait. Listen."

Around the corner, Kade swore and paused to examine the street. The park crouched on the left hand side and buildings lined the other. There were lights in windows, but no sign of life was visible.

The voice came again, making Lana jump.

"Lemar, are you there?"

"I'm a bit busy, Karis. What do you want?"

"I told you," Kade whispered. Lana was staring.

"It's Traskel. He's gotten away. Grindella has gone with him."

"We're married," Kade said. "Technically you're Traskel as well."

Lana looked at him and shook her head.

"Thorn, does he ever quit?"

"Not today." Kade started slowly down the street again, praying he saw the Raiders before they saw him.

"They killed Valal, Lemar."

"What? When?"

"Not long ago."

"Why would they even bother?"

"I sent Valal to..."

"You sent Valal to what? To kill them? He isn't—"

"It wasn't my idea. Reven gave the order."

"To send Valal?"

"Well, no."

"Damn it, Karis. Are you going to tell Marsi?" Lemar sighed. *"Well, there's nothing we can do now. And unless he's just down the street there isn't much he can do either. We're in the warehouse and just about ready to go."*

"A warehouse," Kade said

"Good. I've got people out everywhere but sent Danil Barro down your direction, just in case."

"Well, that's all we can do then. Now let me get on with this."

"Of course. Good luck. Hopefully I'll hear from someone soon, Lemar. I want to go home."

Kade checked their surroundings.

Lana pointed before he had a chance. "There."

A short distance down the street a two metre high stone wall protected a large, two storey building.

Kade gave a quick nod and hurried onward.

"What do you think they're doing?" Lana asked.

"I have no idea." He wasn't sure if he really wanted to know.

There was a vacant block beside the warehouse. Wading through thigh high grass, stumbling in the darkness, Kade made his way away from the street. A scatter of heavy stone blocks littered the wide, overgrown area as if a demolished building was being stolen one brick at a time.

At the rear of the block was another wall and Kade followed it to the one surrounding the warehouse. He looked at the top, wondered how much luck he had left, and scrambled up in the corner to have a look. There were bright lights and packing crates, but that was all he could really see inside the building. It was surrounded by a couple of metres of overgrown yard. Small mountains of scrap and rubbish thrust up from the grass.

With a sigh, Kade glanced down at Lana, pulled himself up and dropped down the other side. While she struggled to follow, he went to the nearest window for a closer look.

There were quite a few people inside. Some were working on something in the middle of the room. Others were standing around talking. None of them looked like storemen.

Kade turned as Lana dropped down to the ground and crept across to his position.

"At least a dozen people inside," he told her. "Probably more. Can't tell much more from here. Any suggestions?"

"Go and get help?"

Kade shook his head. "Even if we had time to find help, I doubt we'd have time to *convince* them as well."

"Well..."

Kade looked at the building. "If we get up to those walkways on the first floor we'd be in a pretty good position."

"To attack? You said there are at least a dozen of them." She shook her head. "Do you have a plan B?"

"I thought that *was* plan B," Kade said. "Plan A involved getting help."

"Right." Lana groped for inspiration. Unsuccessfully. She sighed. "All right. Come on then. This is crazy, you know?"

Kade smiled. "Don't complain; you knew that before you married me." Kade's heart was racing. He looked at Lana, but she was concentrating, her face set. Her fear didn't show on her face.

Not far away, a drainpipe led straight up the wall, passing not far from a window on the first floor.

Kade didn't pause. He knew if he did, it would be all over because Lana was right. But if he gave up now he'd have the Wind Patrol, Skyway Men and the Green Sea Raiders—or whoever the hell they were—all after him. If he reclaimed the array it would at least get one of them off his back. Hopefully. He gripped the pipe and went up the wall. At the window he opened the shutters and slipped in over the sill. He pulled his two pistols from his belt as soon as his feet hit the floor and examined the situation while he waited for Lana. She came slowly then paused for a moment before lurching from pipe to window and scrambling inside.

III

"I see three men with muskets on this level at the front windows," Kade whispered. Obviously they were expecting trouble. "Three loaders with them. And at least 15 people on the ground floor. Two by the door, another four behind those packing crates, three in the back corner behind a low wall and the main group. Could be more."

Lana shook her head. "We can't do it."

"Of course we can." He took the pack from her and pulled out all the weapons. He took the two from his belt. They were all loaded. "Two for you," he told Lana. "We take out the ones on this level first. Then we see what happens."

"As always." Lana checked the weapons and took a deep breath. "Just once I'd like you to lay out a plan step by step, from start to finish." Her hands were shaking.

"You weren't scared in the alley," Kade said.

"I didn't have time to think there."

"Wait a second and you won't have time to think here either." Kade smiled. "Ready?"

Lana licked her lips and nodded. They slowly crept forward, shifting from thick bands of shadow thrown by columns into long dust-filled stretches of light. They paused about fifteen metres away from their targets.

Trying to breathe calmly, Kade lined up one pistol on the floor near his feet and readied two others. Bags of shot and powder were nearby. "I've got the two outside shooters," he said. A nervous nod from Lana as he aimed. "Let's do this."

They fired, one shot each. Before he had even noted the results, Kade had snatched the pistol from the floor and fired at his second target. All three shooters were down. Lana fired her second pistol. She missed, swore softly and quickly started to reload.

It was a few moments before any of the Raiders knew exactly what was happening. Two of the loaders took up the weapons dropped by their shooters and turned to meet the attack.

Kade swapped the unfired pistol from left to right hand and fired again. Then he ducked his head and was reloading all three weapons as quickly as possible.

Lana fired two shots in quick succession and there were no Raiders left on the top level. Down below, men and women had taken cover. Snatching up his gear, Kade did the same thing. He pressed his back against the cold stone of a column as he finished loading. There were still a lot of Green Sea Raiders down there. Too many.

Kade tried to calm his breathing, amazed his hands weren't shaking. Shot whizzed past, smacking into the stone nearby. He fired two shots over the rail, wounding one man and killing another, then scuttled back to reload.

"We're outnumbered," he said.

"It's a bit late to worry about that now," Lana replied breathlessly. She jumped out from the other side of the column and fired a pistol with her left hand.

When Kade fired again, he could see that the men and women below had been moving crates to clear a large space on the floor.

"What the hell are they up to?" A slug pinged of the rail near his head. "Thorn."

He loaded again, then stood up, aimed at a group of five people and fired with both pistols. It was impossible to miss. He ducked back out of sight as the retaliation came.

"Give it up," someone shouted when the clatter had died down again. It was Lemar.

"I give up now and I'll be lucky to live through the week." Kade was reloading. He decided to keep one pistol in reserve, just in case. "Half the world wants me dead."

Lemar laughed. "Arrogant as ever, aren't you Arik. Or Kade. Whatever it is you call yourself these days."

"That's right, Lemar, ten years working as a blacksmith and I haven't changed a bit. You still know everything there is to know about me."

There was a moment of silence. "So, you know who I am?"

"Of course. Even with that hair cut."

Kade noticed Lana staring at him. "You know him?" she asked.

He nodded. "Lemar was a friend, as much as is possible in the Skyway Men anyway, but he abandoned me. Left me hung out to dry."

Across the other side of the warehouse, Lemar laughed. "Abandoned you? You really have no idea, do you?"

Kade ignored him. "It was my last job," he said. "The straw that broke the camel's back in terms of my career with the Skyway Men." He leaned back against the column and closed his eyes. "We were trying to steal the plans for making skyglasses. There are all sorts of fortunes to be made if anyone can get them. Lemar was leading one of the squads. He was supposed to be a decoy at a second building, allowing the other two squads to get into the main offices." He shook his head. "All he had to do was distract the security guards for ten minutes." He looked over his shoulder and shouted into the room, though apparently Lemar could hear the conversation anyway. "Ten minutes. Was that really so hard?"

Lana started to ask a question, but Lemar shouted over the top of her. "We barely even got inside, Kade. Security wasn't the problem, though: there were constables everywhere."

"Constables?"

"I was shot. I wasn't even conscious when the squad got me out of there."

"Grinner said the clean up squad saw you running away before the action even started. He told me they killed you all."

"Another couple of minutes and we would have been dead, but it was the constables." Lemar grunted. "But we wouldn't have been in that situation if you'd come up with a half decent plan. Fall back options. Plan B. Was *that* really so hard?"

Kade couldn't help but laugh. "I was twenty years old and just survived two massive screw-ups. Do you really think the council let me plan anything? When everything fell apart they blamed me, obviously, but I turned in five plans and all of them were rejected. In then end I just gave in and asked Grinner what to do."

"It was Grinner's plan?"

"Of course. I'm surprised you couldn't see his fingerprints all over it. If you'd hung around maybe you would've."

Kade stuck his head out to have another look. There was a small group of people hidden behind a crate. Others were still working to clear the floor, shoving and pushing crates without much luck.

One of the hidden men rose to his feet and fired, almost without aiming. A splinter of stone sliced Kade's face before he could duck back behind the wall.

"Like I said, if I'd hung around I'd be dead."

"And now you've come back for your revenge?"

"You arrogant bastard. It isn't about you. You were just a convenient idiot. I got out and found a whole new life, a new world, and you're going to mess that up as well."

"We thought you abandoned us." Kade shook his head. "We would have gone back for you if we'd known. We would have tried to help."

"You can help us now. Let us go."

"So, suddenly, *I'm* in charge here?"

"You've killed my friends, Kade. I've know Valal, Togan Reef and Vernor Plist, for years but I'm willing to—"

"They were going to kill me."

"Valal was, I admit. That was a mistake, but I didn't order it. And Vernor wasn't going to do anything. He was going to get you off my back, get some information then dump you somewhere out of the way."

"Yeah—"

"Alive."

"Of course he was."

"You've killed friends of mine in the last few minutes, Kade. I just don't want any one else to die when we're so close to our goal. Give us ten minutes and we'll leave this place and you'll never see us again."

"And I believe you. It's happened before."

"What are they doing?" Lana asked quietly.

Kade looked over the rail. The men and women were still trying to move the crates. "Lemar's stalling for time," he said. "That's all I know for sure." Kade jumped up to slow the work down but a flurry of gunshots forced him back behind cover.

"Thorn."

Before he could work out what to do next the front door of the warehouse exploded inwards, killing two Raiders and knocking another off her feet. All the windows shattered. Smoke drifted upwards in slow, lazy clouds.

"Now what?" Lana asked. Her eyes were wide.

A shout from below answered the question for her. "This is the Wind Patrol. Everyone throw down you weapons."

Kade recognized the voice of Danil Barro. "Good luck with that, Sergeant," Kade called in reply, shaking his head to clear the ringing in his ears.

There was a lull as the Wind Patrol men and women, about half a dozen of them, found cover and the Raiders took stock.

"You won't get away with this Traskel."

"It's not me you should be worried about."

"I'll decide that after you are safely locked away."

"Or dead," someone added. "You killed Valal, you bastard."

Kade tried to keep track of what was happening down below. The Sergeant and the other Wind Patrol agents were spreading out more, moving away from the door. There were a lot of people down below but it wasn't easy to work out who was on which side. The main problem was that only Lana was on *his* side. He glanced back at her and tried a smile.

"Let's think about that," he called to those below. "Why would we kill Valal Corri and the guard if we were just going to escape out the window anyway?"

There was a moment of hesitation before Barro replied. "Henas wasn't dead. Just Valal. But what's your point?"

"Don't listen to him Sergeant," someone shouted.

"Why was Corri even there at that time of night, Sergeant? What did Corri do for the Wind Patrol? Would he have been sent to my room without an armed escort?" Someone fired and Kade ducked instinctively. The shot didn't come close.

"Commander Haverik doesn't tell me everything."

"Obviously not. Why don't you get Lemar to tell you what Haverik wants?"

"What?"

"Lemar's a bit quiet at the moment but he was about to tell Lana and I what he and Commander Haverik are up to."

Kade thought he could hear Barro sigh from across the warehouse. "Thorn," the Sergeant shouted. "Everyone just throw down you weapons and come out in the middle of the room."

Kade looked at the middle of the room, at the patch of clear floor Lemar and his followers had been creating. There was a large square cut into the wide rough boards of the floor. "Is that a trap door, Lemar?" He darted to the cover of the next column to get a better look. "This wasn't you final destination, was it? There's a passage or something?"

"We just want to go home," Lemar replied.

"What in Thorn's name is going on?" Barro shouted. His frustration was obvious.

Kade watched as Lemar stood up, empty hands above his head, and walked to the middle of the room as Barro had asked.

"That was unexpected," Lana muttered.

"I just want to go home, Sergeant. Ten years ago I led some friends beyond the Weir. We have battled the Wilders ever since, trying to protect the little bit that we have. It's my home, our home, and unless we take this weapon back with us, it will all be lost."

"You expect me to believe that?" Barro replied. He stepped out into the open as well. He was armed. "You expect me to let you take the array even if I do believe you?"

"I can only hope."

"Everyone, throw down your weapons and come out."

Kade doubted that was going to happen in a hurry but never had a chance to find out for sure.

There was another explosion, this time at a side door. More smoke. More ringing in the ears.

Men came through the doors and through the broken windows. In the next few seconds a wave of gunshots passed around the room. People screamed.

Then silence, apart from the moaning of the injured.

Kade looked at Lana. "Now *that*," he said, "was unexpected."

IV

Kade looked around the column. Lemar and Sergeant Barro had both disappeared. Sensibly. Kade could see quite a few new comers taking up position but he couldn't see enough to work out what was going on. It was getting very crowded.

With a glance at Lana, Kade headed towards the back of the warehouse. Once in the shadows at the corner he crawled towards the edge of the walkway to look.

At least a dozen men and women, all wearing masks. All heavily armed.

Watching the complicated hand gestures the newcomers used to communicate, Kade had no doubt who they were. The Skyway Men.

For a moment he wondered if handing over the weapon would get him back into their ranks. A week ago he wouldn't have hesitated. Now, he looked at Lana, crouching with her back to a stone column, face covered in soot and dust, butterfly tattal gleaming in a stray glimmer of light.

She was scared. He could see it in her eyes and the way she held her two pistols. But her hands weren't shaking. She was here with him because keeping the array out of the hands of criminals was the right thing to do. Kade had never really done anything just because it was the right thing to do.

And the Green Sea Raiders?

Apparently Lemar had found a new life and now he just wanted to go home. Kade knew how he felt. He had mentioned to Lana that the Raiders didn't seem very ruthless. And if Grinner had lied about Lemar being killed, what other lies had he told about the failed operation all those years ago. Kade suddenly wondered why he would even trust the Skyway Men boss to tell him what day it was.

Kade swore to himself then called out to Sergeant Barro. "Situations change, Sergeant," he said repeating the man's line back to him.

"What?"

"Say hello to the Skyway Men."

By now they had taken up their positions but, like every one else, they seemed to be waiting for someone else to start the games.

"How did they get here?"

There weren't that many options. Either they followed Kade or followed the sound of an interesting gunfight. Or maybe they had people inside the Wind Patrol as well. Or maybe all of the above. He was pretty sure Barro didn't care one way or the other at the moment anyway.

"The Skyway Men will kill everyone and ask questions later, Sergeant. Lemar is at least willing to talk. Think about it."

"Well, tonight has gone to hell."

Kade paused to take stock. Three guns, all loaded, and powder for maybe two more shots. And that was it. Not even a dagger. While he crouched in the shadows trying to think, someone decided they'd had enough.

A single shot fired, shattering the quiet. A moment of stillness. Then an eruption of sound. Gunshots, shouting, screaming.

Kade hung back for a moment, heart racing, then stood up and fired. One shot took out a masked woman near the side door. The other thudded into the side of a crate. He ducked back down and started to load. No more powder. The two pistols in his hands plus the back up in his belt.

Stand up again. Aim and fire in one smooth, easy motion. And back down again as a musket on the far side of the room was brought to bear. Kade discarded the empty pistol, pulled the spare one free. He fired the last two shots and didn't know if they'd hit home.

Looking at the useless pistols he wondered if Lana had any more powder. He turned to ask, but the spot she had occupied not long before was empty. Kade searched for her on the walkway then down amidst the crates and shadows and drifting smoke of the main floor. He couldn't see her.

But near he back of the warehouse, behind the low wall in the corner, Kade saw Lemar. He and two other Raiders had discharged their weapons and were frantically reloading as half a dozen Skyway Men moved towards them.

Kade examined the pistols in his hand for a moment and swore, "Thorn." Then stood up and threw them at the advancing Skyway Men. One of the men was hit. All of them were distracted for a moment. He couldn't ask for much more than that. While Lemar and his companions finished loading, he raced along the walkway until he was almost above their position.

Then he had to wait, and hope he wasn't noticed.

He waited until the weapons had all been fired. When the storm of smoke cleared a few seconds later, he could see one Skyway Man gurgling his life out through a wound in his neck. Three more advanced on Lemar; he was the only Raider left.

Kade had to assume Lemar could handle himself for a minute while he took care of the final two men who had ducked back behind a crate to reload. He made his way around the corner of the walkway and swung down to the main floor. He landed lightly and surged upright, snapping one man's head back with a blow beneath the jaw. He dodged a reflex kick from the other, swept his legs out from under him and finished the fight with a kick to the head. It was all over in a couple of seconds but he hurried to help Lemar, afraid he might be too late.

The Raider had taken down one Skyway Man but still fought against two more. Concentrating furiously, he spun and whirled but couldn't keep up. Punches were getting through and he had no time at all to counter. Then he went down, pummeled by the two men. He was still alive but wouldn't be for long. It was amazing he'd lasted as long as he had.

Kade charged in, knocking the closest man unconscious with an elbow to the back of the neck. He turned just in time to save himself from a similar fate. He took the blow on his shoulder and fell back. His ribs screamed at him, his shoulder throbbed, but he didn't have time to think. He rolled away and came to his feet in the corner. Ducked. Punched and spun back out into the clear. He was hit again, reeled, slammed into the small finger of wall. Grimacing with pain he flung out his hand, an unexpected back handed slap that gained him a second so he could find his feet.

"Have you got the array, Jaetin?" came a call from out in the warehouse during a rare quiet moment.

"Not quite yet," Kade's opponent called back.

"Do you need any help?"

"No. This should only take a second." With the mask covering his face, all Kade could see were his opponent's eyes. They were cold and emotionless. Jaetin thought he was going to win and didn't care who got hurt in the process. He probably didn't even care about the men who had been fighting by his side a moment earlier.

Kade could remember when he didn't care. A few days ago.

But that wasn't true. Laro's wife *was* a terrible cook but Kade didn't say anything because he didn't want to offend her. And Laro never shut up, but buy him a beer and he could entertain for hours with stories from a dozen skylands and thousands of years. If you asked he would even let you know which ones were true.

In that moment there was a scream. It sounded like Lana. Kade almost turned to look out into the warehouse and barely avoided losing his teeth. He swayed away at the last instant, had his jaw pounded anyway. Jaetin kept coming, and Kade fell back, pushing a rain of blows aside, trying not to think about Lana, waiting for an opportunity. One punch slipped past his guard, rocking him back on his heels. A kick put him flat on his back on top of one of the unconscious Skyway Men. He struggled for breath.

Jaetin smiled and drew his dagger as he came forward again. "Today's the day you die," he said.

Kade rolled to the side. As he went, he snatched a dagger from the belt of the man he was lying on. The body jumped under him as Jaetin's foot thumped down into its chest. The Skyway Man swore and Kade slashed awkwardly. Missed, but gained enough time to get to his feet.

"I've spent quite a few years not dying. I'm quite good at it now."

"Aren't we all?"

"No." Kade lunged forward. Changed his movement to a slash when Jaetin stepped aside as expected. The blade ripped through his opponent's shirt but failed to touch the flesh beneath.

The weapon snagged and Jaetin slashed a counter-attacked. Kade swayed back at the last moment then stepped clear before he lost his balance. The other man followed, slashing and stabbing with cold-eyed calm. Kade parried, dodged, wincing with each twist and turn as his ribs and back screamed their silent complaints.

"You're the guy from Jasparac, aren't you?" Jaetin said when he finally slowed his attack for a moment. "You've pissed off the Skyway Men. Nobody does that and lives.

When we've finished with you we're going to find your family and kill them too. You're so stupid it's amazing you can manage to tie your shoes in the morning."

"I use buckles," Kade replied. He blocked a lazy lunge, spun away. He almost tripped over a body but managed to keep his feet.

But Jaetin was right. He'd pissed of the Skyway Men years ago and, even if he hadn't wanted to admit it, had always known he was lucky to be alive. His superiors had said they'd contact him when the heat from the mess he'd made blew over. But Kade had known that if they ever came back for him it would be to make sure he never made another mistake again. He'd waited for them to return and give him a new job anyway. "Of course I'm stupid," he said. "All criminals are. But you? You're a criminal who's playing on the losing team."

Jaetin laughed. "Do you really think you can win here?"

Kade snapped out with his foot but ducked into a roll before the kick had even connected. Jaetin was blocking, slightly off balance. Kade hammered at the man's knee with the hilt of his dagger as he went past.

He came to his feet as Jaetin attacked again, knife low. But when the man's foot hit the ground his wounded knee buckled beneath him. He staggered, remained upright, but it was all the opening Kade needed.

He stepped in, feinted low. Jaetin tried to block, but all he did was throw himself more off balance. He lurched forward and Kade shifted his target in one smooth motion. He buried his blade to the hilt in the other man's chest.

Jaetin groaned once then fell forward with a sigh.

Kade breathed deeply, until the ping of shot striking stone nearby got his mind moving again. He threw himself to the ground and took cover behind the small section of wall.

V

They seemed to have reached a stalemate. Men and women were hunkered down behind crates and columns, peering around the edges, once more waiting for someone to make a move. Kade ducked back down to wait with them.

"Give us the cluster and we'll walk away," someone called eventually. "Nobody else needs to get hurt."

The cluster. Kade turned to look. It was lying on the ground behind him, still in the long black box, broken for all anyone knew.

"I'm going to count to ten, then I shoot this girl. She's already unconscious, so it won't hurt at all."

Girl? Kade stuck his head back up over the wall and tried to find Lana. He couldn't see her anywhere. "Thorn." He didn't know what he was supposed to do. Whoever was talking was half way down the warehouse hiding in a cove of crates. There were about six people there, by the looks of it.

Kade considered the pistols, but knew he'd never get a decent shot. "What's the point?" he shouted back. For all he knew she was already dead, but he didn't want to think that.

"Do you really trust a skyland captain to decide what to do with that cluster? Or the Wind Patrol? What could I do that would be worse?"

Kade turned to look at the long black box containing the cluster— the weapon he'd chased all the way from Tribalin. "Huh." He crawled across, found the catch and folded back the lid. The cluster inside was in the general shape of a musket, but bulkier, and made from more than a dozen shining metal boxes of varying sizes and shapes. That many small arrays... He'd never seen anything like it.

The unseen man started to count.

Kade had to stall. "So what will you do with it? Rob some old ladies? Hold up a grocery store?"

There was a moment of silence before someone broke into the expected indignant speech of one of the older generation of Skyway Men. The young members knew it was all about making money but those who had been around for years thought they were righting the inequities of life, lifting up the down trodden and helping those who couldn't help themselves. The Skyway Men were nothing if not predictable.

Only half listening, Kade lifted the weapon, struggling with the weight, cursing at his shoulder. It was easy enough to work out which end was which. He pointed the barrel, a long solid bar of metal, towards a wall and searched for buttons or switches. There was a whole bank of them.

"There's hundreds of boys and girls who would've died alone on the streets. We gave them a home and a family."

The man cleared his throat, obviously trying to reign in his emotions. "Give us that cluster and we can really make a difference." He started to count again.

Kade could imagine them skyjacking a couple of skylands. There would be no need for them to hide any more.

Kade desperately started hitting buttons. The first couple brought no result that he could see. But the third set several of the cells in the cluster to vibrating. The next two had no obvious results either, so he went back to the first. The cluster bucked in his hand and a dark, smoking patch about the size of a coin appeared on the wall.

"Well," Kade said with a smile. "Well, well, well."

The countdown had reached four when he stood up and aimed in the general direction of the voice. Assume any hostages are lying on the ground.

Two.

One.

He picked a likely target, aimed—allow for the kick—and pressed the button again. The weapon bucked in his hand and the beam of light, a moment of brightness, was visible in the dim, dusty air. It hit the crate and burned a hole right through. And as quickly as it had come, the light was gone.

There was a scream. There was swearing. Then three men jumped up, weapons raised.

Kade stared stupidly as they aimed and didn't duck until the very last moment. Shot whizzed over his head, striking the back wall of the warehouse. And a few seconds after that, he stood up, fitted the cluster into his shoulder and fired again.

A second dark hole appeared in the crate. There was no scream this time, but more swearing.

Kade cleared his throat. "Are you willing to renegotiate?" he shouted.

"Go to hell," came the reply. "You just killed these hostages."

Kade came out from behind the wall, cluster still nuzzled into his shoulder, muscles quivering, body aching. It was heavy, but he kept the muzzle trained on the crates and fired several quick bursts of light. Someone stood up. Kade was slow to react but kept calm as the other man fired and shot passed close by. When Kade fired back a black hole appeared in the stranger's shirt and he crumpled to the floor.

Another couple of shots fired into the wood.

There was no reply. Neither the verbal nor the lead varieties.

Kade stood silently. Waiting. Smoke drifted up from the holes in the timber.

"Looks clear," someone called. "Everyone there is down."

Kade swore, torn between a slow, careful approach and rushing forward to see what had happened. He prayed that Lana was still alive. He prayed that he hadn't killed her. He took several steps closer and nothing happened. Another couple. Finally, he dumped the weapon on the floor and ran to the crates.

"Lana." He leaned into the hidden space, searching. "Lana."

"What?"

"Lana." She wasn't there. There was one female hostage, still breathing, with short hair and a bird tattal on her neck. Kade looked around and saw Lana coming from the other side of the warehouse.

"You didn't think I was in there, did you?" She was holding two pistols. One of them was still loaded.

"Well, he said..."

"He said there was a female hostage and you automatically assumed it was me?" She smiled.

"Shut up, would you."

"Don't you have any faith at all?"

He shut her up himself, pulling her close and kissing her.

A moment later, she pulled away and Kade's heart almost stopped. His first thought was, *That's what happens when you offer a part of yourself to someone...*

But Lana spun, raised her pistol and fired.

Ears ringing, Kade turned to look. In the cove of crates, a Skyway Man slumped to the ground as a pistol fell from his lifeless fingers.

"Thank you," Kade said. "You don't seem to have trouble shooting people any more."

"It isn't all that hard to shoot bad guys." Though the look in her eyes said otherwise.

After a couple of seconds, Danil Barro cleared his throat. Kade took a moment to get his bearings. There were Wind Patrol men and women close by. They were all armed, and they were all staring at him.

"You killed Valal?" Danil asked.

Kade nodded. "We—"

Danil held up a hand. "He was working with... Lemar?"

Kade nodded again.

"And he was going to kill you?"

A third nod. "Apparently that order came from someone else. Lemar wasn't happy about it."

"And Karis Haverick is with them as well?"

"Yes."

"You can't believe him, Sir?" one of the Wind Patrol said.

Danil stood and breathed for a moment then gave a small shrug. "Not sure that we have a lot of choice. Going by the evidence..."

"What evidence?"

"Why was Valal there? Even if he had a good reason, why kill him? Why not just wait until he left? And, like Kade said, why kill Henas if they were going to leave via the window anyway?"

"But—"

"No. We aren't going to let anyone go, but the first thing we're going to do is..."

Kade looked around when Danil paused. They seemed to be on their own in the warehouse. The Skyway Men were all dead, and the Green Sea Raiders had disappeared.

"Where the hell are they?" someone asked. "Where's the weapon?"

Kade looked where he had put down the array, but it was nowhere in sight. The trap door in the floor was obvious enough. A couple of men pulled it open, revealing the dark mouth of a shaft beneath. If the Raiders had climbed down, they were gone now.

"Let them go," Kade said, turning to Danil.

"What? Not a chance."

"If they are going beyond the Weir, do you really want to follow with a handful of men? They have a bit of a head start now so..."

"We can't just let them go," Lana said. "You can't be serious, after all we went through."

After all we went through? Kade had spent ten years thinking his only real friend had betrayed him. And he'd been happy when Grinner told him Lemar had been killed. Instead of mourning his friend he'd been hating him. He spent ten years wondering how things might have been different if Lemar had done what he was supposed to do. Everything had been Lemar's fault.

He shrugged. "You go after them if you want. I doubt you'll have much luck."

"Why's that?" Lana asked.

"If they're going beyond the Weir then they're moving into their world, a world we know absolutely nothing about."

"But they have the weapon."

Kade shook his head. "Guns don't kill people," he said. "People kill people."

"What?"

Nothing had been Lemar's fault, and Kade should have known better. He knew who was to blame, for the mistakes and for the lies. Grinner was a cold and ruthless man; even ten years ago he'd been taking more and more power away from the Council, leading as he wanted to lead no matter what others said. And he didn't let anyone stand in his way. The more Kade thought, the more he wondered if Grinner had wanted him to fail all those years ago.

"You should be more worried about what's happening on the skylands," Kade said. "I'd rather that weapon in Lemar's hands than a dagger in Grinner's."

And every second he delayed, the further away Lemar and his followers were.

Kade had failed again. After chasing the array across the world, he had failed. He couldn't help but smile.

Epilogue

"We don't need the cluster," Lemar said as he moved carefully to the front of the line.

"So we went through all that for nothing? People died. And Vernor might never speak again. For nothing?"

The weapon was lying on the ground at the base of the ladder. Lemar took one last look at it in the half-light. Apparently Arik had chased it all the way from Tribalin to stop it falling into the wrong hands. "We went down there to get away from this world, Donar. So how come we're now trying to take the worst of it back with us?"

"We're doing it because we want to live," Donar said.

Lemar nodded. The woman, Lana, was right; it wasn't difficult to shoot the bad guys. Working out who the bad guys were was the hard part. Was he the bad guy beyond the Weir? He'd led his followers down there and found a piece of land he liked. They built some houses and cultivated some land. Then more people had joined them and they'd spread further.

Were the Wilder's just protecting their homes from invasion? Did they lie awake at night wondering if their territory would be stolen next? Had anyone tried to talk to them? Had anyone bothered to ask?

Lemar touched the lump on his forehead. It was probably the least of his injuries, but at the moment it hurt the most. "Maybe there are other ways to live," he said. Light flooded the passage as someone lit another lamp. "Come on, there's some people we have to talk to."

Please help support
independent writers and publishers.
You money is wonderful.
So are your reviews,
comments, mentions, tweets,
emails, blogs, likes
and deliveries of chocolate.

ABOUT THE AUTHOR

Scott J. Robinson grew up in a small town in rural Australia, the kind of place where you had to make your own fun. And from a young age, his idea of fun was to create strange worlds and populate them with interesting people.

He now lives in a different small town, with his wife and three children, and still enjoys creating strange worlds. Though now, he actually finishes some of the things he starts. When not writing he enjoys photography and camping and recently retired from an amazingly mediocre cricket career.

For more information visit
www.tengama.com

<u>The Age of Heroes</u>

Rawk is one of the great Heroes. He has travelled the world for forty years, hunting exotic creatures, battling magic and fighting evil wherever he found it. But he has been fighting mostly mundane battles since Prince Weaver outlawed magic. And with no great deeds left to be done, Rawk is afraid he'll soon be the old man in the corner of the tavern, dreaming of the good old days and telling tales for anyone who will buy him a drink.

But when a huge wolden wolf is spied from the walls of Katamood for the first time in a decade, Rawk is the man the city looks to once more. He'll save them. He always has.

Rawk will fight to ensure the Age of Heroes doesn't slip away into history, but what if the good old days aren't quite as good as he remembers?

<u>Tribes of the Hakahei</u>
Book 1: The Space Between
Book 2: Singing Other Worlds
Book 3: When the Time Comes
Book 4: A Different Kind of Heaven

Kim McLean is just another tourist visiting Sherwood Forest when aliens attack on the back of giant bats. She didn't think her day could get much weirder after that, until she follows an elf and a dwarf through a magical gateway to another world.

Then, as the endless alien hordes keep coming, she gets involved with bureaucrats and soldiers, governments and people who should know better, and she starts to wonder if her definition of weird needs to be revised.

All she knows for sure is that it's up to her to save the human race.

Travelling to distant worlds and different universes, she gathers strange companions and uncovers long forgotten secrets as she tries to end the death and destruction.

But the war was being waged long before Sherwood Forest was attacked and Kim soon suspects that they aren't even fighting the right enemy.